Graziella Simeone Adwan

The time of the Malier

Ludmilla

Book one

Youcanprint

Title | The Time of the Malìer. Ludmilla
Author | Graziella Simeone Adwan

ISBN | 979-12-22766-05-8

© 2024 - All rights reserved by the author
This work is published directly by the Author through the self-publishing platform Youcanprint and the Author holds all rights to it exclusively. No part of this book may therefore be reproduced without the prior consent of the Author.

Youcanprint
Via Marco Biagi 6, 73100 Lecce
www.youcanprint.it
info@youcanprint.it
Made by Human

Preface

I spent the night waking up from one nightmare after another. I lost count of how many times my mind was dragged, by an invisible hand, to the rock where Cecilia's lifeless body lay.

This story has all the elements of the most harrowing nightmare, a novel that begins with a series of assumptions only to upend them all. It draws us into its labyrinth, pulling us from one side to the other until we are utterly disoriented, powerless to resist what unfolds before our eyes.

We start reading, believing we're about to solve a case that seems straightforward enough, but the deeper we go, the more our certainties crumble.

We soon realize that the lives of the inspectors involved are anything but ordinary, and they will guide us through a novel that makes us feel a wide range of emotions, especially outrage and terror.

From the outset, however, we wonder who Ludmilla is, the one already hinted at in the title, who only gradually reveals herself to us. Her character is both fascinating and unsettling. We sense her presence even when she's absent, as if she's lingering just behind us, slowly becoming an obsession.

Within her class, Ludmilla had the dubious reputation of being the most feared. They called her a 'witch,' and the other girls were afraid of her. Some claimed they'd seen her kill small animals in the schoolyard; others said she could cast spells with a single glance. In all of this, I was the needle balancing between the quiet life of the rest of the class and the world Ludmilla and I inhabited. Yet, the needle always turned in her favor.

The author has expertly woven together the intricate web of relationships between the characters, connecting everything in ways that are nothing short of astonishing. It feels as if life itself is shuffling its cards, playing a sly game to lead people down paths it has laid out for them, altering everything they once took for granted.

Alongside Ludmilla is Cecilia, the innocent victim of the story. A vulnerable child for whom we cannot help but feel compassion and tenderness, she captures our hearts to the point where we deeply empathize with her experiences.

Her death defies everything we understand as humans, challenging the natural laws, creating new ones, and leaving us bewildered. It's a death to be unravelled, one that combines the macabre and the fantastical, a blend of the unknown and horror.

The work thus becomes pure adrenaline, pushing us to test our limits and go beyond them, driven by a curiosity to solve this complex and original mystery.

Nightmares consumed my mind. I could smell the stench of a decaying corpse, overwhelmed by disgust, which was compounded by pain. Radiating pain, beginning in my chest and spreading throughout my body, so intense it made me nauseous. Then, all that pain ceased, and suddenly, I was hovering over a bottomless chasm. All I could see was darkness. A darkness that took the shape of a terrifying creature: a hulking, poorly dressed man with long, shaggy hair and bloodshot eyes.

Fear is one of the strongest emotions in the novel because the reader cannot help but feel it as they witness everything that transpires.

What's most intriguing is that this fear remains plausible and well-founded, precisely because the author masterfully manipulates our thoughts, delving into our fears, shaping imaginary worlds that are both fascinating and terrifying.

The ability to study not only the psychology of the characters but also to anticipate our own reactions is a standout feature of the work. It plays ahead of us, predicting our responses and turning them into something else entirely.

As we delve into the heart of the novel, we can't help but marvel at the author's vivid imagination, their talent for blending real human beings with more fantastical ones, leaving an indelible mark on our minds.

Creativity is not limited to the ingenious and mind-bending plot, which merges various genres—from thriller to fantasy to horror. The characters feel tangible and real because they are embedded in a familiar reality, one filled with work and emotional dilemmas, where life is constantly shifting, leaving us lost and bewildered.

"Ludmilla" is only the first volume of a unique saga that already promises to be unforgettable.

1

The hilly area was closed to traffic. A digital sign indicated a landslide and directed drivers to an alternative route.

I showed my ID to the officer at the checkpoint.

"You're welcome, Inspector Diletti," he said with a smile. I returned the greeting with a quick salute before moving on.

It was pitch black, and the rain was pouring down. I could have been at home, in bed, or watching a TV series, but the pandemic had forced many people into quarantine, including my deputy inspector, Andrea Pancaldi.

I arrived at the cemetery gate, cursing under my breath when I realized I didn't have an umbrella. I dashed out of the car and took shelter under the porch.

A man approached me, holding an umbrella.

"Marino, what are you doing here?" I asked, puzzled.

"Why the look?" he replied, raising an eyebrow.

"I thought it was just a landslide; no one mentioned any casualties."

"And you? What's your excuse? Is the state police so well-funded that they send an inspector for a landslide?"

"Do you live on Mars? Haven't you heard of COVID?"

"Ah, so you're running on half capacity, too."

"Even worse..." I muttered, annoyed. "Now tell me, why are you here?"

"The landslide took some coffins with it. Two of them opened, and someone has to take the remains to forensics. As you can see, even on Mars, COVID has arrived," he added sarcastically.

We headed off, sharing the umbrella, toward the area cordoned off with tape.

"Keep back!" shouted a firefighter. "Oh, it's you, Inspector. Good thing you're here. For now, let's move; this rain could cause another landslide." We moved under the shelter of one of the 'burial tunnels.'

"The landslide hit a house, which is currently unreachable."

"Are you saying we have to stand around doing nothing, even if there might be people to save?"

"That's all we can do. In this darkness and weather, the helicopter can't fly, and as long as the rain keeps up, the ground is unstable and slick. We can't even reach the coffins," he shouted, running off.

I looked at Marino Piano, feeling dejected, and picked up my phone.

"Boss, sorry for the late hour, but it's a mess here, though there's no sign of a homicide, at least on the surface."

"Then why are you there?" he asked, irritated.

"I'm asking myself the same thing, but Inspector Vari was kind enough to offer assistance. Remember, with COVID, staff numbers are dwindling..."

"I get it, I get it... If there's nothing for us, head back to bed. Give me a report in the morning. Good night."

"Doctor, come here!" someone yelled.

By that point, I was wide awake, and nothing was going to put me to sleep. I decided to follow Marino.

Marino Piano had been my first love. We were teenagers when we started dating, a relationship that lasted throughout high school until it ended. As we grew older, I realized I had to choose between pursuing my studies and career or living the life of an unhappy housewife. I chose the former.

By chance, over a decade later, we found ourselves working on the same murder case; a typical quarrel that escalated into a fatal stabbing. Back then, I was in the operations and emergency response unit, and Marino was an assistant at the forensic medicine institute. When he recognized me, I could see the old pain I'd caused him, but time had already begun to heal the wounds.

It wasn't difficult to build a new relationship based on friendship and mutual respect.

"Hey, Inspector, lost in thought?" Marino said, taking my arm.

The halogen lamps lit up the area of the landslide, revealing a body near one of the coffins.

"I'm Dario Bonelli, the cemetery caretaker," the man said, approaching us.

"I'm Inspector Maria Diletti."

"I've printed the chronology of the burials from this year, but none recent enough to explain the intact body we've glimpsed down there."

"Thank you," I shouted, as the heavy rain drowned out other sounds.

I glanced around, but Marino was nowhere to be seen. "Where's Dr. Piano?" I asked an officer.

"I saw him go into the cemetery office."

"And where's that?"

"Follow this path straight ahead. See that building over there? Those are the offices."

"Thank you!"

"Inspector, here, take this."

He handed me a rain cover, still folded.

"God bless you!"

I walked briskly toward the offices, but halfway there, I saw Marino coming out.

"Why are you all suited up?"

"They've assured me a safe route to reach the body."

"Give me a suit, I'll come down with you."

"Not a chance," he said firmly, heading straight for the firefighters waiting with their harnesses.

I got as close as I could to try to pass the barrier, but they stopped me. I settled for a spot where I had a nearly perfect view of Marino already at work.

The rain stopped, and the dim light of dawn began to break through the thinning clouds.

"Inspector," Marino Piano called out, "I'm afraid this has just become your case."

2

I slipped into my polypropylene suit and descended to join Marino.
"It's the body of a little girl. Look at her neck; it seems like she was attacked by a dog."
"My God! How could a little girl end up here?"
"That's for you to find out. As soon as we get the go-ahead from the Commissioner, I'll take her to the institute," Marino replied.
"Inspector, have you lost your mind?" a voice shouted.
"Speak of the devil," I said to Marino with a smirk. "Commissioner Spatafora, it's safe; you can come down, too."
"Get a move on, and fast!" he barked.
I complied. A tense Spatafora would only make things harder for us.
"Our fearless inspector. What's the situation?"
"The body is that of a girl around ten years old, with a clear dog-bite wound, which seems to have caused her death. Dr. Piano will provide a more detailed report after the autopsy."
"What are you waiting for!" he shouted again. "Remove the body!"
He handed me a signed document authorizing the removal, then walked off.
I stood there, the paper still in my hand, deep in thought. Spatafora's arrogance and sense of superiority never failed to sour my mood, but my thoughts drifted beyond that body, which seemed so out of place at the landslide site. Where would this lead us?
The ringing of my phone snapped me out of my reverie. It was my deputy.
"Hey, love, how are you?"
"Negative swab, I'm back on duty."

"Perfect timing. See you at the office. Welcome back."

Deputy Inspector Andrea Pancaldi had been the love of my life for about 20 years. We had never talked about living together or getting married—we both weren't suited for that—but the love, friendship, and respect we shared kept us together in a wonderful relationship.

"Why don't you stop by instead of heading straight to the office? Just to confirm the swab is really negative. I'll be waiting," he teased.

I let Celeste know that I'd be stopping by home to change, then headed to Andrea's.

3

"Hello Pancaldi, welcome back," echoed the greetings from colleagues.

"Diletti and Pancaldi, my favourite team. How are you, deputy inspector?" the commissioner greeted us.

Adelmo Celeste, besides being my direct superior, was also an old and dear friend. Our families had known each other since high school—one of those rare friendships where both sides married and stayed together into old age. I won't deny that both families had, at times, hoped to see us end up together, but we were just good friends, more like siblings, and you can't have anything but a familial bond with a brother.

"Any news from Piano?" I asked.

"None yet, but since you were on site, what's your take?"

"I think the girl's body was hidden in that coffin, and fate intervened so we would find it. Have there been any reports of missing children?"

"None, at least not in the last two months. Thank God."

"It may be thanks to God, but this is going to be the case of the year," I said gravely.

"Oh, it certainly will be. Mara Mezzani is already on the case."

Mara Mezzani was a journalist who never quite made it into the big papers. She had started her own blog, which had gained a following among conspiracy theorists, a crowd that had grown during the pandemic. She could stir up quite a mess with a case like this.

The phone on the desk rang, pulling us out of our thoughts about Mezzani.

"It's Dr. Piano," whispered Celeste, motioning for us to stay seated. "What can you tell us, my friend?"

"There's a lot to discuss; it's better if you come here in person."

"We're on our way." Celeste hung up, sighing.

We headed to the service car, where a young officer was waiting to drive us.

The forensic institute in Turin was housed in a newly renovated wing of the 'Molinette' hospital, known as 'Wing 13.' The fourth floor was home to the autopsy rooms—four of them, to be precise—and the cold storage, but area 4, reserved for unidentified bodies, was in a basement that wasn't part of the renovated section.

The elevator opened onto a dimly lit corridor, where Marino Piano was waiting.

"Where are we?" Celeste asked, his voice tinged with unease.

"We're in the old containment rooms of the former psychiatric ward. Now it's more like a storage hole. We brought the girl's body here for two reasons: firstly, because she is unidentified, and secondly, to keep journalists from spinning their own stories."

"What do you have for us, doctor?" Celeste cut in.

"Nothing you're going to like, but come in."

He led us into the autopsy room. The body, still covered, lay on the table.

Marino pulled back the sheet. The sight of that poor child, with a deep laceration across her neck, made me gag. I quickly covered my mouth.

"Are you alright, Maria?" Marino asked, concerned.

"I'm fine, thanks."

I didn't intend to throw up, but looking at the girl's face left me uneasy. I had the unsettling feeling that I knew her.

A tune from the computer on the desk interrupted Marino, drawing his attention.

"Excuse me," he said, heading over, "just what I've been waiting for. The body was identified through the fingerprints I sent to Codex." He scanned the screen and continued, "What I'm about to tell you won't be easy to hear."

"Don't keep us in suspense," Celeste urged.

"Better if you sit down."

We took our seats around his desk, hanging on Marino's words, anticipating what he was about to reveal.

"Cecilia Donadio, born in Turin on 15 March 1975, died in Turin on 23 June 1986."

I couldn't contain my emotions and slumped back in my chair.

Marino's slaps and the voices of Celeste and Andrea calling my name brought me around.

"Welcome back, what's going on?" Celeste asked, suspicion in his voice.

I tried to collect my thoughts before speaking.

"Cecilia Donadio. I knew her well. We went to the same school. She died in the Piazza Vittorio fire, at the 'Two of Spades' disco. Do you remember?"

"That was thirty-six years ago. How can this corpse be so old?" Celeste said, his voice hoarse.

"That's the least of it," Marino said, sitting down. "I'll get to the most important part now, but first, I'll fetch some coffee. Maria, you look too pale; you need something to perk you up."

"I'll come with you," Celeste offered, rising from his seat.

I was left alone with Andrea, who immediately pulled me into his arms.

"Feeling any better?" he asked, gently stroking my cheek.

"No, I'm not. An old wound I thought had healed has reopened."

Marino and Celeste returned, and the latter handed me a small cup of coffee from the vending machine. I drank it, feeling a bit more steady.

"I'll get straight to the point," Marino began. "The fact that the body is so well-preserved isn't entirely strange. It depends on the environmental and soil conditions, whether it was exposed to air, and other factors that can mummify a body instead of letting it decompose. Still, this case would be a contender for the Guinness World Records in mummification. The real issue is that the wound—or rather, the bite—that caused the girl's death wasn't from a dog. It was human."

We were stunned, staring at Marino, waiting for further explanation.

"Human, but there's more. The dental imprint, clearly visible on one side of the wound, matches that of a boy or girl—DNA will confirm this—around the same age as the victim. About ten, maybe eleven."

"Dr. Piano, what are we dealing with here?" Celeste asked.

"Your guess is as good as mine," Marino replied, dejected.

A ping signalled the arrival of a message. I read it.

"They've confirmed that Cecilia's body was buried there, and the case was closed as an accident. The coroner determined at the time that her neck wound was caused by a detached strobe light: the glass sliced through her right carotid artery, leading to death by exsanguination. She was the only one who didn't die from the fire itself. The other victims—I've forwarded you the death certificates—perished from burns or smoke inhalation. Thirteen young girls in total."

"We can only hope to find someone who was involved in the original investigation still alive. I'll ask Spatafora," Celeste muttered, looking up at the ceiling and clenching his fists.

We said our goodbyes to Marino Piano and returned to the service car.

During the silent drive back to the station, I sank deep into my thoughts.

15

4

I was born and raised in Turin, a city as beautiful as it is enigmatic.

Situated exactly halfway across the northern hemisphere, on the 45th parallel, between the Po and Dora rivers—interpreted as the masculine and feminine—Turin is considered an important energy hub.

The city's mysterious energies, esoteric symbols, and unresolved dark events were often the subject of animated discussions among young enthusiasts of the occult.

My family owned a small business that did well enough to allow me to attend a private religious school. It was seen as a security for the future by my father and a path to a life in the presence of God by my mother.

I vividly remember my first day of school. The short car ride, with my parents doing nothing but praising how lucky I was to attend such a prestigious institution. Silent, I gazed out the window, watching the landscape change as the car climbed the hilly road. At one point, my father turned onto a side road that led into a forest. Anxiety gripped me. I made a clumsy attempt, hoping the car would turn back, and started crying in despair, begging to go home.

After passing through the woods, we found ourselves in front of a gate that, to me, seemed to lead straight to the devil rather than to school. I imagined the car being sucked through the infernal gate by a whirlwind that would transport us to another dimension. I tried my theatrical crying again.

But soon, I was standing in front of the institute's entrance, held firmly by my parents.

A group of little girls was gathered around a woman with a gentle expression and a kind voice—Miss Adelina Della Carnia, the teacher. She approached us and introduced herself.

Encouraged by the teacher, I joined the girls, who were still singing in a circle. Two of them let go of their hands to welcome me into their game.

"I'm Ada," said the girl on my right. I stared at her, mouth agape, as I had never seen such a tall child.

"I'm Ludmilla," sang the girl on my left.

"I'm Maria," I replied, following the rhythm of the circle.

Out of the corner of my eye, I saw my parents leaving, but I was no longer afraid.

Teacher Adelina led us to the classroom, encouraging us to choose any seat we liked.

"Maria!" I turned to the sound of the voice. The girl with the unusual name was inviting me to sit next to her. "We could be desk buddies, if you'd like."

That moment marked the beginning of our friendship. We became inseparable. Ludmilla immediately considered me her best friend, the only one, as she put it, with whom she could confide and sleep peacefully between two pillows.

Her family was very small, just her and her grandfather. She used to call him Grandfather Robert. I never met her parents; she said they were archaeologists traveling the world, discovering ancient treasures.

Ludmilla's life was governed by a series of rules that I found incomprehensible: no school cafeteria due to health reasons, she followed a strict diet of only a few foods because of allergies; no going out in the evenings; no contact with animals; and she was exempt from religious classes and mass. She seemed to live in a state of grace.

I was fascinated by her peculiarities, even though she could be quite harsh at times. Her mood swings led to several arguments during our friendship. She could shift from a refined 19th-century lady to a rough-

and-ready 20th-century dockworker, especially if pressured on matters she deemed unworthy of discussion—like bringing other friends into our circle of trust.

At school, Ludmilla was one of the top students, bested only by Ada, the tallest girl, who received more praise because she attended religious classes and mass.

In her relationship with the rest of the class, Ludmilla held a negative reputation. They called her a "witch," and the other girls were scared of her. Some claimed to have seen her kill small animals in the schoolyard; others said she could cast spells with a single look. In all this, I was the needle balancing between the quiet life of the rest of the class and the world Ludmilla and I inhabited. And yet, the needle always pointed in her favor.

Five years of primary school passed, and the end of the 1986 school year arrived, signaling the transition to middle school. The school council, made up of teachers and parents, decided to organize a big party at one of the city's clubs, the 'Two of Spades.' The invitation was set for the afternoon of Friday, 27 June. Everyone received an invitation card except Ludmilla. I remember her grandfather coming to my house, explaining what had happened and pleading with my parents not to mention it to anyone—Ludmilla was not to know she hadn't been invited. Shortly after Mr. Robert, as I called him, left, Ludmilla called me to apologize, saying she couldn't attend the party because her parents would be back that very day. I knew it was just an excuse, but I had sworn I would never tell her the truth.

I awaited the event without much enthusiasm. I disliked the girls in my class, but given the promise I made, I couldn't voice my thoughts.

Fate took matters into its own hands, and on the day of the party, I woke up with a fever. I spent the day in bed, either sleeping or watching TV. Several times in the afternoon, I heard my mother talking excitedly on the phone. I didn't know what was going on, and I was too dazed by the fever to care.

The next morning, my mother woke me with a breakfast tray, and I immediately noticed her tear-streaked face.

"Why are you crying, Mum? I'm feeling better."

"Thank God you're better and here, alive and well. Something terrible happened," she managed to say between sobs.

My grandmother entered through the bedroom door.

"Grandma!" I exclaimed. "When did you get here?" I was so happy to see her that I forgot my mother's tears.

"My dear, I arrived this morning, but I let you sleep so the fever would pass," she replied, embracing me warmly.

The idyllic moment was interrupted when the two women sat down on my bed.

"There's something terrible you need to know," my mother said, still sobbing. "The party yesterday..."

I abruptly pulled my hand away from hers. "I don't want to know anything about it."

"Listen to me," she insisted. "There was an accident. Many of your classmates died."

She told me about the fire and how devastating it had been for a group of ten-year-old girls. I didn't cry; I was too angry at all those girls, and deep down, I almost wished they had all died. In a twisted way, they got what they deserved for being so mean to my best friend, who was mercifully spared by not attending the party. These dark thoughts quickly gave way to guilt, and I was soon overwhelmed with despair.

The funeral was a collective ceremony held in the institute's chapel, attended by city officials and thousands of people—families, friends, and onlookers. Ludmilla was absent.

I had spoken to her on the phone in the days leading up to the funeral. She seemed busy, and when I asked if she would attend, she avoided the question. I tried calling her on the morning of the funeral, but it was no use. I assumed she was out with her parents. She called me that evening.

"Hi, Maria, we can't see each other anymore. I'm leaving with my parents."

It was a cold shock.

"Just like that, out of the blue? You didn't say anything..." I protested.

"You were busy with your friends. But now I have to say goodbye. Goodbye."

She didn't give me time to respond. The line went dead.

And that was how my friendship with that extraordinary girl came to an end.

I spent the following days feeling melancholic and angry, unable to understand how Ludmilla could be so rude. A seaside holiday helped me move on, and I gradually forgot about her.

5

"We have arrived." Someone shook me out of my daze, snapping me back to reality as I got out of the service sedan and entered the police station.

"Inspector Diletti, there's a man asking for you—he says his name is Giovanni Donadio. I've put him in the waiting room."

"Thank you, Calabrò. Have him come to the commissioner's office in five minutes."

"You got it, Inspector."

We entered Celeste's office, just in time to welcome the man.

"Please, Mr. Donadio, this is Deputy Inspector Pancaldi, Commissioner Adelmo Celeste, and Chief Inspector Maria Diletti."

"I'm here because I heard someone on TV talking about what happened to my poor daughter's remains. That same person mentioned the name Inspector Diletti, and then I remembered I might know her," he said, swallowing with difficulty, "and then... I found this in the mailbox just this morning as I was leaving to come here." He laid a half-torn blue envelope on the desk.

"I apologize, I tore it in a fit of anger..."

"Have a seat, Mr. Donadio," I said, moving a chair from under the desk.

He looked at us with a mix of fear and hesitation, visibly shaken.

"You're right, Mr. Donadio, you do know me. I went to the same school as Cecilia; we were even in the same class," I replied, trying to put him at ease.

"May I read it?" asked Celeste, another tactic to help the man feel more comfortable.

"Of course, Commissioner," he replied, his voice quivering.
"Let's see..."

"My dear Mr. and Mrs. Donadio," Celeste began to read, "it pains me to reopen a wound, which I believe never truly healed, regarding the death of your beloved daughter, Cecilia. I have come to learn of the infernal abyss that consumed delicate Cecilia, but you should know that beings of a sanguine nature live among us, whose cruelty inflicts suffering on those they encounter. One such being approached your Cecilia, and the seed of madness led her to her end. Poor victim of what she did not understand. She felt no pain. A friend."

We all fell silent. The only sound was that of Giovanni Donadio's quiet sobbing.

"When did you say you received it, Mr. Donadio?" Celeste finally asked, breaking the silence.

"This morning. I was supposed to go to the cemetery office to handle some paperwork, but after reading this, I just couldn't. Once I gathered my strength, I came here."

"The letter is addressed to Mr. and Mrs. Donadio. I assume your wife knows about it, correct?" I asked.

He swallowed hard before answering. "My Elvira has been as good as dead since that damned day."

"Explain yourself, Mr. Donadio," Celeste prompted.

"That afternoon is burned into my memory like it was yesterday. I was against that party—don't ask me why. Just a feeling I should have listened to. Elvira and I accompanied Cecilia to the party. I don't need to describe how happy she was. The club had a small room adjacent to the dance floor, directly connected to the outside via a security door, and we parents stayed there once the girls were inside. We waited, chatting about this and that to pass the time. I remember there was also a boy who had accompanied his sister because their parents couldn't. He sat quietly, off to the side, playing one of those electronic games that were popular back then..."

"Do you remember his name?" I asked.

"No, but I remember him saying he was preparing for the entrance test to the Carabinieri academy. His sister was the only one who made it out safe."

"I think I know who you're talking about—Luca Perri, right? Antonella's brother."

"Yes, Maria, that's right." He paused.

"If you feel up to it, please continue," I encouraged him.

"Of course, sorry. Suddenly, we heard a strange noise coming from the ballroom. Some of us went to see what was happening. A girl, who I was told wasn't invited, had arrived at the party, causing a commotion among the girls who tried to drive her away. One of the men decided it had gone on long enough. He went into the ballroom and tried to persuade her to leave, first calmly, then by force. He dragged her into the small room, closing the door behind them. You know, sometimes people can become beasts. The adults, including my Elvira, started yelling at her, 'You witch, get out of here!' Someone dragged her outside and pushed her onto the pavement. I voiced my disapproval and tried to leave, even urging my wife to come with me, but she insisted I was the one in the wrong. I went outside, hoping to find the girl and comfort her, but she was gone. I decided to take a walk, just to clear my head. I didn't go far—my Elvira was near the end of her pregnancy with our second child, and I thought it was just hormones making her act out like the others. I had parked the car a few streets away, intending to sit and have a cigarette. But I never got the chance. The blast was so loud, it felt like a bomb. I didn't know where it came from, but I had a bad feeling and ran toward the club. When I turned the corner, I saw little girls running, some screaming, and others on fire. It was hell on earth. I tried to get inside, but people held me back. The flames were so high, shooting out of the doors like tongues of destruction. In all that chaos, my Elvira went into labor. The police, fire brigade, and ambulances arrived, and one of them took her. I lost track of time. I was sitting on the curb, beyond the cordoned-off area, when I saw that boy holding his sister's hand. Both were covered in soot and coughing, but they were alive. That gave me hope: maybe the fire was under control, maybe the girls were safe. But my hopes were crushed as they started bringing out bodies, laying them on the ground and covering them with white sheets. Then I saw her—a firefighter carrying her. I pushed past the barrier, breaking free from a policeman's grasp, and threw myself over my little girl's lifeless body. You know, she hadn't been touched by the flames."

"Why don't you take a break, Mr. Donadio. Can we get you something?" I interjected, seeing he was struggling to continue.

"Maybe a glass of water."

I got up, fetched a small bottle of water and a glass from Celeste's minibar, and handed it to him.

He took small sips, bracing himself to go on.

"The flames had spared her, but her neck..." He took a deep breath. "It was almost severed, so much so that when I hugged her, it felt like she would come apart. A policeman made me let go and pulled me away. That's when I thought of my Elvira. I didn't even know where they had taken her. I asked around, and a firefighter told me to check with the police patrols. An officer radioed the operations center, and they said Mrs. Donadio had been taken to the maternity hospital. There was nothing more I could do there—Cecilia would have understood. She was a conscientious child. So I went to the hospital. When I got to the obstetrics ward, a nurse asked who I was looking for. When I said my name, she went pale and told me to wait while she called the head doctor..." He lowered his head, starting to sob again.

"Mr. Donadio, you don't have to tell us everything today. We can come see you tomorrow, if that's alright."

I had seen many desperate people, but none like him. Mr. Donadio was not just in despair—his expression was pure terror.

"Yes, that would be best. Come tomorrow. I'm just going out for groceries, but you can come by anytime. I'll be waiting." He got up and left.

I watched as he walked out, shoulders hunched, head bowed, like a man carrying an unbearable burden.

"What do you make of this letter?" Celeste asked.

I reread it carefully. "It could be from the killer, or from someone who knew. It's filled with cryptic language, clearly intended to create confusion. Let's have the experts analyze it and see what they find."

"Are you two going to think it over?"

"Of course."

I took the letter from Celeste's hands and sealed it in a plastic bag.

I checked the time—it was well past lunchtime, and my stomach was grumbling.

"How about a quick sandwich, and then we head back to Marino Piano?" I suggested to Andrea, feeling tired.

"Sure..."

"You don't have to eat if you're not hungry," I added, knowing full well he wasn't talking about food.

Andrea didn't say it, but I knew he felt a pang of jealousy toward Marino, aware of our past and the bond we still shared. I decided not to push it and headed for the exit of the station.

6

Marino turned the letter over in his hands, occasionally placing it under a violet light. He puffed out a breath.

"Nothing visible to the naked eye, not even on the envelope. Let's hope they licked the seal," he commented, holding up the envelope.

"Anything else?"

"Not for now. I'll need to conduct more in-depth analysis. It will take a couple of days. I'll call you," he said, dismissing us.

"Your coroner friend is always so pleasant," Andrea muttered sarcastically.

For the second time that day, I chose not to engage in an argument.

The phone vibrated, and Celeste's number appeared on the screen.

"Boss?"

"I spoke with Spatafora. He's looking for a certain Carlo Delbono, the inspector who conducted the investigation into the 'Two of Spades' fire."

"He's all we have?"

"It seems the coroner from that time has passed away. Start with Delbono, and we'll see where it leads."

"Send me his contact details. We're just leaving Marino Piano's, so if he's available, we can go see him."

"Talk to you later."

He hung up, and moments later, a message arrived with Delbono's phone number.

"Hello?" answered a voice after just two rings.

"Inspector Carlo Delbono?"

"Strange to be called 'Inspector' again. Yes, it's me. Who am I speaking with?"

"I am Inspector Maria Diletti from the Homicide Section. Commissioner Spatafora provided your contact information."

"Go on."

"I was hoping we could have a face-to-face conversation if you have the time."

"This is unexpected, but yes. May I ask what this is about?"

"Does the fire at the 'Two of Spades' ring any bells?"

A moment of silence followed. "Come over. I'll be expecting you."

I tossed the car keys to Andrea. "You drive."

Carlo Delbono lived not far from the forensic institute, but city traffic made the journey twice as long as expected.

The former inspector was a refined man, with an arrogant smile that made him look much younger than his eighty years. He greeted us with courteous but distant manners, clearly suspicious.

We took seats in an exquisitely furnished parlour, where no expense seemed to have been spared.

"Alright. What can I do for you?"

"We have reopened the 'Two of Spades' case..."

"Really?" he interrupted, eyebrow raised.

"I assume you've heard about the landslide on the hill and the coffins that ended up in the valley."

"Of course, but I fail to see the connection."

"One of the coffins contained the remains of a little girl who died in the fire—Cecilia Donadio. Does that name mean anything to you?"

"Yes, I remember, but the connection still isn't clear." I handed him the two expert reports—the one from 1986 and the current one. He read through them carefully.

"Well, where do I fit into all this?"

"Unfortunately, the coroner who performed the original autopsy passed away a couple of years ago. We were hoping you could provide your insights. I imagine you would have followed the autopsy during the investigation."

"Inspector, those were different times. We didn't work closely with forensic medicine, and we certainly weren't allowed to attend autopsies. But I can tell you that Professor Lamberti, God rest his soul, was a highly regarded professional. He probably didn't have the techniques available that we have today. Mistakes happen."

"You were still in charge of the investigation. What was your perspective on what happened?"

"The fire brigade determined there was no malicious intent. The electrical control unit wasn't designed to handle sufficient current; it overloaded and caught fire. The venue was closed down, and the owner was put on trial, found guilty for not upgrading the electrical system. Once there was no evidence of foul play, the investigation was closed. The poor girl died by chance; if that chandelier hadn't fallen, she might have survived. But, come to think of it, there might be someone else worth talking to. There was a boy, whose name I can't recall, who ran into the fire to save his sister. They both made it out."

"We'll get in touch with him. Thank you for your time."

"Don't mention it. Sorry I couldn't be of more help."

"Yeah... too bad," I muttered.

"Well, that was a waste," I said to Andrea as we left the building. "Though, if you ask me, he brushed us off rather smoothly."

"Maybe, but I think he just didn't want to dwell on an old case."

"I don't know... it feels like there's something he's not telling us," Andrea insisted.

"Alright, tell me about this suspicion of yours," I prodded.

"What if someone covered up the evidence?"

"Why would they do that?"

"Think about it. Different times or not, a bite is still a bite. How could the coroner mistake it for a cut from a chandelier?"

"So, you think Delbono knows the truth, and that's why he hurried us along?"

"I don't know, but I wouldn't rule it out. Look, maybe Piano can tell us more about Dr. Lamberti. I'd imagine they crossed paths."

"I'll give Marino a call."

I scrolled through my contacts and dialed Marino.

"Bit early to ask me about the analysis..."

"Actually, that's not why I'm calling," I interrupted.

"Alright, then shoot."

"Did you know Professor Lamberti?"

"Of course, he was my lecturer during my specialization. Why are you asking about him?"

"He performed the autopsy on Cecilia Donadio."

"From the way you're talking, I assume you have a copy of the report. Can't you read it anymore?"

"I know we have a copy, but... it's a long story. Care to discuss it over dinner?"

"Fine, but don't tell me I'll have to put up with your deputy... oops, am I on speaker?"

"Sure, Marino, let's tolerate each other for the greater good," Andrea responded, his sarcasm barely masking his irritation.

"See you later," I said, ending the call.

"If you'd rather be alone, I can stay home..."

"Are you trying to pick a fight?" I replied, irritated.

Thankfully, Andrea stopped provoking me. Marino never missed an opportunity to be less than tactful, and I still couldn't understand what it was about my relationship with Andrea that bothered him so much. It was Marino who had distanced himself when we reconnected years ago. He was one of those men who liked to keep women at arm's length, available at his convenience. He'd have loved for me to be a casual lover, but he'd picked the wrong woman for that.

I called Celeste and told him about our meeting with Carlo Delbono, as well as Andrea's suspicions. I asked him to join us for dinner, so I wouldn't be stuck between the two of them. He agreed.

"Celeste will be there, too. How about we ask Pepe to make a paella?"

"You never say no to Pepe's paella. Good idea."

7

"Professor Manlio Lamberti was one of the pillars of modern forensic medicine," Marino said, pausing to take a forkful of paella, which he swallowed almost like water. "But around 1990, he suddenly stopped working in the field and devoted himself entirely to teaching. According to student stories, it was quite abrupt. I can assure you he was a tough guy, a rare kind of professor—strict, but so knowledgeable and engaging that he made you love the subject. That's why it seems unlikely to me that Lamberti would have made such an obvious mistake. But the autopsy report is signed by Dr. Mauro Chioggia."

"What can you tell us about this Dr. Mauro Chioggia?" asked Celeste.

"Honestly, nothing. I've never heard of him or met him at a conference, which is quite odd. But I can find out."

"Please do," I urged him.

He picked up his phone and dialed a number.

"Valerio, my friend, sorry for the late hour, but I'm working on a rather tangled old case. Do you know a Dr. Mauro Chioggia?" He put the call on speakerphone, motioning for us to stay silent.

"No, I don't know him."

"His signature is on an autopsy from 1986, and I need to get in touch with him."

"Should be easy. Just do an online search in the medical register."

"I'm doing it as we speak. It says no professionals match the search parameters."

"That could mean two things: removed from the register for various reasons or deceased."

"Can you dig a bit deeper with your usual sources?"

"I know who I can ask. If we're lucky, I'll have something in less than an hour. If not, I'll call you tomorrow."

"I owe you one."

"Tomorrow night, I'll crush you at Burraco. That's enough of a reward for me. Later."

"Thanks again," Marino said, ending the call.

"What would lead to disqualification?" I asked.

"Some doctors request removal to focus on other specialties or because they're going to work abroad. There are also disciplinary actions, but in that case, the search should have returned a result, so we can rule that out."

"Is there no general register for medical graduates?"

"There is, but it's not open access. That's probably what my friend Valerio is looking into."

"I have to ask, Marino. Do you have any theory of your own?" Celeste inquired.

"I'd like to give the benefit of the doubt to whoever performed that autopsy. I can only imagine what the poor girl's body must have looked like. Her neck was likely so battered, with extensive swelling, that it would have been difficult to distinguish between a cut and a bite. Plus, I think the rush to close the case played a major role. As for the ex-inspector's claim that Lamberti was present, even though his signature isn't there, I think he's simply mistaken. The forensic institute must have been a mess with how many victims? I don't remember."

"Thirteen," I said, still affected by the number.

My phone, which was charging, began to ring. I stood up to answer it. The number was unfamiliar, and considering the late hour, it was unlikely to be a call center.

"Hello?" There was heavy breathing on the other end.

I put it on speakerphone.

"Who is this?" I asked loudly.

"Creatures of sanguine temperament live among us, hidden and quiet, but to search for them means death. Inspector Diletti, abandon your investigation and put poor Cecilia Donadio's body back in the ground, but first, purify it with fire." I stood there, frozen.

Andrea grabbed the phone from my hands. "Who are you?" The line went dead. Silence filled the room.

I remained motionless, and Marino guided me to sit down.

Celeste immediately called someone.

"This is Celeste. Veneziani, I need you to trace a call."

"Aye aye, Commissioner."

"Inspector Diletti's phone. Two minutes ago, incoming call. Do it now."

Celeste came over and sat next to me, taking my hand.

"You've been threatened."

"I hadn't noticed," I replied sarcastically, trying to deflect. I knew where this was headed.

"Tomorrow, I'll request an escort from the commissioner."

"No way."

"Don't be childish."

"Don't put me under escort. I'd just evade them. Instead, it means Andrea Pancaldi will be staying with me for a while. Agreed?"

Celeste sighed but conceded. Andrea's grin widened, and Marino shot me a teasing look. I had to resist the urge to smack them both.

Marino's phone rang.

"It's Valerio," he signaled us to be silent again.

"I can only tell you this: no database lists a Dr. Mauro Chioggia, mah..."

"Go on," Marino urged.

"Well, I found a tidbit on Manlio Lamberti. He was subjected to disciplinary proceedings, suspended from the register for five years, from 1986 to 1991, and never returned to the field. He chose to teach instead."

"I'll have the records of the disciplinary action requested."

"Wait, I'm not done. He was declared dead in 2020, after disappearing during a hunting trip in 2010 in Romania. I've sent you the newspaper article and the death certificate by email."

"I'll let you beat me at Burraco. You've been fantastic. Thanks, man, I owe you."

"How is it possible that the autopsy report is signed by a ghost?" Andrea asked.

"Could that be the reason for the disciplinary action?" speculated Celeste.

"It's up to us to find out," Marino replied, preparing to leave. "I might be able to help by making a call to my friend, the president of the Medical Association. If he's in a good mood, he might let you peek at the records without having to wait for the usual bureaucracy. But no promises."

"Thank you, Marino," I said, walking him to the door.

He kissed me on the cheek, waved a quick goodbye to the others, and left.

"You two, go finish your conversation with Donadio tomorrow," Celeste instructed. "I have a feeling things are going to get rough. We'll need to track down everyone who was at the event. I'll try to get a complete list by tomorrow afternoon. I think it's best to bring them to the station," he ordered as his phone rang.

"Veneziani?" He listened silently, then gestured at me, his expression troubled. "You won't believe this, but the call came from Romania. The signal was picked up and routed to the nearest tower in Italy from the Constanta area, on the Black Sea."

"Romania, twice now. Could that be a coincidence?" I mused aloud.

Celeste gave me a concerned look, scratching his brow.

"Deputy Inspector, don't let her out of your sight for a second, and if she gives you trouble... shoot her," he finished with a smirk.

"Alright. See you tomorrow, late morning," I said, walking Celeste to the door and bidding him goodnight.

8

We left the house together. By now, Andrea, my self-proclaimed protector, had taken over the guest room, "but only so as not to invade your privacy," he teased, mocking me.

We headed towards Donadio's house, stopping first at our usual café for breakfast. That's where I saw her for the first time. As I struggled to swallow a mouthful of croissant, I noticed a woman across the street. She was minding her own business, yet for some inexplicable reason, she caught my attention.

"Do you know her?" I asked Andrea.

"I don't. Do you?"

"Not at all."

"Then why are you staring? She's just standing there, probably waiting for someone."

"Maybe so, but her face is... I don't know... intriguing..."

I took a long sip of cappuccino and tried to pull myself together, convincing myself I was being paranoid.

Andrea went to the counter to pay the bill. We said goodbye and stepped outside.

I got into the car, trying to act indifferent, but I still glanced at the pavement in front of the café. She was gone.

Donadio's house was in an old building in the center of Turin. Finding a parking spot was a nightmare, and after several curses, Andrea decided to place the magnetic flashing light on the car roof and parked in front of some rubbish bins.

"Let's see them try to give me a fine."

I didn't comment, leaving him behind as I made my way to the building entrance.

Mr. Donadio opened the door without asking who was buzzing, but as we entered, a suspicious man stopped us.

"Who are you here for?" he asked, sounding arrogant.

"We're here to see Mr. Donadio. He's expecting us."

"Poor souls," he said, shaking his head. "The daughter died a second time. That's why you're here, isn't it?"

"For what?" I asked curtly.

"The... the... landslide," he stammered, backpedaling. "I suppose she's not going anywhere..."

"But I didn't do anything," he whimpered.

"I just need to ask you two questions," I said, pulling out my badge.

"Officer, I'm sorry, I didn't mean to be rude."

"Inspector Diletti. And this is Deputy Inspector Pancaldi. We'll speak later."

"C-c-certainly, at your service."

"Your name?" I pressed.

"Giuseppe Marenzi, at your service," he said, bowing with an exaggerated flourish, like a character from a Goldoni play.

I entered the lift, irritated.

"You're wicked. The poor guy was going to crap himself," Andrea commented, amused.

"I detest meddlers and know-it-alls."

"He's a porter," Andrea teased, drawing me closer.

Donadio was waiting at his door.

"Have a seat, and forgive the mess. The lady who helps me with cleaning left for holiday yesterday."

"No worries," I replied.

"Come, I'll introduce you to my Elvira."

The dim light from a table lamp gave the room a ghostly feel. Donadio went to the window, pulling up the blinds, then walked over to a single bed and sat down beside the woman. Her posture was stiff, and her vacant stare didn't change even when he took her hand and gently caressed it.

"Elvira, dear, look at these people; they've come to see you."

For a moment, she seemed to respond, but then she started screaming and shaking. Her movements were violent and erratic. Donadio quickly returned to the window and lowered the blinds.

"She's been like this since that damned day. Only the darkness calms her."

We were stunned. No one should have to endure such torment.

"Come, let's sit in the living room. Would you like some coffee?"

"Don't trouble yourself, Mr. Donadio," I said.

"No trouble at all. I've modernized; I only drink coffee from capsules. Simple."

He disappeared for a moment, returning with three cups on a tray.

"Help me remember where we left off. It's madness here, with little time to think about the outside world. And age doesn't help..."

"You were at the hospital," I said, trying to make him comfortable. "But take your time, we're not in a hurry."

"Everyone seemed to want to avoid me. A nurse told me to wait for the head physician. I didn't have to wait long. A kind man came over and led me to his office. I could see the desperation on his face. He took a deep breath and told me the truth: my baby was stillborn, and my Elvira was in shock. Initially, they assured me she would recover. She had lost two children on the same day, and it was normal for her mind to shut down—a defense against the unbearable pain. But years passed, and my Elvira never woke from her stupor. At first, she repeated one word: 'Beast.' After that, nothing."

"In your opinion, Mr. Donadio, why did your wife initially say 'beast'?" I asked.

"At first, I thought she'd seen something, or someone, but the investigation found no evidence of foul play or intruders. The psychiatrist who treated her said her mind had created a figure to blame—the 'beast'—as part of her defense mechanism."

"And you found this explanation satisfactory?"

"No, Inspector, I always believed my Elvira saw something, but that her pain prevented her from telling me. Yesterday's letter confirmed it."

"Thank you very much, Mr. Donadio. We'll put everything on record when we're back at the office. I'll need you to come to the station to sign it."

"No problem, but may I ask—my Cecilia's been taken to forensics. Why?"

"It's standard procedure. You'll have her back in her resting place soon," I said, bending the truth a little.

"I'll see you to the lift."

"No need."

The porter's lodge appeared to be closed. We rang the bell at the guardhouse several times, but no one answered.

"If he thinks he's being clever by hiding, he's mistaken. I'll have him escorted to the station."

"The door looks open," Andrea said quietly.

"Mr. Giuseppe, are you there? This is Deputy Inspector Pancaldi."

"We're coming in!" I shouted, but something was blocking the door.

"Can you see what's in the way?" Andrea asked, pushing harder.

"There's someone down!" he yelled.

"Who?"

"Looks like the porter. I can only see his feet."

"You stay here and call Celeste. I'll try the guardhouse window."

I ran to the window and tried to force it open, but it was locked from the inside.

"Andrea, can you get the door open?"

"No, the body's blocking it, and I'm afraid of injuring him."

With the butt of my gun, I smashed the window, shattering the glass. I climbed over the counter and entered the lodge.

I immediately saw the body lying on the floor. I knelt down, stunned—it had been decapitated, and the head was missing.

"Andrea, go around; we can't move him. He's dead."

His clothes were soaked in blood, which had pooled near a lower section of the floor, making it hard to spot at first.

"Jesus Christ, Maria, a little warning!" Andrea exclaimed, catching sight of the corpse.

"In my bag—hand me the gloves."

I pulled out my phone and began taking photos and videos. There was no trace of the head; it was gone. Oddly, there were no blood trails leading away from the body, where there should have been. I checked his pockets—no handkerchief, no receipts, no phone. Had the killer taken it? Maybe he never had one, given the landline on the counter. I picked up the handset and pressed redial. Nothing. No numbers were saved.

Forensics arrived, and a technician approached.

"Good morning, Inspector. Please tell me you haven't touched anything," he said with a hint of arrogance. I didn't dignify him with a response. "Do we know who it is?" he continued.

I stepped aside, revealing the body.

"He was decapitated?" he exclaimed.

"Nothing gets past you," I said, stepping back.

I resisted the urge to snap at the rude technician and exited the lodge.

Celeste and Spatafora arrived shortly after.

"Where are they?" asked Spatafora.

I shrugged and walked out the door. I needed air—the place had become a gas chamber from the forensic chemicals. Marino and his assistant arrived in the van, and I saw him stepping out.

"I hear there's not much left to study," Marino greeted grimly.

I returned inside with him and joined Celeste.

"Are we sure it's the porter?" asked Celeste.

"Not absolutely, but the clothes match. It's the same outfit he was wearing when we entered the building. I'd planned to ask him some questions, but when we left and rang the bell, he was already dead."

"Have you spoken to the residents?"

"I don't think anyone has noticed anything. It's a quiet building, full of hard-working people. No one's come through that door in the last hour."

Celeste sighed, as if bracing for whatever was to come.

The forensic team completed their work and signaled they were done.

"You may proceed," said the technician with whom I had argued earlier.

Marino knelt beside the body, and I placed a hand on his back.

"What kind of weapon are we looking for?" I asked.

"Maybe none. More likely, it's a person—someone big and strong enough to tear a head off with his bare hands. That's who you're looking for," he said, pointing at the neck. "See here? These aren't marks from a blade. The head was removed by dislocating the neck vertebrae, and then," he pointed closer, "these are bite marks. Once the vertebrae were dislocated, the killer tore through the tissues, a cannibal."

We stared at Marino, stunned and horrified.

"This could be the same person who killed Cecilia. The modus operandi is similar," I said, my stomach turning.

"He's refined his technique and strength since then," Marino replied. "I'll be able to confirm more once I've completed the analysis."

He signaled his assistant to bring the stretcher over for the body.

"I'm heading back to the station. Keep me updated. Commissioner, you're coming with me," Spatafora said, walking off, with Celeste following closely behind.

9

The drive to the police station was silent and quick, as most drivers were at lunch. Andrea slowed down, turning on the indicator to enter the service car park, when I noticed her again—the woman from earlier, sitting at the bus stop across the street. She seemed to blend in with the other passengers, but I was sure it was her.

"Her again!" I exclaimed, tugging on Andrea's sleeve. He had to brake abruptly, narrowly avoiding hitting the car park wall.

"Are you crazy? You want to kill us?" he shouted, trying to pull free from my grip.

"Look!" I pointed towards the bus stop, where she was still seated.

Before Andrea could reply, I opened the door and jumped out of the car.

The street was suddenly bustling with traffic, making it impossible for me to cross.

"Nooo...," I groaned as I saw the bus pulling up.

Instinctively, I reached for my holster, thinking to draw my gun and stop the bus from leaving.

A hand clamped down on mine, stopping me.

"Are you out of your mind?" Andrea hissed in my ear, keeping me in place.

The bus loaded passengers and departed, the platform quickly emptying.

"Let's go after it," I urged him, my frustration boiling over.

"Stay still, or I'll handcuff you," he snapped, trying to keep me calm.

"Get back in the car," Andrea ordered.

I glared at him but obeyed, knowing he was right.

"You want to tell me why you're so fixated on that woman?"

"I don't know, but I have this feeling I know her, and I'm sure she's trying to find a way to approach me. Yesterday she was near the café, and today she's across from the station. She's following me, and when she sees I'm not alone, she disappears."

"I don't know, Maria... but this case is going to drive us all crazy," he muttered, doubt creeping into his voice.

We walked into the police station just in time to hear Celeste cursing, having just been informed that the press had already gotten wind of the incident.

"How is this possible? The body was still warm, and she... this... this...," he hesitated, avoiding a harsher insult, "already claims to know who the killer is." He slammed his fist on the desk. "Come in, why are you just standing there?"

We sat quietly, letting Celeste vent his frustration.

"You do know, don't you, that a huge pile of crap just fell on us? So big that we might drown in it," Celeste fumed as he sank into his chair. "Well? Don't you have anything to say?" he taunted, daring us to respond.

We kept silent, knowing that anything we said would only fuel his outburst.

My patience, however, was wearing thin. I left Celeste's office and went to mine, only for my phone to vibrate. It was Marino.

"Marino, have you finished Marenzi's autopsy?"

"Listen, Maria, something terrible has happened," he said, his voice grave.

"What is it, Marino?"

"The body... Cecilia Donadio's body..."

"Marino, for God's sake, speak up!" I raised my voice.

"It's been stolen..."

"What did you say?" I shot up from my chair.

"The girl's body, it was stolen. I think it happened while we were dealing with Marenzi's murder."

"How could this happen?"

"I don't know, Maria, I just don't know..."

"I'll have Celeste call in every available unit. We're on our way."

I hung up and, in a fit of frustration, threw my phone on the desk.

I rushed back to Celeste's office. Andrea was still there, in the same spot, looking like he wanted to tear something apart.

"They stole Cecilia Donadio's body," I blurted out, waiting for Celeste's inevitable reaction.

"I must have misheard," he said, his hands clenched into fists. "They stole... what?"

"That's enough!" he thundered, slamming both fists on the desk. "How the hell did they manage to steal a body..."

"Maybe... while Marino was preoccupied with Marenzi's murder," I suggested cautiously.

"Are you telling me no one else was in the forensic department while Marino was out? There are about thirty people working there, plus guards who rotate around the clock." Celeste's face was flushed, and he was breathing heavily, as if he'd just run a marathon. I feared he was on the verge of a heart attack.

"Marino Piano is waiting for us," I said softly, avoiding his piercing gaze.

Andrea was the first to leave the office, muttering that he'd wait at the car.

"It's no longer just a pile of crap; it's a wall—a tsunami of it. We'll never wash this off," Celeste continued to rant as we walked to the car, his tirade only stopping when we got in.

We drove to the forensic institute, and Andrea flashed his badge at the guard, who promptly raised the barrier. Marino was waiting for us by the side entrance, looking as if he'd seen a ghost.

"What's going on, Marino?" Celeste demanded.

"Nothing makes sense. No one saw anything," Marino said, bewildered.

"In broad daylight, Marino? How is that possible?" Celeste persisted, his face turning red again.

"The only possibility is that someone hid inside last night and managed to sneak out with the body after the night guard finished his last patrol. At that moment, the guards sign out, and their fingerprints activate the system connected to the cameras. During that minute, the cameras reboot to save the recordings. I had a DVD of the recording prepared."

There was a moment of tense silence before Marino led us to the central entrance, where the guardhouse was located. The guard handed over the DVD.

"You've got twelve hours of footage. Good luck," he said, smirking.

I snatched the DVD from his hand and left, suppressing the urge to punch him.

"Marino," Celeste said, "go back and deal with Marenzi's case. I'll speak with the commissioner. We need to keep the disappearance of Cecilia Donadio's body under wraps, at least for now. And you two," he said, glaring at us, "lock yourselves in the office. Watch every second of that recording, and I forbid you from arguing," he added, pointing directly at me.

"Aren't you coming back with us?" Andrea asked.

"No. I've already called Calabrò to pick me up. I'm going to speak with Spatafora in person."

"Alright, then we'll head out," Andrea said as we drove off.

"Twelve hours of footage... I haven't watched that much in ages," Andrea grumbled.

"Let's split it between four people—three hours each. It'll go faster," I suggested.

"Sounds like a plan," Andrea agreed, relieved.

Back at the office, I called two colleagues: Aldo Panerai and Federico Cosma.

"Guys, we have twelve hours of video to go through. It'll be quicker with four of us. Can you help?"

"Sure," Panerai replied.

"I'm in," Cosma echoed.

"Great. Take the DVD to Veneziani so he can split it into four and send it to us. Thanks."

I organized my office, making it comfortable for all of us, and ordered snacks from a nearby café, realizing how hungry I was. But my plan fell apart when the office phone rang.

"Veneziani here. I need you to come down."

"I'm on my way."

I left without explaining, noticing the confused looks from the others. I knocked on Veneziani's office door.

"Come in, Inspector."

"What's the issue, Veneziani?"

"The DVD is empty."

"What do you mean?"

"It didn't record anything, as if there was a system blackout. Sorry, Inspector."

"Thanks, Veneziani."

I returned to my office, seething.

"The DVD is empty. Someone's playing games with us."

Without waiting for a response, I called Celeste, but he didn't answer. So, I called Marino.

"Marino, do you know the guard who gave us the DVD?"

"Yes, Davanzi. He's been here a few months, replacing Remo, who retired. Why?"

"He gave us a blank DVD."

"He must not have known. I'll head to the guardhouse and check. Give me 15 minutes."

He hung up before I could argue, already anticipating my impatience.

The office phone rang again—it was the café delivery.

"Cosma, could you grab the food?" I asked.

"Inspector," Panerai said, "these recordings sometimes fail or get corrupted. Copying them can erase the data."

"Thanks, Panerai. Let's hope that's all it is."

Cosma returned with our food, and we ate while waiting for Marino to call.

It wasn't long before he did.

"I have bad news. The recording doesn't exist."

"What do you mean?" I asked, irritated.

"The system froze from 6 PM yesterday until 6 AM this morning. It rebooted only when Davanzi came on duty."

"Then why give us a DVD?"

"He probably didn't check it."

"Fine... we're back to square one. Is forensics done with the surveys?"

"Yes, but they didn't find any unusual prints."

"Just like Marenzi's gatehouse..." I said, ending the call.

"Are we ever going to get anywhere?" Andrea asked, sounding defeated.

"Listen," I turned to Cosma and Panerai. "Tomorrow, Celeste wants the list of names from the 'Two of Spades' incident on his desk. Can you handle organizing the interviews?"

"Of course. Any tips?" Panerai asked.

"Don't make it sound like an interrogation. We don't want them to shut down with 'I don't remember.'"

"Got it, Inspector. We'll head out now."

Andrea and I were tidying up the office when Cosma returned.

"Sorry, but on our way out, we heard an emergency call from the forensic institute. Squad cars are heading there. I thought you should know."

"What now?" I muttered, frustrated.

The sun hadn't set yet, even though it was 9 PM on that hot June evening. The car was warm, and I threw my sweater onto the back seat, turning up the AC.

I noticed Andrea glancing at me.

"Keep your eyes on the road."

"Red light ahead," he replied, nodding toward the windshield.

I said nothing, lost in thought, until we took the turn leading to the institute. A squad car sped past, sirens blaring, and Andrea cursed.

"Idiots. Didn't they see our plates?"

We pulled up to the entrance, and an officer signaled for us to stop. I stepped out, showing my badge.

Another car arrived behind us—Celeste and Spatafora.

"Will we ever be free of this nightmare?" Spatafora whispered, uncharacteristically somber.

An ambulance was parked near the guardhouse. I approached, noticing two paramedics tending to someone. It was Davanzi, sobbing as one of them took his blood pressure.

"What happened?"

"Inspector, I've never seen anything like it," he cried.

"Is he alright?" I asked the paramedic.

"Just shock and fright. We'll do an ECG, and if it's clear, he'll be sent home to rest."

I thanked her and turned to go inside, but a man in a white suit stopped me.

"We meet again. Today's been a long one, huh? But if you're going in there, you'll need to suit up."

I glared at him, biting back a retort.

Suiting up, I stepped inside. On the console, in full view, was Giuseppe Marenzi's head. I clamped a hand over my mouth.

"Don't puke in here. We still need to do the bio-surveys," the technician warned.

I was about to lash out but decided against it, leaving the room to avoid disrupting their work.

I ran into Marino. "I came as soon as I was called. They interrupted my Burraco night," he said, irritated.

"Tell me about it. I was ready to relax on the couch with a glass of wine."

"With your bodyguard," he teased, walking away.

"Lovely," I thought sarcastically.

I joined Andrea, Celeste, and Spatafora, who were deep in discussion.

"This has to be seen as a warning. They didn't bring it back out of kindness," Spatafora said.

"Have you spoken to the guard?" Celeste asked.

"No, he was being treated when we arrived. I'll check now."

"Mr. Davanzi, can you tell us what happened?"

"I was supposed to finish at 10 PM, but my colleague asked me for a favor..."

"Was this arranged in advance?" I interrupted.

"He asked this morning at shift change. I still live with family, so I'm happy to help those who have their own."

"Do you know why he needed the change?"

"No, ma'am... I mean, Inspector Diletti. I just do my job."

"Go on."

"We were to switch at 10, but from the station, they activate the alarm once we report that our inspection is complete. If they don't hear from us, they call to check. Sometimes doctors stay late, so we alert them not to set the alarm."

"So you did your rounds and reported in?"

48

"Yes, I have my mobile... but I phoned and then stepped out for a cigarette."

"How long were you away from the guardhouse?"

"The round takes about fifteen minutes. I checked that lab doors were locked, firebreaks closed, lights off. Called the station, then had a smoke. About twenty minutes. Routine."

"And once the alarm is set, no one can enter, correct?"

"Yes, that's right. We enter through the side door to avoid triggering it."

"Alright, Mr. Davanzi. No vacations for now—I might need you again."

"Understood, Inspector. I'm not going anywhere."

I returned to the trio as Celeste was venting.

"Listen to this," he said, holding his phone, tuned to a news channel. "This is a nightmare."

"I'm reporting from the entrance of the Institute of Forensic Medicine, where a night watchman discovered the severed head of Giuseppe Marenzi, murdered earlier today in his own home. Authorities are tight-lipped, but what were Inspector Diletti and her deputy doing here? We asked around and found that a family connected to the 'Two of Spades' fire in 1986 resides nearby. But that's not all. Cecilia Donadio, the girl in question, was buried in the cemetery that collapsed. What ties these cases together? Why was Marenzi's head found here? Are the authorities hiding something, or are they just groping in the dark?"

From Turin, I'm Mara Mezzani."

"I'm going to arrest her," Celeste fumed, only to be stopped by Spatafora.

"Don't be foolish, Commissioner. That sensationalist doesn't have anything concrete. We're done here for now. You all need rest. Goodnight."

"Celeste, let's give you a ride home," I said, as we made our way back to the car.

10

The next morning, I arrived at the police station more tired than when I went to bed, a few minutes late and alone.

"Where's Pancaldi?" Celeste snapped. "What part of 'you must not be alone' is unclear to you?"

"Good morning to you too, Celeste. Come on, don't overdo it. Andrea had to stop by his place to grab a change of clothes. He hasn't had the chance yet."

"Alright, fine, but it's useless with you anyway. Cosma and Panerai told me you already briefed them on how to proceed with the interviews."

"Yes, I did that yesterday afternoon."

"Let's go to your office; maybe we can have a quieter discussion there."

I offered Celeste the chair behind my desk and sat in the chair opposite, knowing full well that his need for 'quiet' meant he wanted to grill me.

"Shall we wait for Andrea?" he asked.

"If you don't mind," I replied.

"Well, I have a quick call to make. I'll be right back," he muttered, leaving the room.

I took the opportunity to call Cosma and Panerai.

"Can I ask you to try reaching Captain Luca Perri?"

"Inspector, to interview the captain, we need the commissioner's approval," Cosma replied.

"Then get it, and in the meantime, keep going down the list Celeste gave you."

"Alright, Inspector. We're heading to the station now. We have two interviews this morning: Sister Ada Garzina and Sandra Venerato."

"Ada Garzina became a nun?"

"You knew her, Inspector?"

"Didn't Celeste inform you? I knew all those girls. We were in school together. I was supposed to be at that cursed party, but a fever kept me home."

"Damn, Inspector. No, nobody told us. I'm sorry; these are wounds that should never be reopened."

"Thank you, Cosma, you're always kind."

Celeste returned as Cosma and Panerai were leaving.

"I asked them to go straight to the police station and seek permission to speak with Captain Luca Perri."

"You did well, assuming your superior allows it. You know how tricky dealing with the Carabinieri can be." He smiled, lightening the mood just as Andrea walked in.

"Are we having a meeting?" Andrea asked, sarcastically.

"Sit down," Celeste said, cutting to the point.

"Maria, I want your perspective."

I took a moment to organize my thoughts and tried to present them clearly.

"A little girl was bitten to death during an incident, but this was only discovered thirty-six years later, by chance. The initial autopsy report stated that the cause of death was exsanguination from a cut to the right jugular, caused by a strobe light dislodged due to toxic fumes from the fire. The case was closed as an accident, and the owner was fined for not upgrading the electrical system. It would have ended there, but thirty-six years later, part of the cemetery where she was buried collapsed. Her body was exposed, requiring it to be taken to the Forensic Institute for identification. Marino discovered that the cause of death was not what the original report claimed—she was murdered. So, we have: a murder concealed for decades, an inaccurate autopsy, a letter confirming to the family that the murder happened, an inspector who remembers nothing or pretends not to, a coroner who doesn't exist, another declared dead, and a recent murder with similar decapitation. Plus, an unknown figure leaves us Marenzi's head as a warning to drop the case. Before that, they called and threatened me. Conclusions? Unfortunately, none."

Celeste looked at me, tired and aware that despite all the details, we had no clear path forward.

The office phone rang, and I answered.

"Marino? I'm putting you on speaker," I said, to avoid unnecessary questions from those present.

"I finished checking the letter paper. There's nothing on it besides Donadio's prints and yours. Have you not heard of gloves?"

"Cut it out, Marino. Get to the point," Celeste scolded.

"It wasn't a joke. Anyway, on the envelope, besides your lovely prints, I found Marenzi's too."

"Anything else?" I prompted.

"Yes. I confirm that the footprints in the cold room and autopsy room are all ours. Whoever acted wore gloves—no signs of wiped-off prints. Same goes for the guard room. That's all I have for now. I'll update you once I know more about the bites on the girl's neck and Marenzi's."

"Thank you, Marino."

"Well, we know one more thing," Celeste said. "But it's just more crap added to the pile."

I stormed out, slamming the door. Andrea, seeing my frustration, raised his arms in surrender.

"He's worse than a child when he's angry," I muttered.

Screams echoed down the corridor. We stepped out to see what was happening. Two officers were struggling to restrain a man.

"Inspector, please, this man is asking for you. We tried to tell him you were in a meeting, but..."

"Mr. Donadio!" I exclaimed in surprise. "Let him through."

I gently took his arm and guided him into the office.

"I had to find out from the television that my Cecilia is gone. They took her away from me. What am I supposed to do now?" He looked at me, his face twisted in sorrow. Then, clutching his chest, he gasped, "I can't breathe..." His knees buckled, and Andrea rushed to support him. We laid him down, trying to keep his head steady.

He was pale, his face sharp like a blade. I checked his pulse—nothing.

"Someone call 911!" Celeste yelled, bursting out of his office.

"Mr. Donadio, answer me," I pleaded, slapping him gently.

I tried CPR, but it was no use. Giovanni Donadio died right there, the moment he heard his daughter's body had disappeared.

Another murder. Because whoever started this mess was responsible for his death, too, I thought angrily.

I ran out of the station, needing air, and lit a cigarette.

"Another one? You'll smoke yourself to death," Andrea commented.

"Leave me alone, Andrea. Go back inside." I walked a few steps away.

The ambulance arrived, but the paramedics could only pronounce him dead.

I glanced around, looking for an ashtray, and there she was again—the woman. Standing across the street, she smiled and gave a shy wave. Before I could react, everything went black.

Someone was slapping me awake. "Welcome back," a male voice said.

"What happened?" My head throbbed.

"You fainted and fell flat. You're lucky you didn't break your nose, just got a nasty bump. You'll need to come with us for some tests."

"No way. I'm just stressed, working too much, eating too little. Nothing a good meal can't fix."

"But you hit your head. You need an MRI," the paramedic insisted.

"Where do I sign?" I said curtly.

"Your choice," he sighed. "Anto, get the refusal form."

Andrea handed me a cup of hot tea.

"Here, this might help."

"Thanks," I said, sipping gratefully.

"Maria, what's going on?" Marino's voice came from behind.

"Just exhaustion playing tricks on me."

"You need time off. I'm suggesting it to Celeste," Marino said.

"Dare, and I'll shoot you," I replied, managing a wink.

Andrea helped me pick up my things, and we rejoined Marino, who had started examining Donadio's body. Celeste handed him the doctor's report from the paramedics.

"Acute myocardial infarction... they should lose their license," Marino scoffed.

"Explain yourself, Dr. Piano," Celeste pressed.

"Smell that bitter almond scent? It's cyanide, homemade."

We all stood there, stunned, watching Marino as he calmly continued examining the body.

"Any more surprises, Doctor?" Celeste asked, his face livid.

"Unfortunately, yes. But they don't concern poor Mr. Donadio."

"Then if you're done, let's move to my office."

"Give me a moment to have the body taken away," Marino replied, then followed us.

"Maria, are you up for this, or would you rather go home? It wouldn't be a bad idea," Celeste asked as we entered his office.

"Why does everyone care so much about my health? I'm fine, end of discussion," I snapped.

Celeste shot me a disapproving look but sat down, muttering under his breath.

"There are too many victims now. Someone wants this to end. But who, and why?" Celeste wondered aloud, rubbing his forehead before taking a sip of water.

Marino entered, a report in hand.

"I've got the bite analysis from both Cecilia Donadio and Giuseppe Marenzi. No DNA in either case. We couldn't investigate Cecilia further for obvious reasons, but on Marenzi, I can say there's no sign of a struggle. He seemed to let himself be killed. And before you ask, the toxicology report came back clean, but without DNA, we're stuck."

"How is it possible there's no DNA from the bites?" I asked.

"It's as if the killer sterilized the area, removing any chance of genetic detection."

"So you found other material in the wounds?"

"No, it's just a deduction."

The situation was exhausting. Every lead seemed to lead nowhere.

A knock on the door interrupted us. Cosma peeked in.

"Can I come in?" he asked hesitantly.

"Of course, get on with it," Celeste said, irritated.

"There's a problem..." Cosma began reluctantly. "There's a name on the list, Ludmilla Geoana. She doesn't exist in any registry—alive, transferred, or deceased. She's nowhere. What should I do?"

"That's not possible," I retorted. "I knew her. We went to school together for five years. Damn it, she exists or existed."

"Excuse me, Inspector, but look at this," Cosma insisted, handing me several papers.

They were results from database searches across Italy—nothing.

"Have you tried requesting school records?"

"I was planning to, but I wanted permission first. I'll need a warrant."

I turned to Celeste. "We need that warrant quickly. Can you ask Spatafora?"

"Sorry to interject," Andrea cut in, "but remember the Frassi case? We don't need a warrant for school records. You can apply directly to the Ministry of Education. They have records for all students from primary school onwards."

"You're right. I hadn't thought of that," I said, then turned back to Celeste. "But still, ask Spatafora. We need to expedite this, and bureaucracy isn't our friend."

"It's clear someone is trying to mislead us. We need to figure out what's behind this before it slips out of our grasp entirely. Find Ludmilla Geoana. She can't have just vanished. Now, everyone, get back to work," Celeste urged, dismissing us.

11

In the midst of all the chaos, I decided to take care of Mrs. Donadio. Since the couple had no relatives, it was easy to get the judge to appoint me as her legal guardian. I found an excellent care facility for her, where she would be well looked after. The entire police district got involved; Mr. Donadio had, in his way, left an impression on everyone's heart.

That morning, Celeste had a scheduled meeting with Spatafora at the police station. He asked me to accompany him, so I instructed Andrea to join Cosma and Panerai to continue with the interviews—it was crucial to wrap them up.

Instead of his office, Spatafora was waiting for us in the security room.

"I apologize, but here we can be sure no one will overhear us," he said, suggesting there was a mole within the police headquarters who had tipped off Mara Mezzani about confidential matters.

"I spoke to the Ministry attaché, but there's bad news. Apparently, a fire at the Turin Superintendency in 1986 destroyed records from public schools for that school year. However, it didn't end there. The following year, when students enrolled in middle school, they cross-referenced the names of those who passed their exams to try and undo the damage. But, despite their best efforts, Ludmilla Geoana's name still doesn't show up. I have a warrant ready here, which you will use at the school—somewhere, that name must be found."

"What about our request to interview Captain Perri?" I asked.

"Inspector, the captain has been working with the joint homicide section in Romania for years, which makes him practically unreachable. I can't exactly pick a fight with General Giffoni over it. Let's see what the other interviews yield, and if we come up empty, I'll find a way to get you in touch with Perri."

"If there's nothing else," Celeste said, "we're heading to the school. We should have an update in a few hours."

"Sure, go ahead, and good luck," Spatafora replied.

"Always live the wolf!" I said, a response I knew would irritate him, given Spatafora's disdain for animal references.

Romania again...

It was rare for me to do fieldwork with Celeste, and I found it exciting. It reminded me of our days patrolling together—good times.

"I'm calling Cosma; he should have spoken with Sister Ada Garzina yesterday."

"And what does she have to do with the school?" Celeste asked, puzzled.

I motioned for him to wait, as the call connected.

"Inspector?" Cosma answered.

"Cosma, did you manage to speak with the nun yesterday?"

"Yes, but she's not just a nun—she's the Mother Superior of St. Martyr's School, and she has quite a presence."

"Really? And how did she react to your questions?"

"She deflected all of them, hiding behind the fact that she wasn't present at the party. But I can tell you this much: she still has a very negative opinion of that Ludmilla. I swear, Inspector, Ludmilla has even started haunting my dreams."

"Tell me about it... Anyway, thanks, Cosma. Talk soon."

We began walking up the slope that led to the school. I pressed my nose against the car window, lost in thought.

"Do you remember when I used to pick you up with your parents to go swimming?" Celeste said suddenly.

"I do. Good times—carefree," I replied.

We were received by Sister Ada herself.

"Maria Diletti! What a pleasure to see you. Did you bring your husband for a visit?" she greeted, smiling.

"Inspector Maria Diletti. And this is Commissioner Adelmo Celeste. We're not here on a social visit, and he is not my husband," I corrected her.

"But we do have a search warrant," Celeste added, with a mischievous smirk.

"A search warrant? For what?" she said, her smile fading.

"Just a precaution, really. But if you cooperate, we can tear it up," Celeste offered, attempting to barter.

"Please, have a seat," she said, reluctantly leading us inside.

The school interior hadn't changed since I left it. Even the pupils, still an all-girls institution, looked the same. Ada sat us down in her office, doing her best to make us feel comfortable.

"I'm at your disposal. What do you need?"

"Enrollment and attendance records from 1980 to 1986," Celeste said, as I stood in the corner, trying to avoid making Ada uncomfortable by leveraging our familiarity.

"But those were our school years, weren't they?" she said, catching on.

Exactly what I'd hoped to avoid. I simply nodded.

"I'd say you're in luck. In 2000, we digitized everything. We have records going back to 1947," she said, her tone shifting to a more formal pitch.

"Then let's get to the computer!" Celeste said eagerly.

"Yes, but we need to head to the offices. My computer here doesn't have access to the registration folder. But, if I may ask, what are you looking for? Did I say something suspicious to your colleagues yesterday?"

"Mother Superior, it has nothing to do with yesterday. We are looking for Ludmilla Geoana's records," I explained.

Ada's face turned pale but quickly composed itself.

"And why come to us when you could check the superintendency?"

"We have our reasons. Is that a problem?" Celeste snapped, cutting off further evasion.

Ada stood up, and we followed her to the bursar's office.

"Sister Margherita, please assist these officers with whatever they need," she instructed a young nun sitting at a computer.

"Welcome, have a seat. I'll just finish what I'm doing, and I'll be right with you," the nun said politely.

"I'll leave you to Sister Margherita. I have other tasks to attend to, but I'll return shortly," Ada said, excusing herself.

"What can I help you with?" Sister Margherita asked.

"We need to access enrollment and attendance records from 1980 to 1986," Celeste repeated.

"Enrollment records are no problem, but we no longer have attendance logs. We're only required to keep those for five years."

"Give us what you can, Sister Margherita. Thank you," Celeste replied.

The nun began typing, and a few seconds later, the system beeped as it loaded.

"Here are the records starting from 1980. Would you like to handle it yourself, or should I assist you?"

"Please, Sister. Your expertise would be much appreciated," Celeste said, with a smile.

"I'll print everything out for you. It's just a few pages."

She returned shortly with the documents.

"Here you go. Feel free to use my desk. I'll be over there, working, if you need anything," she said, before stepping aside.

We skimmed through the printed names.

"Here she is: Ludmilla Geoana, enrolled in first grade on June 6, 1980. Then every subsequent year, until June 15, 1985—her last year," Celeste whispered.

"Sister, we're done. Can we keep these pages?" I asked, knowing she would likely comply.

"Of course. Anything else I can assist with?"

"No, Sister, you've been more than kind," Celeste said, bowing slightly.

As we left, we ran into Ada in the corridor.

"All done already?" she asked.

"Couldn't have been easier, thanks to Sister Margherita," Celeste replied.

"Then if your task is complete, I suggest you take your leave," Ada said, leading us to the exit.

"Right, let's not overstay our welcome," Celeste quipped, stepping out first.

"Maria, only you seem unaware of the darkness surrounding Ludmilla. She will answer for it one day, before the Lord."

"Sister Ada, that's a heavy accusation without evidence. Perhaps you know more than you're letting on?" Celeste said, his tone turning stern.

She glanced at me, seeking support, but I avoided her gaze.

"I... I didn't mean anything by it. Just a thought. I apologize," she stammered.

"That was a clear accusation, Sister, but let's leave it there. Do not leave Turin," Celeste ordered.

"I'm afraid that's not possible. Tomorrow morning, I'm being taken to the Vatican."

"You'll have to cancel, or I will arrest you," Celeste said, his tone firm.

Her defiant look met his unwavering stare.

"Next time, inform us before you make any travel plans," he said, leaving without another word.

"What do you think she's going to do at the Vatican?" Celeste asked, as we walked out.

"No idea—maybe a spiritual retreat," I replied.

"Why does she hate Ludmilla so much?"

"Not just Ludmilla. She was an unconventional child—kind, but shy. Very beautiful, well-dressed, articulate, and always top of her class. Ada was always second. They competed in everything: grades, answering the teacher first, even being the first to enter the classroom. But they were still just kids. The rest of the class sided with Ada, except me, Ludmilla's only friend. And whenever there was a scapegoat, it was Ludmilla."

"Seems like there was a lot of madness and spite," Celeste remarked.

"We're talking about ten-year-olds, Celeste."

"Wasn't it Marino Piano who said the bite marks could be from someone around that age?"

"Yes, he did, but he couldn't explore that hypothesis further after Cecilia Donadio's body disappeared. You're not seriously buying into the cock-craving nun's words..."

"Cock... what?" he laughed.

"I'm starving. Let's grab lunch at that place near the 'Gran Madre'."

"Yes, let's," he agreed.

After a divine meal at Matteo Ferrero's, our spirits lifted.

"So, how does a person just vanish? It's impossible," Celeste mused.

"We're missing something crucial. But if we figure it out, we'll have this case in the bag," I said.

"Do you also have doubts about Ludmilla?"

"No, but I'd like to talk to her, hear her side. Maybe she saw something that day..." I paused, then a thought hit me. "What if she was put under protection? Could that explain her disappearance?"

"Why would they protect her?"

"She was there. Maybe she saw the killer. Maybe he's still out there, and maybe he's killed again."

"Protected for thirty-six years? Unlikely. But if they changed the family's identity... Maria, you're brilliant!" He stood and planted a kiss on my cheek.

"We need to bring Carlo Delbono in, but this time to the station. Agreed?"

"Fine. I'll handle it, and I'll speak to Spatafora about obtaining access to any relevant documents. This won't be easy," I warned.

After a delightful coffee and liqueur, we took a walk to digest. The sun had started to set, casting a golden hue over the Murazzi. Suddenly, Celeste's phone rang, and he stepped aside to take the call, leaving me to check my messages.

One message stood out, from an unknown number:

"Inspector, I warned you. You are crossing a line, and there will be no going back. Painful changes await you. Take this chance, slim as it is, to forget about Cecilia Donadio. A friend."

My vision blurred as I read the final words. I could hardly breathe as I fought back tears of rage. Whatever it took, I would see this through, even if it cost me my life.

Celeste ended his call, noticing my distress. "Maria, what's wrong?"

I handed him my phone.

"This is a direct threat. I'll assign you an escort and pull you off the case."

"Don't even think about it! I'll accept the escort, but you're not taking me off this investigation," I snapped.

"Maria, this is serious—your life is at risk!"

"Celeste, I'm the only one who can see this through to the end."

"Fine. But let's head back and have Veneziani trace that message. It won't be easy..."

I said nothing more, and Celeste, understanding me well, left me to my thoughts during the ride back to the station.

"Veneziani!" Celeste barked as we entered.

"What's wrong?" Veneziani asked, startled.

"This," Celeste said, thrusting my phone toward him. "Find the origin of this message. Get whatever you need to do it."

Veneziani nodded, taking the phone, and I headed back to my office, declining Celeste's gesture to follow him.

I dialed Andrea.

"It's me."

"What's going on?" he asked, his tone tense.

"He sent a message this time."

"I'm coming to you. Nothing is adding up here, and I need to be with you."

"Inspector?" Cosma said, peeking through the door.

"Come in."

"There's Panerai too."

"Both of you, come in."

"We finished the interviews, but... nothing new came up," Cosma began. "Most of them barely remember the day, and two are dead. Sara Delvecchio, who passed away from breast cancer in 2001, and Amanda Di Corato, who died in a mountain accident in 2010 in Romania."

"What did you just say?" I asked, my voice cracking.

"Uh... Amanda Di Corato, died... in Romania, in 2010."

I couldn't believe it. "What the...?"

I quickly called Celeste. "Get in here right now!"

"What's going on?" Celeste asked, barging in.

"Cosma, repeat everything to the boss," I instructed.

"You think she was with Lamberti?" Celeste asked after hearing Cosma out.

"It's possible, and we need to investigate."

"I was just talking to Spatafora. He said he has contacts in the prosecutor's office and expects to give us good news soon."

"Thank you, Cosma, Panerai. Dismissed."

"How are you holding up?" Andrea asked as he entered.

"I'm fine. But tracing that message won't be quick. Meanwhile, there's another interesting lead. Amanda Di Corato, one of the girls, died in Romania. In 2010."

"Romania again. It's like a death trap. If you want to die, head to Romania," Andrea quipped, trying to lighten the mood.

"Can I shoot him?" Celeste deadpanned.

"Here, take my gun," I chuckled.

"I'm going home," I said, grabbing my things.

"Not alone," Celeste reminded me.

"Who's my escort?"

"Calabrò and Armando."

"My house is big, and there's a spare room with a bathroom. But they're not staying outside, scaring the neighbors."

"They have to stand guard outside, that's non-negotiable," Celeste said, firm.

I hurried to shower once I got home. The cold blast of water jolted me awake. Andrea had probably turned on the water in the other bathroom, messing with the temperature—typical.

As I stepped out, still muttering under my breath, I couldn't help but smile at how absurdly protective Andrea was being.

Later, I set the table and handed out plates of rice salad to the officers on duty, who seemed grateful.

"Celeste summoned Carlo Delbono for tomorrow morning," I told Andrea.

"Do you think he'll reveal anything? If he even knows anything?"

"You weren't convinced last time," I reminded him.

"It was just a feeling," he muttered, mouth full of rice salad.

As we cleared the table, Celeste's call came through.

"You nailed it, Maria. Ludmilla Geoana and Robert Du Jardin entered witness protection on July 29, 1986. Through unofficial channels, Spatafora learned they were relocated to... Romania. You're not going to like this, but there it is."

"Romania? Why? This means the one threatening me could be them. How do we handle this, Celeste?"

"There's only one way. Go directly to Romania and speak with Captain Perri. He was the one who terminated the protection order in 1993."

"Will you authorize the trip? Of course, Andrea would come too."

"If Spatafora gives the green light, you can leave soon," Celeste agreed.

"We'll return with the solution in hand. You're the best, Celeste!"

"Thank me later, let's see what the commissioner decides."

I spent the night restless, adrenaline coursing through me, and when Andrea found me at six a.m., I was barely awake, head on my laptop.

"Get up, you're drooling on the keyboard," he teased.

"I don't drool," I protested, wiping my face.

"It's eight o'clock."

"Damn, we're late!" I yelled, jumping up.

We made it to the station just before nine, and I dashed to Celeste's office.

"Well?" I asked breathlessly.

"Good morning, Inspector," he said, grinning.

"Yes, yes, good morning," I said impatiently.

"We're booking your flight and hotel," he said, finally.

"Thank you! Thank you so much!"

"Just remember, if this trip yields nothing, it's my neck on the line. If that happens, I'll take it out on you. Understand?"

12

Flying has never been one of my favorite activities. I've always thought "flying" is a verb unsuited for humanity. My composure typically disappears as soon as I'm forced to board a plane, but fortunately, they didn't skimp on bourbon upon request.

Andrea laughed when he saw me ask for the first bottle.

"Do you know who will be waiting for us?" he asked.

"Captain Perri himself."

"What an honor... escorted by a carabiniere..."

"Stop fooling around," I scolded, asking the stewardess, who was serving snacks, for another bottle of bourbon.

"You're the only Italian I know who copes with nerves using bourbon."

"You don't know what you're talking about, my dear," I said proudly, holding my little bottle.

After a five-hour flight, including a layover in Frankfurt, we landed in Constanta, on the Black Sea. As soon as we stepped off the plane, a wave of stifling heat hit us. I heard Andrea mutter a few choice words. We retrieved our luggage and made our way to the exit, scanning for our escort. Suddenly, a familiar voice called out.

"Maria Diletti, my goodness... you're still the same!"

"Luca Perri, and you haven't changed a bit! What, did they preserve you in formalin?"

We shook hands, and I introduced Andrea.

"Follow me; someone's waiting in the car. Like everywhere else, parking at the airport is a racket."

Luca took my trolley and led us to the exit. The Romanian police car was parked nearby. As we approached, the officer driving it got out to open the trunk, greeting us with a military salute. We returned the gesture, and I told him to stand down.

"I'll take you straight to the hotel. You probably need to relax a bit. Agent Istrate will pick you up in about two hours and bring you to my office. I'm sorry we can't talk right away, but I'm tied up with a case that's eating my soul. I have to interview a witness."

"So you don't miss out on stress here either," I quipped.

"You have no idea, Maria."

The 'Hotel de charme' that the police had arranged for us was a gem, located on a central street.

"This area is quiet and close to the sea. Just a few steps, and you're on the Faleza of Constanta," Luca said, winking at my confusion. "Faleza is the seafront. Congratulations, you've learned your first Romanian word," he teased.

Luca walked us to the reservation desk, apologized again for having to rush off, and left. Once the check-in was sorted, a very young bellboy led us to our room. The elevator opened onto a corridor with magnificent mosaic floors and views through the windows. The room didn't disappoint: understated luxury blending various styles seamlessly.

"Tonight, I propose a colossal bender!" Andrea declared.

"Deal, but first, let's meet Luca Perri."

After a quick shower and unpacking, Officer Istrate returned to pick us up. We arrived at a building with a courtyard, where Perri was waiting. "Welcome to my kingdom." I looked around, puzzled.

"Where are we, in a churchyard?" I asked, noticing the priests coming and going.

"My office is inside the curia. Follow me."

We entered through the door Luca had come from, finding ourselves in a dimly lit corridor. I observed Luca closely; he looked much younger than his years, considering he was at least five years older than me. His office was a small, cluttered room with a desk, an outdated computer, an old rotary phone, and shelves crammed with files, books, and notebooks.

Next to the computer was a book that stood out, covered in leather and richly embroidered with golden threads. I picked it up.

"How beautiful!" I said, admiring it.

"Do you have a thing for old books?"

"Yes, especially the bindings and covers—they're true works of art."

"You'd be surprised; this country hides immense treasures. But let's get down to business," he said, cutting me off.

Andrea handed him the folder containing our documents: analyses, autopsy reports, photographs, and everything else he might need.

"The strangest part is that my sister maintained, until her death, that Cecilia Donadio was murdered."

"That's news to us. Most of the witnesses barely remembered anything; some are dead, and others only remembered the animosity they felt toward Ludmilla Geoana. Only your mother told us that your sister Antonella claimed to have seen Ludmilla engulfed in flames, and that a flying man saved her."

"A flying man..." Luca let out a dry laugh, then opened a desk drawer and took out a piece of drawing paper, stored in a plastic sleeve. "Look," he said, handing it over.

The drawing showed flames with several figures lying on the ground, one standing, another curled up against a wall in a fetal position, and a third figure, drawn in black, kneeling beside the girl, its head bent toward her neck.

"When did she make this drawing?" I asked, astonished.

"A few months before she died. She was a diving champion with a bright future ahead of her. I still can't fathom how it happened. One dive was her last—she lost her balance and hit her head on the edge of the board. By the time she fell into the water, she was already dead."

"I'm so sorry." Despite my sympathy, I couldn't help but wonder why a promising diving champion had died from something as simple as losing balance. But I didn't voice the thought.

"The day she gave me this drawing, she told me she'd had a nightmare. She dreamt of the fire and Cecilia asking her for help. I begged her not to show our parents the drawing and promised I would handle it. At the time, I was in the academy."

"And did you investigate?" I asked.

"Not really. I just made her believe I was, to reassure her. But it didn't matter—she died."

There was a knock on the door. A stout man in a shabby robe appeared.

"Allow me to introduce Father Vesta, our soul-saver."

The priest shook my hand, and a shiver ran down my spine, as if a cold wind had just brushed against me.

"Inspector, I sense you are very tense. Your soul is shrouded in darkness."

What was this creepy priest talking about? I pulled my hand back.

"How dare you! You don't even know me!" I snapped.

"Her soul is clouded because they have come for her. Do you think you're here of your own free will?"

"That's enough, Father Vesta," Luca interrupted sharply. "Leave the inspector alone." The priest bowed and left, leaving a palpable chill in his wake.

"You have to excuse him. Father Vesta is... unique, with a deep understanding of the occult. Sometimes, listening to him isn't a bad idea," Luca said, sighing.

"Do you know Ludmilla Geoana?" I asked, my tone cold and direct.

Luca's eyelid twitched, and he stiffened.

"It was I who ended their witness protection status—hers and her grandfather's."

"Her grandfather?"

"Yes, Mr. Du Jardin, her grandfather." Luca's green eyes narrowed. "So, of course I know her. Her father, Dorian Geoana, is the Romanian equivalent of a police commissioner for Constanta."

"Explains a lot," I muttered.

"I'd say we're done here. I have other matters to attend to," Luca said, getting up to show us out.

"Don't trouble yourself; we know the way," I said, annoyed.

As we made our way down the corridor, I gestured for Andrea to stay quiet, fearing we might be overheard. Then, we were intercepted by Father Vesta.

"Would you join me in my office? A gesture of peace—I recognize I overstepped earlier."

If Perri's office was a cubicle, the priest's was vast. I marveled at the shelves stretching to the ceiling, crammed with books. A hidden door between two bookshelves swung open.

"Please, follow me," Father Vesta said. "Don't be afraid."

The smaller room had no windows, only the hum of the ventilation system. It was cool and comfortable, perfect for reading. At an antique lectern was another richly decorated book.

I leaned closer to read the title: Successio principum eiusdem stirpis sive sanguis familia.

"It's Latin," I said. "The succession of rulers from the same family by... blood?" I turned to Father Vesta.

"Yes. It means the sequence of rulers from the same bloodline."

"What's the significance?" I asked.

"This book lists, in alphabetical and chronological order, the dynasties—extinct and still active—of non-human beings. The only creatures humanity truly needs to fear."

I couldn't help but laugh.

"Something funny, Inspector?"

"Forgive me, Father, but you want me to believe that this ancient manuscript lists the names of... what? Demons? Witches? Something else?"

He handed me white gloves.

I put them on and, with reverence, opened the book. It was filled with names, repeated year after year, some crossed out, others added. Each name was preceded by a number, the last being 10,437. I glanced at Andrea, who looked amused.

I placed the book back on the lectern and realized we were all rubbing our temples.

"It's the air. The ventilation modifies the oxygen to maintain the right humidity. Three people add too much carbon dioxide," Father Vesta explained. Once outside, we felt better.

"Father Vesta, we're completely lost. I think I speak for Deputy Inspector Pancaldi as well," I confessed. "We've handled gruesome cases before, even cannibalistic serial killers and terrible vendettas. But this... this is beyond anything. Please, tell me something," I pleaded.

"My duty, my children, is to warn those who come into contact with the dark world. No one stumbles upon the sanguine world by accident. A sanguine creature has been searching for you, and it has found you; it wants to reveal itself. Why, I don't know. But perhaps you, my child, if you dig deep into your subconscious, can find the answer."

I hesitated... his words...

"That's enough for today," Andrea interrupted firmly. "The inspector needs rest."

"Be careful," Father Vesta said, grabbing his arm. "If you stand between the creature and Maria, you will pay the price. Take care. You can always find me here."

He handed me a business card and blessed me.

Finally, we stepped out into the open air. The sun was bright, and despite the heat, I sought refuge in Andrea's arms. Across the street, Officer Istrate's car was still parked. He lowered the window and beckoned us.

"I'll take you to the hotel," he said in his broken Italian.

"Thank you, but we'll walk. It's such a nice day," I said.

"I have orders," he insisted.

Annoyed, I called Luca Perri.

"Tell Officer Istrate he doesn't need to escort us."

"He is your escort. You're not here on vacation," Luca snapped.

"No way." I hung up. "Officer Istrate, you may go. I'm still your superior, even if not Romanian. Go, we don't need an escort. That's an order."

We walked away, ensuring we weren't being followed, and reached the seafront.

"After everything we heard this morning, I'm starving," I said.

"Same. Let me check my app for a restaurant."

"No, let's just pick one," I said, pointing.

"How about Mircea's? Looks good."

"Let's try it." I took Andrea's hand as we found the entrance down a side street.

The place had a cozy ambiance, with soft music, the aroma of good food, and waiters in traditional attire.

"Welcome!" they greeted us in Italian, as if we had it stamped on our foreheads.

I smiled, amused. Wherever you go, they always greet you in your own language.

We asked to dine outside.

"We have tables on the terrace—you'll love it," said the waiter.

The terrace was stunning, offering a gorgeous view of the sea. The sun and sea breeze lifted my spirits, clearing my mind.

As we settled, our waiter brought a plate and a bottle.

"You must try the pálinka," he said, smiling.

"But it's alcoholic," I protested.

"It's served ice-cold," he insisted.

"Well, if it's cold, that's different," Andrea replied.

"It's basically plum juice," the waiter said with a sly grin.

We let him choose the menu, and soon he returned with two dishes: zacuscă de fasole (bean dip) and salată de vinete tocate (a kind of baba ganoush made from eggplant), served with homemade bread and white wine. Everything was delicious, and we ate in silence, toasting frequently.

Then Andrea's phone rang. "It's the boss. Why is he calling me?"

I pulled out my phone, realizing it was completely dead.

"Damn, no battery!"

"Answer it," he said, handing me his phone.

"Celeste, it's Maria."

"Where's your phone?"

"It died, but as soon as we landed, we got swept up by Perri and this strange priest."

"I got a call from Spatafora, who said Perri told him you refused the escort. Tell me that's not true."

I hesitated, and Celeste started shouting. I held the phone away from my ear, waiting for her to calm down.

"Are you done?"

"Don't even think of talking back! I'm not willing to argue. The escort is mandatory. If you refuse, pack your bags and come home. Now."

"There was a misunderstanding," I said quickly.

"Good. And for God's sake, charge your phone!" he barked, then hung up.

"We've gained an enemy: Luca Perri," I muttered, handing back the phone.

"We had that enemy the moment you questioned the Romanian police," Andrea pointed out.

We paid and stepped outside. The poor Officer Istrate was still there, getting out to open the car door.

"Please take us to the hotel," he said.

"Thanks," we replied in unison, amused by his Italian.

Back at the hotel, we collapsed into the room, slightly tipsy and exhausted. It was already six o'clock. My phone chimed, signaling an incoming message: Tomorrow at nine a.m., Commissioner Geoana is expecting you. —Luca Perri.

"Well, it seems he doesn't hate me that much," I laughed as Andrea slipped into the shower.

"Since we're not allowed to go out alone, how about we grab a drink downstairs at the hotel bar?" he called out.

"I'm too tired, and I have a headache from the alcohol. I'll take an aspirin and try to sleep. Maybe I'll join you later."

As Andrea finished his shower, I crawled into bed, relishing the cool air-conditioning and queuing up a movie on my tablet, hoping to clear my mind before the next day.

13

I was woken by loud knocks at the door. Annoyed, I assumed Andrea had forgotten his key card. The knocks became more insistent.

"Just a damn minute!" I snapped, dragging myself to the door, still half-asleep.

Standing outside were two figures. One of them was Officer Istrate.

"Officer Istrate, what can I do for you?" I asked, puzzled.

"Inspector Diletti, this is Officer Eliade; he speaks your language." The young officer greeted me with a slight bow.

"Inspector Diletti, you should come with us to the station."

"Alright, give me a moment to inform Deputy Inspector Pancaldi. He's downstairs at the piano bar."

"I'm afraid there's no time for that. You must come now." Something in his tone made me uneasy.

"Can I get dressed?"

"Of course, we'll wait outside."

I closed the door, instinctively pulled open the blackout curtains, and was hit by blinding daylight. Checking my phone, I realized it was ten in the morning. I had slept for eighteen hours.

"Andrea?" I muttered, searching the room and bathroom, but he wasn't there. His clothes were still in the closet. I felt a sudden unease. If he had taken off on some personal mission, he would have to answer for it. I dressed quickly and ignored a call from Celeste, heading out to meet the officers. They escorted me to the station, which was only a short drive away.

Waiting for us outside was a man, a striking figure. As I got out of the car, I was taken aback by his presence.

"I am Chief of Police Dorian Geoana. Inspector Diletti, I presume?"

"Yes, that's correct." I stuttered, almost entranced by his presence. He spoke perfect Italian, and his voice was deep, melodic.

He extended a hand, and I took it, feeling as though I was gripping a piece of cold, smooth marble. He was nearly two meters tall, with black eyes that seemed to draw you in, high cheekbones, and full lips. But then it struck me—if he was Ludmilla's father, shouldn't he be over seventy years old? Yet he appeared much younger, almost ageless. My mind was struggling to make sense of it all.

"Can I offer you something?" he asked.

"A coffee, perhaps."

He picked up a phone and ordered two coffees, his movements graceful and precise.

"Will someone tell me why I'm here?" I asked, trying to maintain my composure.

"When was the last time you saw Deputy Inspector Andrea Pancaldi?"

"Why do you ask?" I countered, suddenly suspicious.

"You asked why you were brought here, so I'm telling you."

"Then tell me," I retorted, my patience fraying.

"Deputy Inspector Pancaldi's papers were found in a rubbish bin."

My heart skipped a beat.

"Was he harmed?" I demanded, my voice rising.

"We don't know yet. That's why we need to ask you some questions. Let's start again: when was the last time you saw Deputy Inspector Andrea Pancaldi?"

"Around four in the afternoon yesterday. We had a long day, and back at the hotel, he wanted to go to the piano bar, but I was too tired and went to bed. I didn't plan to sleep for eighteen hours. Honestly, I don't understand how that happened. I only woke up when the officers knocked on my door. That's when I realized Andrea wasn't in the room."

"Did you take any sleeping pills?"

"Of course not. It was four in the afternoon, and I just wanted a nap. We'd been up since four in the morning, and we arrived on the ten o'clock flight."

"Did you have a headache when you woke up?"

"I still do."

"I believe someone sprayed a narcotic in your room to keep you asleep longer."

"Why would someone do that? Nothing seems to be missing, not from my things or Andrea's."

"Were you and Deputy Inspector Pancaldi just colleagues, or were you also a couple?"

"Yes, we've been together for fifteen years... almost twenty."

"Captain Luca Perri gave me all the documentation on the investigation you and your deputy are conducting. I won't lie—it makes me uneasy to learn this way that two Italian police officers are in Romania investigating murders that occurred outside your jurisdiction."

"We were authorized by Commissioner Spatafora..."

"With whom I have a strong friendship, which makes this situation even more infuriating. But there's no point crying over spilt milk, as you say."

"More or less, yes."

"Have you noticed anything unusual since you arrived?"

"No, apart from the fact that Captain Perri assigned us an escort. We were alone in the restaurant."

"Your country, my dear inspector, is safer. Here, people disappear every day, often for trivial reasons: a watch, a handbag... Sometimes we find them, but many just vanish. Forever."

His tone was gentle, almost fatherly, and I couldn't help but start to cry. He handed me a handkerchief and stepped away to take a call. I tried to compose myself, but panic gripped me. Where was Andrea? Was he safe?

After a few minutes, Geoana returned with a paper in hand, which he handed to me.

"What is this?" I asked, looking at the Romanian text.

"They found Deputy Inspector Pancaldi. He's fine."

I leapt from my chair. "Where is he?"

"A patrol spotted him standing in front of a gate. They tried to approach, but he fled."

"What do you mean, he ran away?" I demanded, anxiety bubbling over.

"I think it would be best if you return to the hotel," he said, leaving it at that.

Fortunately, the office phone rang, and he was forced to sit back down. I seized the opportunity, asking for directions to the bathroom, and slipped out of the station unnoticed. I needed to be alone, to think.

I walked quickly, deep in thought, but a noise snapped me out of it. I looked around, disoriented, feeling lost. The noise disappeared, but I could still feel someone's presence. I continued walking, listening intently. Then I heard it again—footsteps, matching my pace. A chill ran down my spine. When I twisted my ankle and had to slow down, I decided to turn and confront whoever was following me. But no one was there.

Convinced I was imagining things, I limped back to the hotel. I hoped Andrea would be there, waiting, but the room was empty. Disappointment washed over me, and I slumped onto the bed, trying to call his phone, but there was no answer. Geoana had warned me that Andrea's phone was likely stolen.

Unable to sit still, I went outside, and there she was, standing across the street.

"Maria!" she called, her voice instantly recognizable. Memories of childhood flashed before me like a movie reel.

"Ludmilla?" I whispered.

She approached to hug me, but I stepped back. "You know you're a suspect in the murder of Cecilia Donadio?"

Ludmilla hesitated for a moment before responding, "I know, but now is not the time for that. We need to focus on finding your fiancé."

"Deputy Inspector Pancaldi," I corrected, trying to stay professional.

"Yes, your boyfriend. Is that accurate?"

"That's not your concern," I said, choosing to remain guarded, even though part of me longed to reconnect.

Ludmilla's expression hardened, resembling the same stony look I'd seen on Dorian Geoana's face earlier.

"You can arrest me if that's why you're here," she said.

"I'm not here to arrest you, but to understand. Ludmilla, you might not realize this, but there's a trail of murders linked to the one you witnessed."

"I will tell you everything you want to know, but first, we need to find Deputy Inspector Pancaldi," she pleaded.

"Alright, but promise me you won't try to escape. And one more thing: why were you following me in Turin?"

"I wanted to talk to you. I knew what was happening, but you were always with someone, and I didn't want to intrude. And yes, I promise I won't run away. I would never do that, now that I've found you."

This time, I allowed her to hug me. When she took my hand, I was shocked by how cold and smooth it was—just like Geoana's. She noticed my reaction.

"I promised to tell you everything," she said.

My phone rang. It was Luca Perri.

"Yes?" I answered, stepping away from Ludmilla.

"I have bad news. A disfigured body was found with Deputy Inspector Pancaldi's badge."

I struggled to breathe, fighting back a scream as my legs buckled. Cold hands held me steady.

"Maria, what's wrong?" Ludmilla's voice echoed.

I felt as if I were in a vortex, unable to focus, unable to speak, barely able to stand, held up only by Ludmilla's support. I had the sensation of being lifted. I clung to Ludmilla, my cheeks wet with tears.

"Maria," Ludmilla's soothing voice whispered, "Andrea is not dead."

I looked up, barely comprehending her words.

"Why would Captain Perri lie about something like that?" I managed to say.

"He didn't lie," she said, her tone firm. "Please, there's no time for explanations. We need to go."

I pulled away, trying to regain my composure. "Where's my phone?"

"You dropped it," she said, handing it back.

"I need to call Captain Perri."

"Not now. Please, let's go."

We left the doorway where she had hidden me, stepping out into the warm afternoon air. I took a long, deep breath.

"I have a car parked one block away. If you can't walk, wait here, and I'll come back for you."

"I'm coming with you."

We walked in silence, but Ludmilla occasionally smiled at me, a smile I couldn't help but return. There was something hauntingly familiar about her, a resemblance to Dorian that I couldn't shake. Then, without warning, Ludmilla froze, her eyes turning red and her head swiveling in a way that sent chills down my spine. A car pulled up to the curb, and out stepped Father Vesta.

"What are you doing with her?" Ludmilla snarled.

"Father Vesta? We're just walking. What's wrong?" I asked.

"You're walking with evil," he said, his voice booming.

"That's enough," Ludmilla snapped. "Leave us alone. You don't want to see me upset."

Father Vesta didn't back down. "I will not let you manipulate her," he warned.

"No one is manipulating me," I said, stepping forward. "Please, just go."

Father Vesta hesitated, then sighed, lowering his arms. "I'm leaving, but remember, evil is circling you," he whispered, turning back to his car.

Ludmilla gritted her teeth, muttering, "Damn priest."

The car ride was mostly silent. Ludmilla drove while I stared out the window, watching as we left the city center.

"Where are we going?" I finally asked, growing impatient.

"We're almost there. Grandpa Robert is waiting for us."

"Grandpa Robert?" I echoed, bewildered. "Ludmilla, this isn't the time for family reunions. We need to find Andrea."

"Trust me," she said, not offering any further explanation.

We pulled up in front of a villa. I hesitated to get out, unsure of what to expect, until I saw him—Mr. Du Jardin, looking exactly as he had thirty-six years ago.

I got out of the car and hugged him, overwhelmed with relief.

"It's so good to see you again, Maria," he said. "You haven't changed a bit."

"And neither have you," I replied, still in shock.

They led me inside, in a small, elegant living room. And then I saw him: Andrea.

My heart raced as I ran to him, but as I got closer, I froze. He looked like a mirror image of Dorian, Ludmilla, and Du Jardin. I took his hands, feeling the same cold, smooth texture. My mind was spinning as I stepped back, realization dawning.

I thought of the book in Father Vesta's library, his warnings, and the fury I had seen in Ludmilla's eyes.

"What are you?" I whispered, staring at Ludmilla. "And what did you do to him?"

I looked at Andrea, who remained silent, his expression pained.

"Maria," Ludmilla said, her voice controlled, "remember your promise? It's time to trust me. Everything will be clear soon."

I lunged at her in frustration, but she remained calm, almost as if she knew my every thought.

"You know what we are," she said softly.

"I'll ask one last time: what are you?"

She met my gaze, hesitating before finally saying, "Vampires. But deep down, you already knew."

"And what did you do to Deputy Inspector Pancaldi?" I demanded, my voice shaking.

"We didn't do anything to him. But the monster searching for you found him."

I saw the sincerity in her eyes, and my anger gave way to concern.

I turned to Andrea, determined to get answers, but he looked away, turning towards the window.

Robert Du Jardin appeared beside him, gently holding his arm.

"It's not time for him to exert himself," he said. "He's not ready to control it yet."

They disappeared, leaving me alone with Ludmilla.

"Why can't he control himself?" I asked, feeling more lost than ever.

"Come and sit down," Ludmilla said softly, as if trying to regain the control she had almost lost earlier.

14

The noise from outside the room caught our attention. By now accustomed to their way of making an entrance, I wasn't surprised to see Dorian Geoana appear.

"I hope I didn't frighten you," he said with a mocking tone.

I arched my eyebrows. "Nothing scares me anymore," I replied coldly.

He stepped closer, his expression turning serious. "I'm glad nothing scares you anymore, but if you want my advice, stay afraid. It might just keep you alive."

"Are you threatening me?"

"I'm warning you—enough blood has already been shed."

Then he turned furiously to Ludmilla. "I hope you're satisfied with the trouble you've caused us all."

"I didn't mean to, Dad. But letting him die... it wasn't an accident, an illness, or a personal choice. A vampire monster killed him," Ludmilla replied, meeting her father's gaze defiantly.

"Why did Robert take Andrea away?" I asked, hoping to diffuse the tension between the two.

Dorian swallowed and began to speak. "The deputy inspector is still fresh. During the adaptation phase, a non-blood vampire is very dangerous. It takes almost nothing for them to attack. They're hungry... they need blood... human blood."

"Did he have to kill someone?" I growled.

"No, we're well equipped. We don't need to kill humans. We have, let's say, cruelty-free blood supplies."

"Cruelty-free?" I laughed, though I knew there was little to find amusing.

"Blood banks, willing donors, animals—but that's not enough during the adaptation process."

"So, I take it there are people who know about your existence?"

"Oh, many more than you might imagine."

"What would drive someone to willingly become vampire food?"

"Money, of course," he replied with a smirk.

Of course... "So the transformation happens after being bitten by another vampire?" I asked.

"Not always. Some of us are born with the vampire gene, in which case adaptation occurs spontaneously around the age of ten or eleven and completes about ten years later. It's a long and painful journey, but it's ours—we can't change that."

I took a moment to process what Dorian had said. Everything started to make sense.

"It was Ludmilla's inability to control her thirst that led to Cecilia's death. It wasn't a deliberate murder," I concluded, almost relieved by the realisation.

I looked into Ludmilla's eyes and saw her suffering. I felt pity.

"Even after all these years, the memory is still vivid in my mind. I just wanted to attend that damn party... so I ran away from Grandpa's control. I didn't expect to be insulted and laughed at by a bunch of adults. The worst was Cecilia's mother. She dragged me out of the small room where they were gathered, shouting at me: 'You're a witch, get out!' I still didn't know what I was, let alone my strength. I managed to get into the ballroom, thinking I'd have fun with my classmates. I was wrong. 'What are you doing here, you witch?!' they shouted. One of them threw me to the floor... it all happened so fast. The rage I felt gave me the strength to break free from the girls holding me down, stomping on my body and face while others kicked me. I escaped and hid between two sofas. It wasn't long before they found me. I saw Cecilia approaching with a broken bottle neck, threatening to cut my throat. Overwhelmed by rage and fear, I grabbed the weapon from her hand and drove it into her throat. Blood started spurting out—it was the first time I smelled it. I remember Grandpa's face—distraught, grief-stricken. It was the last thing I saw before I lost consciousness. Later, I learned that I had bitten Cecilia's neck so violently that I had her windpipe in my mouth. I felt rage and shame for what I discovered I was, and I didn't rest for years."

"How did the fire start?"

"I had to clean up the mess Ludmilla made." I looked up to see Robert had appeared. "The screams of the other girls alerted the parents and the bouncers, who rushed inside. When I arrived, Cecilia was lying in a pool of blood, and two bouncers were holding Ludmilla to stop her from escaping—or so I thought. But one of the parents had a weapon and was threatening her. At that time, she would have died, as her adaptation wasn't complete. When he saw me, he started shooting wildly. He hit the electrical panel behind the two bouncers holding Ludmilla. It exploded like a bomb, and within minutes the fire had engulfed the entire room. The short circuit caused the emergency doors to lock, trapping everyone left inside the dance floor. In a split second, I had to decide how to hide Ludmilla's bite marks on Cecilia. I pulled down a strobe light, broke some glass, and slashed Cecilia's already battered neck to mask the teeth marks. It didn't work. Then I grabbed my niece and escaped through the back door into the courtyard behind the disco. I made her say goodbye and leave Turin." He paused, catching his breath. "Later, I returned to Turin to make sure the police had no doubts about what happened. I found the forensic pathologist who conducted the autopsy and hypnotised him to tell me his findings. I forced him to change the autopsy report, but that wasn't enough... I had to hypnotise the inspector in charge of the investigation and everyone else who knew, altering their memories... then it was over. They were left with their pain, but I gave them peace of mind. It was the only way I knew to ask for forgiveness."

A thousand questions rushed through my mind, but I chose to stay silent, listening to the scream of horror echoing in my head.

The world was no longer as I knew it—a part of it, unknown and mysterious, had found me, and somehow, I felt it was mine too: I understood it, and I didn't fear it.

"But that's not all," Dorian continued. "From the documents you gave me, it seems that the corpse of the infant Cecilia Donadio shows clear bite marks, inflicted with particular force by someone with an undeveloped dental arch, suggesting a child of about ten years old. The body remains uncorrupted. Cecilia was put in a state of semi-death," he said, reading from part of the autopsy report prepared by Marino Piano.

"What exactly does 'semi-death' mean?" I asked, trembling.

"It means someone plans, sooner or later, to bring her back to life."

It was all too much for anyone... certainly for me. But I found the courage to continue questioning.

"Why would anyone want to bring Cecilia back to life?"

Dorian hesitated, as if debating how much to tell me. I got the impression they were communicating with each other, deciding on their next move.

Dorian finally spoke. "For years, we've been hunting a monster a rogue vampire, a killer who drinks human blood. He rejects the law and kills for sport, often without feeding on his victims. He acts without reason..."

I interrupted, feeling like he was feeding me nonsense.

"He may be a monster, this rogue vampire, but are you expecting me to believe he was in Turin in 1986 and again a few days ago? You insult my intelligence and test my patience."

"If you'd let me finish... you'd see no one is trying to insult or deceive you," Dorian replied impatiently. "May I continue?" he asked.

I nodded, and at that moment, Andrea returned.

"We can continue another time. For now, it's important you two talk."

My heart was racing; being near Andrea made me feel as dizzy as I did around Dorian Geoana. And to think... in fifteen years, I had never felt anything like this. He sat beside me and took my hand.

"I've become a creature of darkness, a monster. I would have been better off dead..."

"Andrea, are you insane?"

"It's true. I am a monster. I don't know how I'll ever come to terms with it, but one thing is certain: I want to kill him with my own hands."

"Andrea, what are you saying? We'll bring him to justice!"

Sadness clouded his eyes—eyes drained of life and hope. He knew there was no going back.

I felt a pang of shame, thinking that he had been granted immortality... and he was even complaining about it...

Then I looked at him. His sad eyes locked onto mine, but suddenly, I saw a flicker of red in his pupils. I recoiled, but he grabbed my hands, pulling me to his chest. He was so strong that any attempt to escape was pointless.

"You see, I scare you," he whispered, letting go.

I took a deep breath and cupped his face, forcing him to meet my eyes.

"I've dealt with paedophiles, rapists, and murderers—I was afraid of them. But you... you're different. I know you'd never hurt me. I just need time to get used to this, and if there's anything I can do for you, tell me—I'm here to help."

I tried to kiss him, but he sprang up and in a flash reached the opposite wall.

"I can't control myself; all I can smell is your blood," he gasped.

"You'll have to learn to control it, and the only way is to face your demons."

"My demons?" he growled. "I am a demon."

He bolted from the room. I tried to follow, but Ludmilla stopped me.

"Give him time. He's scared and doesn't yet know his strength. Maria, you must understand—it takes very little to kill humans; you're as fragile as glass."

Someone spoke behind Ludmilla.

"Maria, when was the last time you ate?"

It was Robert, carrying a tray filled with all sorts of treats. "I know you're a vegetarian," he added quickly.

"Grandpa's a marvel in the kitchen," Ludmilla said, taking the tray from him and placing it on the table.

"So, you eat regular food?"

"If by regular you mean everything but blood, then yes, absolutely."

Satisfied and feeling grateful for Robert's cooking, I went outside to the garden for a cigarette.

"I see you're one of those humans devoted to cancer," Ludmilla commented.

"It would mean that on my deathbed, you would turn me into a vampire..." He didn't respond but sat down beside me on the doorstep.

"Can you tell me what happened to Andrea?" I asked, glancing at him from the corner of my eye.

"It was entirely my fault. I wasn't paying attention, and he saw me near the hotel where you were staying. I could have run, like I did those other times in Italy, but I felt I couldn't anymore. Then he called my name, and I was forced to stop..." He noticed my questioning expression and paused. "If a human calls us by name, our essence compels us to stop, just as we can't enter your homes without an invitation. We don't know why, but it makes us vulnerable to vampire hunters."

"Do vampire hunters actually exist?"

"History, or rather, legends, are full of them. But back to us. When Andrea called me, I had to stop. He approached and told me not to be afraid; he just wanted to ask me a few questions. I agreed. He suggested we go somewhere quiet where we could talk. I knew a café a little outside the centre where we could chat in peace. You and your man are very similar, both skilled at turning an interrogation into a casual conversation... After coffee, we ordered a couple of beers, then more... and more... until I had to run to the bathroom. But I didn't tell him the truth. I couldn't predict his reaction, and it could have been dangerous for both of us. When I got back, Andrea was no longer at the table. I asked the boy behind the counter, and he said he saw Andrea leave with a friend. When he described the friend, I understood everything. The beast had taken Andrea. I tried to track him by scent, but it was no use. So I called my father and grandfather; only they could help. And they did. We found Andrea lying in a playground. He had no papers, no badge. The beast had taken them—those kinds of vampires like to play games. It's no coincidence that someone found his papers in one place and his badge on an unidentifiable corpse elsewhere.

He'd been drained, but there was still a breath of life left in him. We took him to a friendly clinic. They did what they could to save him, but the prolonged hypoxia had damaged his brain. He'd have been a shell for the rest of his life. It was my decision. I had put him in danger. So, I gave him my blood and then bit him. Time was running out, and you could have woken up and started looking for him, maybe even contacting the local police or, worse, Luca Perri. When I entered the hotel room, you were still sleeping, but you were starting to wake up. I hypnotised you so that you would stay asleep and forget you ever saw me when you woke up. Forgive me, but I had no other choice... you know the rest."

"Explain to me: why would it have been worse to turn to Luca Perri?"

"He's a vampire hunter. But because of my father's position, he agreed to a deal years ago: in exchange for sparing families that don't feed on humans, my father would give him the others—the slayers and the azaras."
"What are azaras?"
"Vampires who feed on other vampires."
"The abomination of abominations," I muttered.
"Exactly. And they're the only ones who can kill blood vampires with a single bite."
Before I could ask more, Ludmilla silenced me, placing two fingers on my lips. "That's enough for today. You can't expect to process all this at once. I swear I'll answer any questions you have tomorrow. Tonight, you'll stay over, and I won't take no for an answer."
I didn't protest, though I would have preferred to be alone for a while.
Ludmilla jumped up, beaming. She was still the same little girl, her heart-shaped smile lighting up her face with excitement. She hugged me, almost squeezing me in half.
"Grandpa! Grandpa! Maria's staying at my place tonight—she can't be alone with Andrea yet!" she shouted, sticking her head into the hall.
I tried to go in and grab my bag, but before I knew it, she had it in her hands.
Ludmilla's house wasn't far from the centre, in a charming little square full of bars and restaurants. She parked under a beautiful arched vault, richly frescoed.
"It's the family crest," she boasted.
From there, we entered a smaller courtyard, where a grand staircase began, adorned with arches and random geometries. We climbed two floors, and the entrance to her home was on a balcony that led through a series of areas with wood-panelled and coffered ceilings.

Inside, the place had an air of the past: large spaces, fittings and doors that seemed original. I stood, mouth agape, admiring an early 19th-century console table beside a Louis XIV-style chair, upholstered in silk satin. I adored art furniture, but, alas, my finances had never allowed it.

Ludmilla, noticing everything, proudly flitted about, explaining the origin of every piece of art in the house.

"The common theme throughout the house, as you may have noticed, is Tiffany glass. Lovely, isn't it? But please, sit down and make yourself at home. In fact, consider it your home."

I thanked her and set my eyes on a beautiful, majestic white sofa, complete with a chaise longue and a very old Persian rug. I took off my shoes and sank into the sofa.

The intercom buzzed, and Ludmilla excused herself.

I was alone for a moment, just long enough to remember that, some forty-eight hours ago, I'd ignored Celeste's call. I reached for the bag I had tossed on the chaise longue and picked up my phone. Twenty-two missed calls. Who was going to listen to my excuse now, I thought, running a hand over my forehead.

I clicked on the first missed call notification and waited for the line to connect.

"Tell me you've been abducted by aliens or you're fired!" he shouted. Well, sort of... it was actually about vampires, I wanted to reply. "Sorry, it's my fault. I had a health issue and ended up in hospital," I lied.

I heard him sigh, but he regained his composure. "And how are you now?"

"They're discharging me. I didn't answer so as not to worry you."

"Not even that jerk of a man of yours... at least he could have picked up."

"I wouldn't let them. But let's change the subject. We managed to speak to Captain Perri and Ludmilla Geoana."

"So what?" he said, his tone rising.

"So far, we haven't made much progress, but we're following the trail of who—Captain Perri believes—is responsible for all the murders, including the abduction of Cecilia Donadio's body."

"Fine," he replied, sounding suspicious. "But from now on, I want a report every twenty-four hours."

He ended the call before I could argue.

Ludmilla returned, laden with bags.

"You know, I'm not a great cook, but Pavel, the chef at 'Monastir,' creates real works of art. I had him send over some things for you to try."

She had practically emptied the restaurant and its wine cellar.

"How can someone be born a vampire?" I asked after my third glass of Fetească Albă.

"The same way humans are," she replied, bursting into laughter. "Well, not quite like humans," she corrected herself, adopting a serious tone. "Take me, for example. I was born from a human and a vampire."

"T... t... you... you have a human mother?" I stammered.

"Yes, but sadly, I never met her. She died giving birth to me. I was raised by Grandpa Robert until I began my adaptation, then by Dorian and Adelheid."

"Are you saying Dorian isn't your biological father? Holy crap..." I squinted my eyes and poured another glass of wine.

"No. They adopted me when my mother died... my father didn't want to know me."

She lowered her head, visibly pained.

"So, a human male and a vampire, or two vampires, can also have children?" I asked, trying to shift away from the topic that was clearly distressing her.

"It's possible, but very rare in both cases. Between a human and a vampire, it's only feasible if the human is under twelve or a newly turned human who still has reproductive capability. The same applies between two vampires. Basically, only male vampires can procreate at any point in their lives, and believe me when I say any one of them could have enough children to populate the moon."

"Damn, it's really true that if you're born female, in any species or race, you're at a disadvantage. End of story."

"Absolutely. Males always have the upper hand, especially if they're vampires. For centuries, female vampires barely existed, or there were far fewer of us than males. Most of us were killed because we were mistaken for witches."

"Wait, are you saying that the massacres carried out by the Church during the Inquisition were targeting vampires, not just human women?"

"Oh no, the unfortunate humans met the same horrible fate. The witches were the ones who managed to escape the Inquisition."

I poured myself another glass of wine, deciding that only inebriation could make sense of what I was hearing.

"Witches... they exist?" I was sure she'd laugh at my question. But instead...

"Of course. Although, over time, they've lost their powers, or rather, their knowledge. Today, there are very few, and they stay on the sidelines. Only the worthy can find them. You've met one."

"Really?" I asked, astonished.

"Father Vesta."

I couldn't help but burst out laughing. The idea of Father Vesta being a witch... well, I couldn't wait to tell Andrea. I would probably leave out the part about Luca Perri, though; it felt in poor taste to mention to a newly turned vampire that vampire hunters were on his trail. I laughed again.

"And does he have a crystal ball... a cauldron... make the occasional trip to Vesuvius?" I couldn't contain my laughter.

"None of that... but please, never let him catch you making fun of him..." She couldn't finish the sentence before she started laughing too.

"When can I be alone with Andrea?" I asked, regaining a semblance of seriousness.

"It'll be a few days. It depends on his level of self-control. It's a risk you can't afford to take, believe me. If he attacked you, you wouldn't have time to scream."

"Alright. But there are still a few questions you need to answer, aren't there?"

"Of course. I made a promise, and I intend to keep it."

"How is it that you can walk around in daylight without any problem? I always thought vampires were creatures of the night."

"Mostly, you've read about that in horror literature or seen it in films. Either way, we don't like sunlight—our eyes are similar to those of nocturnal animals. Bright light weakens even the oldest of vampires."

"But you're immortal, right? No one can kill you."

"If no one could kill us, there wouldn't be vampire hunters, would there?"

"Man... I hadn't thought of that. But then, what about the whole immortality thing?"

"It's true. As long as no one kills us. We're immune to disease, accidents, bullets, old age, but not to an azara bite, decapitation, removal of the heart, or a simple ebony stake through the heart. Now you know how to kill me," she smiled.

"I'll keep it in mind," I replied, pretending to be serious.

"Maria," she said, her voice growing more concerned, "the search for the monster is dangerous. You need to listen carefully... you're not dealing with the worst human criminal. He's a centuries-old vampire. He has strength, hypnotic powers you can't imagine, he can read minds, and he can sense human emotions. Even all of us together would struggle to defeat him. So I beg you, be careful."

"I will, don't worry."
"You must be tired. Let's get some sleep," she said, sounding almost motherly.
"Yes, I am tired... but one more question. Adelheid, your foster mother, why haven't I seen her yet?"
"She doesn't live here in Constanța. She prefers her residence in Cluj-Napoca. You'll meet her soon; the search for the monster will start from there."
"Why are we searching in another city?"
"We're not searching in the city. These vampires live in the mountains. According to Dorian, he's already left Constanța and taken refuge in some cave."
"Then I'm going to sleep."
She walked me to the guest room and left, not before giving me a hug.
The phone vibrated, and I saw who was calling: Andrea.
"Love, how are you?" he asked, instead of greeting me.
"How are you? I'm not the one who turned into a vampire," I replied sarcastically.
"I'm better. With every passing minute, I feel stronger and less anxious. Even the thirst has subsided. I managed to eat a piece of pizza—terrible," he laughed.
"I'm not surprised. What possessed you to eat pizza in Romania...?"
"There was nothing better, and I didn't crave anything else. But you've been elusive, Maria. What's going on?"
"Nothing, nothing's going on. I'm just tired, you understand." I tried to evade the question; it was still too soon for me to see him as anything but a vampire, though just days ago he'd been my man.
He stayed silent for a few moments that felt like hours.
"I couldn't ignore Celeste's call," he said all at once.
"Have you lost your mind?"
"I had about thirty missed calls—how could I not answer?"

"You should have," I snapped.
"He told me he'd spoken to you and that you'd been too evasive. He wanted to make sure everything was alright and updated me on a few things."
"Like what?"
"Spatafora. He ordered the exhumation of all the victims from the 'Two of Spades' fire."
"He wants to confirm there aren't more victims killed by the same hand that murdered Cecilia."
"Do you think they'll find the truth?"
"A manipulated version of it, maybe."
"I'll let you rest. See you tomorrow."
"See you tomorrow."
A ray of sunshine woke me, and I instinctively shielded my eyes with one arm. I looked around, disoriented. Wow, what a marvellous bedroom! I thought, as I remembered I was in Ludmilla's house.
Getting up to head to the bathroom was a bad idea. When I looked in the mirror, the sight was worse than I'd imagined: bloodshot eyes, a pallid face, hair tangled beyond belief... if anyone looked like a vampire, it was me. Typical—they always get to look cool.
I stepped into a hot shower, determined to stop worrying about my appearance. After a few minutes, I began to feel more like myself.
"Maria!" I heard someone call from outside the bathroom. "It's me, Ludmilla. I brought your clothes from the hotel and cancelled the reservation."
"What did you say?" I pretended not to understand.
I wasn't used to someone taking charge of my life like this; I found her... exuberant behaviour a bit unsettling.
I came out of the bathroom wrapped in the bathrobe she'd provided. I found her fussing with the wardrobe.

"Forgive me, darling, but it's clear you can't be alone anymore. Consider me your bodyguard, and much more than just armed," she said with a wink and a wide smile.

"Damn!" I muttered.

The few clothes I'd packed before leaving Italy were neatly arranged at the back of the wardrobe; up front, in full view, was a row of new outfits. I ran my hands over them—still new, with tags removed, all in my size.

"I thought you might need something more, considering how long you'll be staying."

"Are they all for me?"

"Who else would they be for?" she said, as if it were obvious.

She picked out cream trousers and a light red blouse.

"Red suits you. It brings out your eyes," she said with a wink, laying the clothes on the bed. "I'll wait for you out there. There are surprises." She left, leaving only the lingering trace of her perfume.

I made my way to the dining room. The table was set for a breakfast fit for a queen.

"Are you planning to feed all of Romania?" I joked.

The familiar gust of wind signalled the arrival of someone non-human.

"Andrea!"

He took me in his arms, and immediately Ludmilla was by his side, ready to step in if she sensed any change in his mood.

"I'm fine," he reassured her.

She stepped back to give us a moment of privacy but remained vigilant.

"So, did you sleep in a coffin last night?"

"Yes, and I had breakfast with virgin blood."

"Stop being an idiot."

"You started it."

"Well, well, I sense a certain lightening of moods," came the trilling voice of Dorian, who had materialised in the room.

I jumped. "I should be used to your sudden appearances by now."

"You will be..."

"Your phone is about to ring," Dorian said, amused.

I raised an eyebrow at him, and then the phone rang.

"Alright, tell me—what does Celeste want?" I asked sarcastically.

"Answer it. It's better that way."

"Good morning, boss."

"Good morning, my ass."

That wasn't quite like Celeste, or at least not always.

"Yesterday, late in the afternoon, the first two bodies were exhumed. You won't believe it... empty coffins."

I was speechless, seeking some kind of reassurance in Dorian's gaze, though he clearly already knew.

"Are you sure?" It was all I could manage.

"No, we're not sure. We actually had nothing better to do. You know, the heat, the boredom... so we thought we'd make up this nice little story and tell it to you... Of course we're sure!" he thundered, making my eardrum ache.

"Sorr... sorry... I didn't mean to..."

"Excuse me? Didn't mean to? What are you even saying? Listen, I don't think you're getting anywhere over there. I think the Romanian lead is wrong... you need to come back."

"You're wrong, Celeste. The right lead is here. If we leave now, the culprit will vanish into thin air."

"I doubt that..."

"Celeste, you've always trusted my investigations. Has something changed?"

I decided to play the professional card.

"I'm giving you forty-eight hours, after which you come back. Or you hand over your badge."

"Understood," I whispered, but he had already ended the call.

"The missing bodies are at rest, peacefully," Dorian affirmed.

I stared at him, not entirely sure I understood.

"We couldn't be certain the other bodies were actually dead. The risk that the damned monster had left them there, ready to be revived, was too high."

"And tell me... were any of them those little girls you mentioned?"

"Yes," he replied, meeting my eyes.

"But... they were just little girls..." I whimpered.

"This is too much for any human to handle. Listen to your commissioner—go home, be safe. And forget about it."

"Did you say that to me alone?" I asked, narrowing my eyes suspiciously.

"Andrea cannot leave Romania, not yet. The initial stages of adaptation are very difficult and dangerous. If anything were to happen, and people found out... you have no idea how many hunters there are, especially in Italy. They would find out about his presence and launch a ruthless hunt. Therefore, Deputy Inspector Andrea Pancaldi will have to die here in Romania, fulfilling his duty. He will die a hero, but that's how it has to be."

I could hardly believe what I was hearing. I hadn't let myself consider that possibility, or rather, I knew in my heart that things would never be the same, but I didn't know how.

"It wasn't supposed to be like this," I mumbled.

Andrea held me close, offering some comfort. "You'll see, everything will be okay," he murmured.

"I'm not going home. I have to find this monster and face him," I declared.

"The minds of some of us," Dorian began, "haven't adapted to living alongside humans. You must understand, humans are easy prey, the most vulnerable and desirable of all. These outcast vampires gather in small groups, acting stealthily and lethally. They prefer slums, where people forgotten by society live. Sometimes, though, they dare to hunt in crowded places, even in daylight. A kind of test of skill. Usually, they're transformed humans who, unable to adjust, choose the easy way out... that of becoming a monster. But the one we're hunting is an ancient vampire, of pure bloodline. Maria, every moment you spend here, your life is in danger."

"It would be in danger at home, too. And on top of that, I'd be alone and worrying about all of you. I'm staying, and if you no longer want to help me, I'll do everything myself."

"You are stubborn," said Dorian. "We'll move to Cluj-Napoca, leaving at dawn tomorrow. Captain Luca Perri will come with us."

"Why does he have to come too?" I asked, frustrated.

"You ask too many questions. Anyway, you're human, and he's a vampire hunter, captain of the carabinieri and head of the most secretive squad there is. He wouldn't allow a single move without your presence. It's his job to protect you."

"I don't need protectors," I protested.

"Exactly because of what you're saying, you need one."

"All we're missing now is a priest..." I mumbled.

Dorian frowned at me but didn't respond to my sarcastic comment, cutting the conversation short: "Tomorrow morning at dawn. Not a minute later." He vanished, and Andrea went with him.

Mechanically, I sat down at the table, determined to drown my frustration in the massive cream-filled croissants that dominated the tray. Ludmilla quickly poured hot coffee into a cup and sat across from me.

We had breakfast in silence, with Ludmilla leaving me to my thoughts. For a while.

"A leu for your thoughts."

"I'd be rich. You know, I have so many questions that I'm afraid of becoming annoying, even ridiculous."

"Don't be. I promised you... honesty."

I sighed, bringing the coffee cup to my lips.

"For example," I began, "how do you not raise suspicion with how you look like you're in your twenties?"

"Dorian is a very old vampire, but he's not of pure bloodline. He was bitten during the Middle Ages when he was in his forties. Let's just say, before people start questioning his youthful appearance, he's got a few more decades."

"And then what?"

"And then... you change your life. It's part of the price of living among humans. You're very focused on appearances... it forces us to move every twenty to thirty years."

"And you?" I pressed.

"I'm very young, your age, which for us vampires means being a teenager. I haven't reached a century yet, but soon I'll have to move on. People are beginning to notice, despite the ageing makeup."

15

Ludmilla sent me to sleep for a few hours, but not before offering me an herbal tea that induced an immediate yet restless slumber.

Nightmares took hold of my mind. I could smell a rotting corpse, a stench that brought disgust, quickly followed by pain. A searing, radiant pain, starting in my chest and spreading throughout my body, so intense it made me nauseous. Then, all of a sudden, the pain ceased, and I found myself hovering over an endless ravine. All I could see was darkness—darkness that formed into a terrifying creature: a hulking, disheveled man with long, shaggy hair and bloodshot red eyes. He was rising, carried by unseen currents, reaching out to grab me, trying to drag me into the abyss. But I fought back, somehow slipping free and running. I was in a forest, running... running... running, until I was out of breath. I stopped and turned, but no one was there. Suddenly, the fear was gone, and the forest vanished, replaced by a field of flowers. I saw Ludmilla approaching, smiling, and she took my hand. "Come on," she said, "you will be well forever." But I didn't understand her words, and terror gripped me once more. And everything repeated itself.

The alarm on my phone woke me up. I checked the time: three o'clock.

We left to head towards Robert's house, where Andrea and Dorian were waiting for us.

Robert was already in the car, sitting in the driver's seat. "You two will come with me, while Dorian and Andrea will be in the car driven by Luca."

I don't know why, but hearing Luca's name irritated me. Maybe it was because when we went to question him, Luca already knew. He knew everything and only made up excuses to brush us off.

"Am I mistaken, or do you dislike Luca?" asked Ludmilla.

"You're not wrong," I replied, still annoyed.

"Luca Perri may be a vampire hunter, but he's honourable and lives by his own code. If he makes a deal, he keeps it. Rest assured. For years, he's been infiltrating the sects of humans who think they're vampires, only to be killed by the real ones. Besides all these excellent references, he's also quite the looker—hot as hell, I'd say. A visual and olfactory delight that stirs my male bloodlust." She finished her sentence with a playful, sultry tone, baring her sharp canines, then burst out laughing.

Robert, who had been watching his granddaughter's playful performance, sighed and frowned. "Ludmilla, aren't you ashamed to talk like a woman of easy virtue?"

"I'm only telling the truth, Grandpa," she replied, sticking out her tongue like a child.

We left the lights of Constanța behind as the car merged onto the motorway, heading towards Bucharest and then on to Cluj. We had about a three-hour journey ahead of us, and the fatigue from a night of nightmares made my eyelids feel heavy as lead. I closed them and drifted into a deep sleep.

I woke up, disoriented and aching from head to toe. I remembered I was in the car, glanced out the window, and saw we were still on the motorway.

The first light of dawn outlined the mountains, while a massive road sign indicated we were nearing our destination.

"Good morning," said Ludmilla. "Just in time to see the revival of the ancient Roman Castrum Clus. The city lies on a plain surrounded by hills and gentle mountains—the Apuseni mountains, which are part of the Carpathian range..."

I didn't let her finish her geography lesson. I smirked at the mention of the Carpathians.

"Should we pay a visit to the Count's house while we're at it?" I remarked, emphasising the last word.

"Clever... but you know he never existed. Pure fiction," she replied, sticking out her tongue playfully.

"There are about four hundred caves in those mountains, most of them inaccessible. The beast is hiding in one of them," Robert interjected, cutting off the playful exchange between Ludmilla and me.

"Well, it doesn't seem easy to me to find the right cave. It's like looking for a needle in a haystack," I replied, feeling discouraged.

"That's why Luca Perri is with us. His intuition as a vampire hunter is rarely wrong."

"Strange thing, though—aren't you vampires supposed to... how should I say... sense each other?"

"You've been watching too many films, dear Maria. We can't sense each other unless one of us wants to be noticed."

"So you rely on the abilities of a human? Strange world you have, I'll never stop being amazed."

I was sure I heard a giggle between them. It was rare to hear them talking or laughing together—they didn't always use words, often relying on telepathy.

I leaned my forehead against the window, enjoying the sight of the city waking up. We sped through the streets and then slowed as we neared a narrow alley.

The car stopped in front of a Gothic-style palace. The main door, set between beautiful pointed arches, began to open. The courtyard was dark, and the car's headlights illuminated a path that veered right, past a garden that must have been stunning in the daylight. The gently sloping road ended in another courtyard, where a gate was opening. As soon as the car halted, the automatic openers clicked, and I got out.

Luca greeted me, squeezing my hand firmly. "Stay calm but alert, and everything will be fine," he whispered.

"Are you alright?" asked Andrea, appearing suddenly and pulling me into a hug. "The guy's too considerate..."

"Stop it," I scolded, freeing myself from his arms.

Ludmilla took my hand and led me to a steep staircase that opened to the doors of a lift. She pushed me inside and closed the doors, pressing one of the buttons.

"I wanted a few minutes alone with you," she said, gripping my hand tighter. "Adelheid, my foster mother, can be a bit distant towards strangers, especially if they're human. She's been prepared for your presence, but she may come off as strange, aloof, even a bit rude. Just ignore anything that might annoy or offend you. She's very protective of anyone important to me... and you are."

"I'll know how to handle it, mainly because I don't have much choice—she could smash my skull against a wall with a flick of her wrist..." I smiled, trying to hide the unease already creeping in.

The lift doors opened directly into the house.

A very young woman with unsettling black eyes greeted us.

"Miss Ludmilla, how lovely to see you again," she said with a slight bow. Then she turned to me, but only glanced briefly before disappearing.

Ludmilla ran down the corridor, and I watched her, reminded of when we were children. This was the Ludmilla I remembered—carefree, cheerful, yet so mysterious.

"She'll never grow up," sighed Robert, with the rest of the group behind him.

He led the way to a 17th-century arched door, decorated with finely inlaid Baroque panels, bearing the same coat of arms I'd seen at Ludmilla and Robert's house.

Robert ushered us into a small sitting room, where a beautiful woman sat on a sofa, with Ludmilla, radiant as ever, beside her.

The woman stood up with old-fashioned grace and extended her hand to me.

"I am Adelheid Geoana. I assume I am meeting Inspector Maria Diletti and Deputy Inspector Andrea Pancaldi." She fixed her gaze on him, then continued with disapproval, "Have you taken enough blood? Don't come here and cause problems with these neophytes who can't control themselves."

'Charming,' I thought. I saw her turn her gaze to me, revealing her bloodshot eyes.

"I don't need to be pleasant, just tolerant of a situation I disapproved of from the start," she added, her tone unpleasant.

I glanced at Luca, who tapped his temple, signaling caution. I understood—one of them was reading my thoughts.

A shiver ran through me, making me tremble slightly. Adelheid noticed and smiled, seemingly satisfied.

"Captain Perri, what brings you to my humble abode? Oh, yes... you're here to babysit..."

Luca approached her, unbothered by her provocation. He took her hand and brought it to his lips. "I'm here because of someone who's caused too much trouble... but it's a pleasure to be in your presence, Adelheid."

I swore I heard her growl as she moved closer to Andrea. "What a masterpiece my little girl has created... I hope I won't come to regret it. It would end in the only way possible." She finished the sentence with a veiled threat.

Dorian stepped forward, gently gripping her arm. "Don't make things worse, Adelheid."

"I apologise for my behavior," she said with a polite smile. "I'm not good at playing hostess; I see so few... humans. I consider this venture very dangerous, dear Maria.

Am I wrong, Captain Perri?"

"I trust the inspector knows how to handle herself. She won't embark on any reckless or dangerous actions," he replied.

"Then everything is fine," he sneered, inviting the vampire guests into another room.

Left alone with Perri, I tried to speak, but he stopped me, covering my mouth with one hand. Then he took out a pen and paper from his pocket and wrote a note: Adelheid hears thoughts, and everyone has highly developed hearing. Learn to whisper and write.

I nodded.

"Of course, the temperature here is very different from Constanța," I said, improvising as I replied to the note. Where is everyone?

Luca gave me a puzzled look but then answered, Refreshing themselves in their own way. They're facing danger, so they need to drink human blood. I brought it to them.

I stood there, mouth agape.

Get used to it, he added.

The first to return was Dorian, who came and sat beside me.

"Robert is bringing breakfast. You both need it. But first, you must listen to me," he said, his expression grave. "Hunting a murderous vampire, especially an ancient and bloodthirsty one, is no easy task for any of us, but for you, it's like walking into death's embrace. One wrong step, and none of us can save you. I know Ludmilla has already warned you, but forgive me if I keep insisting. Are you truly ready for what lies ahead?"

Reluctantly, I nodded. "I promise to be careful."

We set off as soon as we were refreshed. In a very large jeep, we drove into the densest forest I had ever seen—darker even than the Amazon.

Robert had to switch on the headlights; it was pitch black. It began to rain, making the road slick, as if coated in soap.

After bouncing around for what felt like ages, we finally reached a paved road. The constant jolting stopped, and I felt a bit more like myself...

The rain lightened to a drizzle, and the sun peeked out from behind the clouds.

We pulled into a car park, and I was relieved to finally set my feet on solid ground.

"What a ghastly face!" exclaimed Ludmilla.

"I felt like a tennis ball... or better yet, a jackhammer, getting tossed around so much that my stomach ended up in my throat and my boobs down by my feet."

"You can't tell," she laughed, glancing at my shoes.

"Alright, girls, fun's over. Let's go!" Dorian hummed.

We began walking along a path beside the cable car. The rain had stopped, and the sun was shining warmly in the sky.

I paused to admire the scenery.

"At this rate, we'll never reach the president's residence," Adelheid complained, nudging me forward.

"President?" I asked, confused.

"Even we creatures of the night, who can manage quite well in daylight, as you see, have a law-abiding leader," Dorian replied.

"You didn't warn me about this meeting," I said, feeling annoyed.

Luca came over and whispered, "Save your breath for walking."

He gently pulled me along by the arm.

"We're running late. We need to give the humans a lift," Adelheid insisted.

"What does that mean?" Luca asked.

"They'll need to move quickly. We'll carry them on our shoulders."

"You're all crazy if you think I'm going to do something like that!" I snapped.

Before I knew it, Adelheid had leapt in front of me. She hissed like an angry cat, and in an instant, I found myself on her shoulders.

I felt her take off at a terrifying speed. I tried to fight, but she squeezed my legs, making it clear how easily she could hurt me.

"If you don't stop, I'll break them!" she shouted.

The wind lashed against my face, and the speed made me nauseous. I closed my eyes and lay still, waiting for the ride to end.

We finally stopped, and I opened my eyes.

"Never do that again!" I growled.

Luca tried to intervene, but Andrea got there first, coming close to me and hugging me.

"Stay calm and don't get upset," he whispered softly.

I looked at him with suspicion. "Speak."

"Where we're going is forbidden to any human. You won't be able to remember the way back. That's why both you and Luca, but he already knows this, will have to be blindfolded."

I was silent, feeling the anger rise in my throat. I wanted to throw up every indignity at this gang of psychopaths.

"Or I can take the anger out of you myself..." Adelheid clearly heard my thoughts.

I huffed, letting my eyes glaze over.

"I'll take you this time," Andrea whispered.

It was a repetition of the earlier sprint, and suddenly Andrea stopped, telling me to remove the blindfold.

"Bloody hell!" I exclaimed, looking around.

We were inside a sinkhole, surrounded by dense vegetation. When I looked up, I saw a patch of sky so blue it made the sun's rays sparkle on the plants and flowers clinging to the walls, creating a kaleidoscope of light and color.

The path, hidden beneath the grass, spiraled downward like an immense staircase. I moved cautiously, as the rainwater had pooled into slippery puddles on the shaded rocks.

We reached a door that seemed to blend seamlessly with the sinkhole wall.

Adelheid stepped to the front and knocked several times with her pickaxe.

The sound of footsteps on gravel grew louder. A woman, no longer young, opened the door. Her face was pale and damp, her lips pursed to conceal her teeth. When she noticed her hand was stained with something red, she quickly tucked it into her pocket. "Apologies," she said in the melodious voice I was beginning to recognize, "I just finished my lunch."

A gag reflex nearly overtook me, but I managed to push it back.

"Follow me, the master is expecting you."

The bitterness in my mouth made me queasy. I searched for a mint in the pouch at my waist. Andrea noticed and rubbed my arm reassuringly.

The narrow corridor we walked through smelled of damp, mold, and the metallic tang of blood. It was the stench of death, something I'd encountered many times at crime scenes.

A short staircase led us into a large hall, with a conical fireplace in the center. The walls were adorned with large tapestries alternating with stained glass windows, through which only rock could be seen. A long, rectangular wooden table with intricately carved edges stood in front of the fireplace. A gust of wind swept in, and suddenly someone took my hand.

"What a magnificent specimen from the mortal world," he said, bringing my hand to his lips. He inhaled deeply, almost sensually. "It's not every day one encounters such essence."

Seeing my discomfort, he composed himself. "I'm Charles. Some mockingly call me 'President,' but I prefer... 'Father of the Weak.'"

For what felt like the hundredth time in recent days, I felt ashamed of my thoughts. But there I was, staring at a vision of vampire beauty. When his lips brushed the palm of my hand, warmth spread through me, sending a flurry of emotions and sensations that made my head spin. He wasn't very tall, but his face was perfectly shaped, framed by black hair that fell to his shoulders. Unlike the other vampires, he had sky-blue eyes and full, red lips. He wore a long-sleeved shirt and jeans. I couldn't tear my gaze away; he could have asked for my life, and I would've given it without hesitation. Thankfully, he let go of my hand and moved towards the rest of the group.

"Captain Perri, good to see you again. If I recall, last time you parted with a 'See you never again,' right?"

"Correct. Too bad one of your people tried to kill Deputy Inspector Pancaldi," Luca replied, defiantly.

"I have no followers, only a people to care for. Those who err will pay," Charles roared.

"Perhaps, but lately too many of your people... have slipped from your control."

A hiss echoed, and in a split second, Andrea leapt forward, shielding me. Ludmilla moved beside him, covering my exposed side, while Dorian and Robert sprang to shield Luca. Adelheid remained as still as a statue.

Suddenly, I felt weak and terrified, partly because the confusion was still ringing in my ears and partly because, for the first time, I fully understood Dorian and Ludmilla's warnings.

"Let's all calm down!" Dorian shouted, trying to dispel the tension in the room.

"Forgive the audacity of humans. It's fear that drives them," Adelheid said, bowing slightly.

"It was never my intention to harm anyone. In this house, everyone, human or otherwise, will always find refuge, as long as they're on the right side. Sometimes, however, Captain Perri's manners get the best of him."

Charles remained still, watching as Luca stepped forward with his right hand extended.

"I apologise," Luca said humbly.

Charles extended his hand, and they shook on it. I breathed a sigh of relief. Then Charles beckoned Andrea to step closer... and the fear returned.

"It's always a pleasure to welcome such a sociable neophyte. Rapid adaptation often causes serious problems with socialisation. But you... well, it seems you were born to be a vampire."

Andrea didn't respond, simply bowing his head in submission.

Charles placed a hand on Andrea's head, as if formally welcoming him into their world.

"Has he had his first blood yet?" asked Adelheid.

"We would never have brought him here if he was still in adaptation," she replied.

Then Charles pointed a finger at Ludmilla. "You turned a human, despite it being forbidden."

I saw Adelheid and Dorian grip each other, and for the first time, I saw terror in their eyes.

Ludmilla approached Charles and knelt before him. "I never intended to, but I found him half-dead, his neck nearly severed. I met Andrea because I wanted him to introduce me to Maria, my childhood friend. But you know everything... there's no point in boring you with details you already know. I realised immediately that someone had bitten him, and I had no choice but to take him to our friend's clinic, but they said nothing more could be done. Just before he took his last breath, Andrea regained consciousness for a moment. I asked him, and he told me he wanted to be saved. Only then did I give him my blood and bite him." She finished and lowered her head, waiting for Charles' judgment.

I thought about Ludmilla's words; I didn't know Andrea had asked her to save him in a moment of lucidity. I assumed she had misunderstood. I realised I'd been lost in thought, and someone had been listening. It was too late to hide my thoughts.

"Did you understand what Ludmilla was asking you?" Charles asked, addressing Andrea.

113

"Yes, I understood perfectly... and I had no doubts. I wanted to live," Andrea replied, calm and confident.

"So be it. I will present your testimony to the Council," Charles said to Ludmilla. "But you, for now, will remain my guest."

"No!" thundered Dorian, his voice echoing like a storm. "You promised nothing would happen to her."

"And it won't. But I believe she's safer here than with you, chasing Mihail. You know what that entails," he said darkly.

"You must come with us," Adelheid insisted.

"Or would you prefer I bring your accusation before the Council?" Charles threatened.

No one, not even Adelheid, dared challenge Charles' authority. He gave a slight smile, took Ludmilla by the hand, and they disappeared.

"Don't lay a finger on her," Adelheid stammered, her voice laced with despair.

Ludmilla reappeared at the doorway. "Don't worry. I'm safer here than anywhere else. But please, protect Maria at all costs."

I could see Dorian, not far from me, seething. He was shaking but restrained himself from moving.

The old vampire appeared out of nowhere and urged us to leave.

"Blindfold the humans, don't forget," he ordered before closing the door.

"We have a long way to go, and we'll arrive late at night. It would be dangerous. Robert, please go ahead and prepare as usual," Dorian said.

"What, you can't carry us on your shoulders anymore?" I quipped sarcastically.

"For a while, yes. But then we'll have to blend in with the mountain tourists. We'll walk a bit and then camp for the night. Tomorrow, we'll reach the caves."

Luca handed me the blindfold, and I put it on myself, now used to the routine.

Andrea grabbed me, and we began running. We turned right near the second pylon, and then he let me go, telling me to remove the blindfold. Walking as a group of hikers, we continued along a path that seemed, at least to me, to disappear inside the mountain.

I still found myself marveling at the vampires' abilities. In front of me stood a tent, clinging firmly to the rocks like a desert mirage. Robert ushered me inside. The interior was a vision of luxury: ornate carpets covered the rocky ground, and soft cushions were arranged along the walls, creating inviting seating areas.

"This is your room," he said, pulling back a curtain.

At the center was a four-poster bed, and to one side, a finely painted partition with arabesques separated the bathroom area.

"There's even hot water," he added with a wink.

I thanked him, stammering, overwhelmed by such opulence. Robert hugged me gently, like a family member. It was unexpectedly comforting.

I took a quick shower and changed into a warm tracksuit. Despite it being summer, it was freezing at this altitude during the night.

When I returned to the common area, I found Luca lounging comfortably between two pillows. I sank down next to him.

"With each passing day, I'm stunned by so much beauty mixed with so much horror," I said.

"Oh... you haven't seen anything yet," he replied, running his fingers over the fabric of a pillow.

"Can I ask you something?" I continued, fixing him with a steady gaze.

"Of course."

"What happened between you and Charles?"

"I think they told you about the deal between Dorian and me. As in, I'm a vampire hunter. You must be wondering what that really means." I nodded. "I was born with the ability to sense non-human creatures. You have no idea how thin the veil is between us and them, and how often it dissolves, merging humans and non-humans. Among this, there

115

are humans who think they're vampires, witches, werewolves, or other mythical beings. When a human falls into that delusion, they're somehow stopped and treated. But when a vampire falls into that madness, things change. They can recognize a creature on the other side of the veil, but they can't discern its intentions. That's where the arrangement with Dorian and Charles comes in. Charles, however, is an ancient blood vampire, from a lineage that goes back to the mists of time. The laws he enforces are... well, suited to a different era."

"What does that mean exactly?"

"I was born with the gene that drives me to kill every creature of the night, good or bad, without distinction. Charles' role is to protect and enforce the two primary laws: do not turn humans and do not kill other vampires."

"I see," I replied, my words barely more than a pained whisper.

I lowered my head, lost in my thoughts. I had been fascinated by this mysterious, legendary world—at least I thought I had been until a few days ago. But now, I felt the urgent need to return to reality.

Luca sensed my discomfort and handed me a phone. "Call whoever you want. It will give you some comfort."

I thanked him with a nod and dialed my mother's number—the only person I needed to hear.

"Mom, it's me. I know it's an unfamiliar number, but regular mobile phones don't work out here."

"Maria, thank God! You've been unreachable for four days. If it weren't for Celeste reassuring me, I'd be dead from worry, and so would your father."

"You know how it is when I'm on a tough investigation... you should be used to this by now."

"But you've never been this unreachable. I still don't know where you are," she said, her voice trembling as she began to cry.

"Mum, please, you know I can't tell you where I am, but believe me, you need to stay calm... and calm Dad down too. I have to go now, but I promise to call you more often."

I said goodbye quickly. I knew they were worried, and it would be even worse if they knew the truth.

"Family problems?" Luca asked.

"Not problems... they're just old-fashioned, you know how it is."

"I get it... after twenty years of working undercover, my mother has finally resigned herself."

Robert arrived with dinner, followed by Andrea. When he saw me sitting next to Luca, his expression changed. Luca noticed and met his gaze with a challenge.

"Andrea, sit down. We were just talking about Luca's sister," I lied smoothly.

He sat down without a word, but I could feel his tension. I decided I'd have to talk to him before confronting the monster.

The arrival of Adelheid and Dorian thawed the icy atmosphere that had settled.

We all dined together in silence, the cold dinner prepared by Robert speaking louder than any conversation could.

I accepted a glass of their wine and withdrew, but not before signaling Andrea to follow me.

He sat on the bed, wary. He had known me long enough to sense when something was off.

"Maria, speak. Before something happens tomorrow that could change everything between us, I need to know," he said, gathering the courage to break the silence.

I couldn't think. I couldn't find the words. My feelings felt numb, but I still had enough clarity to realize I needed to speak to him. I had promised myself that much.

"I... I... I can't imagine a life with a vampire. A creature that, until a few days ago, I thought belonged only in literature and legends. But that's not even the main reason. I can't imagine growing old with you." I lifted my head to look into his eyes, tears streaming down my face. "Please don't make this harder. Just think—I'm forty-six, and in, say, thirty years, I'll definitely need a diaper and look like your grandmother. Are you sure you won't see me as that? I don't want that, Andrea. We promised to grow old together, to support each other until death, but we hadn't reckoned on this."

"I can be with you for all your life. I will support you, I will comfort you. I love you, and I can't imagine living without you. So, please, tomorrow, after we catch the beast, please, Maria, kill me. I don't want to live like this."

"You're crazy. I will never kill you. And now, please, I need to sleep... we'll talk about this when it's all over."

Andrea left, and I fell asleep like a stone, perhaps thanks to the effect of the vampire wine.

I woke up in the middle of the night, sweaty, with my heart racing and a feeling of panic.

"Oh shit," I muttered, wiping the sweat from my forehead.

"What's going on?"

I spun around at the sound of the voice. "Andrea, what are you doing here?"

"I heard you... you were restless."

"A nightmare. For two nights, my dreams have been nothing but nightmares."

"Do you want to tell me about them? Maybe I can help."

"Andrea, I told you it was just a nightmare. How could you possibly help?"

"You need to have more faith in my new abilities."

He placed his hands on my temples, and I felt as though I was being emptied... like every bad thought was draining from my body, leaving behind only calm.

I woke up still nestled against his chest, and to my surprise, I felt no discomfort. But this must never happen again, I thought.

"Good morning," he said, gently stroking my face.

"Good morning," I replied, rushing to the bathroom.

I lingered there, hoping Andrea would leave. The last thing I wanted was to continue the conversation about us.

I stepped out of the tent as dawn began to break, yawning, stretching, and taking in a deep breath of the cool, crisp air.

Dorian joined me.

"Are you ready?"

"Are you really asking? I want to destroy whatever it is that hurt Andrea. And I need to avenge the innocent lives... and Mr. Donadio," I said, my voice filled with determination.

"Wow, a lot of... important things you have to do. But remember: anger and revenge will be your coffin."

I stood there, frozen, contemplating Dorian's words. He was right.

I am human, a police officer; anger and revenge must not cloud my judgment. I'm going to finish this damn investigation and then go home, I tried to convince myself.

16

We set off again after a frugal breakfast. The road ahead climbed up a mule track scattered with fresh animal droppings. Adelheid, Andrea, and Dorian walked ahead of Perri and me. Robert stayed at the camp; we needed someone ready to send for help if necessary.

"Be careful," Dorian warned, "we are out in the open. Anyone could attack us. Walk among us."

We reached the foot of the mountain without incident. Here, the road narrowed between two high rock formations, with a small stream beside it. We kept to the middle, avoiding the tracks' scent, wary of any stray dogs living in the valleys.

"They could cause us trouble and reveal our presence," explained Luke.

Soon, we arrived at the cave entrance. Adelheid and Dorian sniffed the air.

"It's inside the cave," they hissed.

A bar, with a prohibition sign in the middle, blocked the entrance.

"The summer rains may have flooded some of the tunnels, so for safety, the forest rangers bar the entrances. But hikers ignore the signs, and they often don't come back," Adelheid commented slyly.

"Forgive Adelheid's humour, you have to know her to understand it," Dorian interjected, as usual.

I saw Luca kneel down, his attention caught by something.

"Stop," he said quietly, "look." He held something tiny between his fingers. "A bullet, recently fired..." he couldn't finish the sentence.

A deafening noise cut through the air—a gunshot. I heard the bullet whistle past, and someone knocked me to the ground. My knees scraped against the rocky ground, the excruciating pain making me curse.

"They're shooting!" shouted Dorian.

"Are you OK?" Andrea asked, keeping my head down. "Knees apart, and if the person on top of me would get up, yes, I'm fine."

Andrea had thrown himself on me, shielding me with his body. He moved to the side, allowing me to breathe.

"He's here," growled Adelheid. "We thought he was inside the cave. Damn him."

Luca freed me from Andrea's grasp and, on all fours, tried to push me towards the cave entrance for cover.

A second bullet hit the rock face, lodging in a tiny crack. An angry shout echoed from the direction of the shots.

Luca stood up, spreading his legs for stability as he held his gun.

"Get down, dammit, get down! What are you doing with that gun?" Dorian shouted, lunging at Luca.

She pinned him down, shielding him from the third bullet.

"Inside!" Dorian ordered. "Stay hidden in the cave. Andrea will stay with you."

I hesitated, staring at Dorian, not thinking clearly.

"Inside!" he thundered.

Andrea took me by the arm and pushed me into the cave.

We started moving, guided only by the torch on Luca's phone. The human-carved path quickly became steep and darker. I switched on my mobile phone as well. A drop of water landed on my head, making me shiver, but then something brushed against my cheek. I screamed.

"It's just the air coming through cracks connected to the outside," Luca reassured me.

Suddenly, the corridor opened into a massive chamber filled with stalagmites. A series of steps led even deeper, but at the start of the staircase was an electrical box.

"With any luck, the mountain guards didn't cut the power before the storm," Luca said as he started fiddling with the switches and buttons.

The cave lit up, and our path ended there, at the first step of a deep staircase that should have led us further underground. The rain-formed lake blocked any attempt to proceed.

"Shit!" cursed Luca. "We have to go back." We exchanged disappointed looks, but then a noise startled us.

"Welcome!" echoed a voice, disorienting us.

I focused on a figure perched on a rock across from us, unreachable except by swimming. He had mocked us all and divided us.

"My son, you have become a magnificent vampire," he said, pausing to stare into Andrea's eyes. "Come to your maker. Come, son, join your father."

Luca tried to hold Andrea back. "Don't listen to him. He's hypnotising you. Look at me!" he shouted, to no avail.

Andrea jumped into the lake, and I would have followed if Luca hadn't stopped me.

"He's hypnotised. We can't do anything right now."

I watched as Andrea knelt before the creature. Blinded by rage, I pulled out the gun hidden in my fanny pack and aimed at the stranger.

"Oh, how frightening. The bad girl wants to kill me..." he mocked. Andrea leapt forward, shielding the monster, and snarled.

"What are you thinking?" Luca whispered angrily. "Do you want to get us killed?"

I lowered the gun.

"Maria, listen to the captain, or I will make your beloved kill you," he threatened. But how did he know my name? He moved stealthily, grabbing Andrea by the neck. Terror choked my sobs.

"Leave, or I'll rip his head off... like I did to that meddlesome porter."

I clapped my hands over my mouth to stop myself from screaming.

"Why don't you tell them to come back to us? A good deed will be taken into account by the Council."

I heard Dorian's voice.

We realised that the attack outside had been just a diversion to lure us into the cave and kidnap Andrea.

"How could I give you back a child I love? You two scum wouldn't give me back my child."

"If you don't shut up and let him go, I swear the punishment you'll receive will be the worst torture you can imagine. I will personally see to that."

"Where is Ludmilla?"

"Don't mention her, you vile creature!" growled Adelheid.

I stood stunned, listening to the exchange between Dorian and the monster. He was Ludmilla's biological father. I looked at Luca, who shook his head, silently pleading with me to stay calm.

I turned away and ran to the last step above the water.

"Let him go! Take me!" I shouted with all my might.

"If I wanted you, believe me, you'd be here, begging me for a glance," he replied, spitting in my direction.

Dorian grabbed me, spinning me behind him where Adelheid was ready to hold me. He carried me on his shoulder, like a drunk, preventing me from moving.

"Are you insane?" I felt the vampire's cold breath. "One more outburst, or any other initiative, and I will silence you for a few days. I can do that," she warned.

He threw me toward Luca, who managed to catch me before I fell again. I tried to wriggle out of his grasp, but he held me tight. "Be quiet," he signalled.

For a moment, there was total silence.

I could hear my heartbeat amplifying in my ears, making me dizzy. I stared at the monster, unable to tear my eyes away from his horrifying face, when I saw his expression change. Alarmed, he leapt towards

Andrea, grabbed him like a puppet, and perched on a rocky outcrop. He released Andrea, letting him roll down. I heard the sickening thud of his body hitting the stalagmites and froze. Andrea stood, seemingly waiting for further commands.

A gust of cold wind tousled my hair. "Ludmilla!" I exclaimed.

He gestured with his head to the right.

Charles had entered silently with his army in tow. "Ludmilla, what an honour for your old father to see you again," he sneered, his voice raspy.

It didn't make sense, I thought. That monster was Ludmilla's father. Why hadn't she told me? Maybe there hadn't been time, or maybe she couldn't bear to admit it.

Ludmilla stayed silent at the provocation, showing no surprise, only a pained smile.

"You will die today... father," she murmured.

Two things happened simultaneously: Charles ordered his soldiers to retrieve Andrea, while Adelheid and Dorian, along with other soldiers, launched themselves towards the monster.

"What a terrible, childish mistake." Those words echoed in my ears.

I didn't have time to realise what was happening until I found myself face down on a rock. I heard the bones in my head creak. Then, nothing.

17

The pain in my head woke me up, and I looked around, trying to figure out where I was. The monster had kidnapped me and now stood there in front of me.

"Don't make any strange movements, or I'll kill you," he threatened.

I regained some clarity and raised my head. He was squatting in front of me. His scent was foul, not the floral scent that vampires usually emitted.

"Do I disgust you? Does my smell make you nauseous? It's normal; I don't just feed on humans, I also feed on vampires... they have a, how shall I say, spicier taste."

I backed away, pushing myself with my arms until I hit the rock face. I looked at him with horror. How could such a monster exist? I swallowed hard and lowered my head.

"You attacked my partner," I said cautiously.

"Yes, but I gave him immortality, if he can keep it."

"No, that was Ludmilla, out of necessity. Otherwise, he would have died."

I saw him pause at my words, and then, like a child preparing to tell a fairy tale, he sat down cross-legged and sang, "Oh my dear, now I will tell you a little story."

"But I don't want to listen to stories, no... lies," I found the courage to reply.

"Sorry, but you'll have to listen to me. We have time; you don't think they'll find us easily," he sneered.

My legs and back were numb, and my head throbbed as if it were about to burst. I realised I needed to relax, so I leaned my back against the wall and pulled my knees up.

"If you want to talk, you must do so at a distance where I can't smell your stench."

He growled but moved about a metre away.

"I come from a noble family. My father was the only legitimate son of Mircea I, called 'The Elder,' Mihail; my mother's name was Maria, like my grandmother, and like you, dear. I have no memory of my father; he died on the battlefield in 1420, trying to repel Sultan Muhammad I. I grew up with my mother, who managed to hide me, making everyone believe I was dead. I also had a brother, but it seems he was taken by the Turks during the battle where my father died.

It was clear from the start that my mother couldn't stay at court, so we took refuge in France, in Paris..."

"Why are you telling me all this? I don't care about your life," I interrupted.

"Oh, but you will care..." he replied with a wicked grin. Then he continued. "We arrived in Paris on a warm, sunny day. We immediately sought out my uncle's family, who my mother thought would help us, but they didn't. My mother asked around, and someone told her the man had been killed during a city rebellion and that his wife and two daughters might be found in a brothel. Fortunately, my mother had managed to secure my father's money, which ensured us a more than decent life, allowing us to enter Parisian high society. Meanwhile, my mother remarried a wealthy merchant who was unaware of my essence. The adjustment my mother feared came, and with good reason. It wasn't long before, during a fit of rage, I killed my stepfather. My mother decided I needed someone to guide me through this painful and dangerous time. She found the vampires of Paris, who lived hidden in the sewers, hunted by both humans and the Catholic Church—quite different from life in Wallachia. A vampire of noble lineage sensed my essence and allowed himself to be approached by my mother. His name was Theophile Cambrian, and he became my guardian. From him, I learned all I needed to know about the vampire essence, and he helped me complete my adaptation. But then he had the nerve to enchant my mother, marry her, and they had more children. In the meantime, I graduated in law, and when my mother thought I could fend for myself, she and her new family left France and returned to Wallachia. They left on the day of the summer solstice, when light defeats darkness, escorted by a squad of vampires. About a month later, one of the vampires from the guard who accompanied them back to Wallachia returned with a letter from my mother: he told me the journey had gone well and not to worry about them, to live my life to the fullest. The only thing I lacked was money.

I enjoyed my life as a young lawyer for a few years, but suspicions about me began to grow. One day, while I was feeding on a beautiful girl from the Parisian slums, something distracted me, and she managed to escape. Thus began the hunt for the 'red vampire,' because of my hair colour. But, as it often happens among you weak humans, the hunt quickly extended to all with red hair, human or otherwise. I decided to flee and join my mother and her family.

I left one night, hidden in a wagon loaded with grapes. I paid the merchant so well that, just outside the city of Paris, he even wanted to give me the wagon and its load, but I refused. I travelled by resting during the day and running by night. At that time, vampires couldn't withstand sunlight; it weakened us too much, making us easy prey for hunters and other vampires. We don't know exactly what changed to make us less intolerant to light, allowing us to live more like humans. Perhaps it was an adaptation of an adaptation. After about three weeks, I reached the border between Hungary and Wallachia. I decided to hide in a cave for a few days, preparing to join my mother.

On the first night, I was woken by a disturbing noise. I searched for a hiding place with a good view of the cave entrance. I saw a man, haggard and exhausted, who must have been running a lot. Maybe he was fleeing something or someone. He collapsed to the ground, and I realised that if I didn't help him, he would die. I couldn't allow that—feeding on corpses is like feeding on rotten food. I approached him to smell him; the prey made my mouth water. I positioned myself above him, ready to strike the jugular, which was weakly pulsing, when he suddenly regained consciousness and looked at me. 'Who are you?' he asked in a husky voice.

I got up and decided, for the time being, to let him live. Maybe he could give me news of my mother. I thought he couldn't have come from far, likely from the village where she lived.

I took the canteen tied around my waist to make me look like an ordinary traveller and brought it to his lips. He drank greedily, coughing and spilling some liquid on the ground. I helped him up.

'Where are you from?' I asked. He told me his story: he was being hunted as a deserter. He had escaped by hiding in a mass grave, camouflaging himself among the rotting corpses. I decided to believe him and gave him the gift of immortality, letting him drink my blood and then biting him. I hid him in the deepest part of the cave, where the soldiers wouldn't find him. He underwent his adaptation there, which took several hours. When he returned, he swore eternal loyalty to me. I asked if he knew of my mother's family. He spoke of Theophile Cambrian, who had become the right-hand man of the local lord. I decided to go to the castle.

Needless to say, my stepfather was far from pleased to see me. He denied me entry to the castle and had me arrested, locking me in an outdoor dungeon. I realised then that only a vampire hunter could have built such a prison, where sunlight would keep vampire prisoners at bay. I also discovered the secret he was proud of: he had formed a small army of Azara vampires..." I gasped at that name, and he noticed. "Do you know what an Azara vampire is?" I nodded.

"Good, I don't have to waste time explaining."

He shifted his position, and for a moment, I thought he might drop the act, but he didn't.

"I quickly realised what was happening: the person I thought was a trusted friend was actually carrying out orders. He was the one who had betrayed me and ensured I was locked up. They mocked me!" he roared, throwing a boulder against the rock face.

For a moment, I thought the cave would collapse.

"My stepfather's beast turned me into an Azara, simply by forcing me to drink vampire blood. When I became like him, he freed me and made me the overseer of his Azara squadron. I thought playing along would bring me to my mother. And it did. I found her imprisoned in an oubliette..."

"In a what?" I interrupted.

"An oubliette. It's more than just a prison; it's a sentence to oblivion in a cell deep underground. You don't get out of there—you die there. But I found her still alive. I wanted my mother; I had no intention of letting her die, so I bit her. But even that was planned by my stepfather. I hadn't accounted for my new essence, and when she turned, I couldn't control my Azara bloodlust. I killed her.

Desperate, holding my mother's mangled body in my arms, I begged for death from Theophile's soldiers, but they didn't grant it. Everything had already been decided—a fate far worse than death: they condemned me to excommunication and mummification. I was sealed in an iron coffin on Christmas Day, 1448."

"Evidently, they didn't leave you there for long," I commented sarcastically.

"I remained motionless for an indefinite time. Hunger tormented me for ages, while my body painfully mummified, but my mind stayed lucid throughout. I slipped into comas several times, yet the pain always managed to awaken me... without relief. One thought sustained me through the torment: the day of vengeance would come. And it did.

Suddenly, I felt air rush into my lungs. A team of archaeologists had discovered my tomb, and the fools opened it... I devoured them mercilessly, but left one alive. I forced him to answer my questions. It was 1916, and I was in Cluj-Napoca. Imagine, half a millennium sealed in a coffin." He spat on the ground, his eyes flaring. I feared he was about to attack me, but he calmed down and continued. "I wandered for a long time, living alone in the mountains and plotting my revenge against my stepfather, whom I imagined was still alive.

World War I began. I joined the volunteer rescuers, a perfect way to find food. I wandered among the dying, easing their pain as they passed away—they even thanked me. One day, after I had finished feeding, I noticed a man watching me. I lunged at him, but he pushed me away with force. Only a vampire could do that.

'You need to stay hidden, or do you want to get caught? They'll notice you soon enough. Nice to meet you, brother, I'm Sebastian.' We became friends. It had been so long since I'd interacted with someone like me that I wasn't willing to lose him. I followed him on his raids among the peasant villages. He disliked the blood of dying soldiers: it was tainted, with a taste of gunpowder residue.

The war ended. One evening, in a bar, we heard about America and the opportunities it offered. We decided to leave.

It wasn't difficult to secure first-class tickets on one of the finest French ships, the 'Beau Soleil.' My imagination, vivid as it was, could never have conjured such beauty. I spent my nights on the top deck, enjoying the sight of the sky, the sea, and the elegant humans. I sampled them, but to my disgust, they tasted sour... undrinkable, especially the women. It was the era of radioactive creams, you see? What can I say, we vampires are fortunate to be immune to radioactivity. But we managed—we couldn't dine solely in restaurants, so we adapted, drinking only from men who didn't use cosmetics.

The ship docked in Louisiana on the afternoon of my birthday. I took it as a good omen. We headed to New Orleans, where Sebastian claimed to have contacts. The address was 1039 Royal Street, where an eccentric Frenchman greeted us: elegant, wealthy, and mysterious. Within hours, he organized a welcome party, and before long, the house was brimming with the city's most influential figures. He introduced us as his distant Romanian cousins and spun tales of our childhood adventures... which, of course, never happened. Every night was a party, and Jacques—yes, that was his name—was the best host I'd ever seen. He answered every question with wit and intellect, and it was rumoured he spoke at least ten languages. His best party was for his birthday; he invited a dance troupe from New York, mesmerized them before their performance, and at the end, they all offered their necks to him. 'Please, friends, drink directly from the source,' he declared, bowing."

"My God... you're a monster," I muttered, nauseated.

The creature's eyes bore into mine, as if searching my mind. Then, the usual sarcastic smile returned to his face.

"My God? If you added up all the murders committed by every vampire on Earth, the total would still be less than the deaths in the name of that God you pray to."

He fell silent, massaging his face, which was covered in pustules. I felt revulsion, and tears began to slide down my cheeks. I was exhausted.

He resumed speaking. "We enjoyed ourselves for a long time. Jacques was the god of entertainment and incredibly wealthy. He showed us how to make money. Sebastian had a few family assets, and Jacques helped him sell them at astounding prices. With the money, he taught us to invest in the stock market. In no time, we became very rich, and we decided it was time to leave Jacques' accommodations. We bought a house in the same French Quarter and began hosting our own parties.

One day, Jacques asked us to invite a new friend to one of our gatherings. We agreed willingly.

Theophile Cambrian had found me. He showed up at the door as if nothing had happened and offered me his hand, which I couldn't refuse.

Later that evening, he approached me and asked me to step aside for a private conversation. Reluctantly, I told him to follow me to my study.

'Dear stepson, I hope everything is all right between us,' he said with a smug grin. In that moment, I remembered what he had turned me into... an Azara. I think he had forgotten. I struck him so quickly he didn't even realize it. He brought his hand to his neck, but the wound didn't heal, and the blood gushed out. I drank eagerly and then bit off his head. But Jacques did not forgive me, and I was forced to leave New Orleans. Sebastian didn't follow me either, but he gave me the name of another vampire who could help: 'Go in my name, he will listen to you.'

Benicio Della Puebla was a wealthy landowner and an ancient blood vampire. He was pleased to learn that Sebastian, the son of his great friend, had sent me to him seeking shelter. I was honest from the start and told him why I had to leave New Orleans. Benicio lived in a magnificent neoclassical mansion, perched on a small hill, surrounded by the wealth that built his fortune: sugar cane. He offered me a job, which I accepted, even though I had my own money. It was to seek out and train wandering vampires, teaching them compassion. Benicio Della Puebla was a compassionate vampire who had learned to drink blood without killing humans. You might wonder why I took on such a role..."

I didn't dare breathe, let alone respond, so I just shrugged.

"I was bored to death pretending to be a compassionate vampire, but Benicio's rules were ironclad. Disobeying them would mean a return to the iron coffin. I found solace in the errands he sent me on to the city to buy supplies. Mostly, it was a distraction for those who speculated about the strange happenings on the plantation. In the city, I became known as 'Benicio's Stranger,' and enjoyed a certain freedom among the brothels near the river port. Along the Mississippi's banks lived the city's outcasts, hopeless paupers. Among them, I was free to indulge my true nature. I could drink without anyone noticing.

One day, I was walking near the estate when I encountered a peculiar woman driving a stunning Rolls-Royce Silver Ghost. I stared at her, dumbfounded. I realized she was like me, and she admitted she had been turned by a stranger about fifty years prior. Her name was Vicky, and she proudly claimed ownership of the northernmost sugarcane plantation in Louisiana. She didn't mince words: she hadn't met me by chance but had come with a proposition. She wanted a vampire trainer, but unlike Benicio, she wanted them bloodthirsty. It didn't take much to convince me. That very day, I left the estate and snuck away.

I joined her at the river port, where her boat, the Oasis of the River, was docked. My life became thrilling and intense again, like it had been in the days of New Orleans. I made peace with my Azara vampire nature, though I doubt they even knew what that meant in that part of the world—but they would soon learn. With Benicio, my thirst for vampire blood was stifled by the compassion I was forced to display, but with Vicky's vampires, it was different. I had to teach them to be ruthless, to crave human blood, to fight. Once, exasperated by a vampire's feigned compassion, I lost patience and bit him. When he died, Vicky realized the cause and demanded an explanation. I gave her one, and it thrilled her so much that she made me head of the estate.

Then Prohibition came, and with it, the financial difficulties of running a sugar plantation. Without converting production to refining, the authorities would have destroyed everything—burning down the crops, sometimes even the house. I had no intention of sacrificing myself for a world that didn't belong to me. I returned to Europe.

Setting foot back in Paris brought me immense joy. I settled down."

He noticed that I was staring at my shoes, my knees drawn up under my chin, with a look of obvious boredom.

"You'd better listen to the rest of my tale... Hmm... let me think... not that you have a choice," he sneered.

"You've answered your own question. I have no choice. I'll listen, but you can't force me not to be bored," I retorted, matching his rhyme.

"Oh, believe me, I could force you."

133

"Well, go ahead then, so I can listen with enthusiasm," I challenged him.

"What pleasure would I get from that? No, you'll listen and be bored... and I'll enjoy knowing just how bored you are. But, believe me, at some point, you'll beg me to continue."

I shifted my gaze back to my shoes, waiting for him to go on.

"I settled in one of the city's most prestigious hotels, frequented by writers, philosophers, and scientists. I felt at ease among them and was able to control my instincts. One evening, during one of my many conversations with other men, a stunning woman entered the hotel bar and sat alone at a small table. Despite being in libertine France, where much was tolerated, a woman alone in a bar still drew attention. I thought instantly that she would be mine, in every sense. But just then, someone came through the door, and a gust of wind lifted her hair, releasing a wild scent. A vampire. She noticed and flashed her fangs, but I tried to calm her by moving to sit beside her. Her clear eyes reflected my face, and I was captivated as we talked about everything and nothing. She soon cut the conversation short and asked me to leave.

The city at night offers intense sensations, and we were both excited and hungry. We strolled down the Seine, where the majestic river banks welcomed tourists, artists, and businessmen by day, but at night became a refuge for the homeless. We chose at random: a man for me, a woman for her. We were swift and deadly, leaving no trace. Satisfied, we left the riverbank and returned to the city streets. We soon realized we were being followed. Alarmed, we started to run, but it became clear that whoever was chasing us was a creature like us. They kept up with us easily, impossible for a human, so we ducked into an alley, ready to confront them.

The street was empty, though a few windows were still lit. It was dangerous for us. We stood still, waiting for the creature, who soon arrived. He was enormous, dressed like a gentleman, complete with a cane and top hat, which he courteously removed. He advanced slowly, cautiously, like a cat, and offered me his hand; I reciprocated, but he didn't let me touch him. With lightning speed, he swung his cane, striking my forearm. The impact was so strong I felt my bones creak. Another blow, aimed at my neck, sent searing pain through me, and I collapsed.

I managed to look up, and now there were three attackers, all holding iron sticks. One of them, the shortest, planted his boot on my chest, keeping me down. My attempts to plead were useless. And then I realized—Adelheid, my companion that night, had disappeared, or so I convinced myself... What a fool I was..."

He scanned the last word letter by letter, but I was still in disbelief, still turning over the name I had heard: Adelheid. I tried to speak, but he silenced me by moving closer and covering my mouth with his hand.

"You can't talk now, let alone ask questions," he said firmly, removing his hand. I sighed in relief, though the stench from that hand was the same as death.

"I was alone and injured, mostly unaware of what was happening to me. My priority was to get back on my feet and find Adelheid. I was terrified at the mere thought of her being a prisoner of those violent vampires; they were going to hurt her. I ran through the city streets, trying to follow her scent, but found nothing. Anger took over, and I lashed out at anyone who crossed my path. Just outside the town, I caught a faint whiff of her essence, which grew stronger as I continued. Suddenly, she emerged from behind a hedge. I ran towards her, but her face was twisted into a monstrous grimace. 'You will die today,' she hissed.

She opened her mouth, extending her canines, and grabbed my head, pushing it to the side to expose my jugular. For a moment, I thought she was also an Azara, and that I would die from the bite, but so would she. I didn't fight back. But she stopped and stared into my eyes. 'You killed your mother, you damned monster. She was mine too.'

I was speechless. My sister was standing before me, and clearly, she still didn't know that a few years earlier, I had also killed her father. I somehow managed to calm her down, and for a few minutes, we talked quietly. She told me she was the only survivor among her siblings and that she was searching for her father. I explained how my mother had died—by my hand—but only because her father had turned me into an Azara. At that word, she recoiled and fled. I never heard from her again.

World War II devastated Europe. Not that I cared much, but it provided me with shelter and sustenance. It was during this time that my most ambitious idea came to me: an army of my own. I transformed many dying people, enchanting them to follow me as their supreme leader. I wanted humanity at my feet, but I underestimated the bloodlust of the newly made vampires. They destroyed entire regiments and, bored by the blood of soldiers, turned on civilians. In no time, they could have eradicated humanity, already weakened by war.

I was forced to ask Charles for help. He set things right but imposed a new excommunication on me. He declared me free game, allowing any vampire to kill me. I spent years on the run, and it was thanks to the cultural advancements of humans that I regained my freedom. Humans were no longer inclined to believe in the hidden world of supernatural beings; they reduced us to mere legend.

I returned to living among humans, stopped feeding on them, and instead perfected the art of vampire hunting. It was a quiet period, and I resumed my career as a lawyer. One day, after winning an important case, the firm rewarded me with a trip on the Orient Express, the most beautiful and luxurious train in the world. The opulence of it all—elegant businessmen, affluent heiresses—made me appreciate immortality. It's fascinating to see the rich, full of pride in their wretched lives, convinced they can take their wealth beyond death. But the fascination turns to joy when you watch them die.

On board the train, I resumed feeding on humans, creating a competition with myself: I would feed and charm them into forgetting the bite. Before long, everyone on board was sporting long scarves around their necks—a sight that amused me.

In Trieste, the train made a prolonged stop due to a demonstration that prevented departures. Many passengers left the carriages to stroll and smoke. I did the same. While lighting a cigarette, through the coils of smoke, I saw her. She appeared like a goddess, accompanied by a porter carrying her luggage. She glanced back at me as she boarded a carriage with the help of a train attendant. I had to calm myself, suppressing the lust that surged within me, and locked myself in my suite.

I saw her again, sitting at a table in the dining car. I tipped one of the waiters generously to deliver an invitation to my table. She accepted. She sat across from me, gazing at me flirtatiously. She exuded a burning perfume, her thick, jet-black hair gathered in a soft knot at the nape of her neck. Her face was a perfect oval, her complexion pure white. She moved a lock of hair, revealing her throbbing jugular. I gripped the chair, my nails digging into the wood as I fought to calm myself. She introduced herself as Rachel, from a wealthy French banking family... now fallen on hard times. A hint of sadness colored her voice. I introduced myself as Mihail Basarabi, a lawyer from the Paris Bar. She listened, spellbound, to my tales as a man of the law. 'I'll be bold; we hardly know each other, but a lawyer could help me recover my family's inheritance, lost during the war.' I couldn't wait to make her mine.

Rachel was lively, and the fine wine served onboard loosened her up. I escorted her to my suite, intending to quench the fire in my throat, but I failed. I hadn't felt carnal desire in ages; life hadn't given me time to consider such appetites. She sensed my inexperience and took the lead, pulling me into a whirlwind of passion that, for a few moments, made me forget how intoxicating she smelled.

We decided to disembark in Istanbul and stayed there for a long time.

One day, what should have been the happiest day of my life turned into my worst nightmare: she told me she was pregnant. My joy faded as I found myself forced to reveal my nature to her. I was certain she wouldn't understand. But she did, and with astonishing simplicity, she said, 'I always suspected.'

Her belly grew, and I searched for ways to ensure a safe delivery. I had heard stories of women who hadn't survived. I sought advice from an old vampire, who assured me that times had changed. Women no longer died during childbirth, but he also warned that after the child was born, the mother would need to be enchanted or turned. The choice was hers. I remembered my mother, who had survived childbirth without any issues. I trusted in the sweet logic of fate.

I returned to Istanbul after two days. As soon as I entered the house, I sensed something was wrong. The air was thick with unfamiliar scents, and Rachel was nowhere to be found.

Now, you should know that one of my vampiric abilities is to discern scents, much like animals do, and I'm never wrong. Adelheid had been there. I cursed her with all my might. I turned to Rachel's father, Robert Du Jardin. There was no love lost between us, but I decided he was the only one who could help me without betrayal. I told him everything, including my true nature and that our son, his grandson, would likely share it. Perhaps I charmed him unintentionally, but he was the one who asked to be adapted. Robert was born to be a vampire; he is balanced, to the point of never having drunk human blood violently.

I know I've been talking for a long time, but we're almost at the end... dear."

That "dear" made my skin crawl. Yet, somehow, he had managed to intrigue me, even make me pity him. I think he sensed it, grinning in a way that made me regret my empathy.

"In a few days, Robert was revitalized and ready to execute the plan we had devised. My sense of smell and his grief for his lost daughter led us to Italy, to Turin. We couldn't enter the city without Adelheid's bloodhounds finding us. I killed a few of them but had to stop; they captured Robert, who was still not strong enough to defend himself against older vampires. I let them take me. They transported us to a secret location and separated us. One night, I was awakened by heart-wrenching screams, followed by silence and the cries of a newborn. I thought I was losing my mind. I was weak, given very little blood, but my captors didn't seem to know about my Azara essence. I attacked the hand of one who offered me my meager blood ration through the bars. I bit him. When he realized the wound wasn't healing, he looked at me in terror, and I seized my chance. I convinced him I could help him recover, but only if he cooperated. That's how I learned Rachel had given birth but died. And that I was the father of a child I would never see."

Robert convinced Adelheid and her companion Dorian to let me live. On the day they released me, they made me swear that I would never be seen again. Robert accompanied me out of the prison, vowing to protect Ludmilla forever."

He abruptly finished his story and his expression shifted. I watched as he turned, and in a fatherly tone, said, "Come forward." Terror gripped me, and I almost stopped breathing.

Oh no, no, no... I blinked, hoping it was just a vision.

Cecilia led a group of children who emerged from the rocks, silent and fluid. In her walk was the elegance of a predator, imbued with a demonic charm. As they approached, I couldn't help but study them. They moved awkwardly, as if weighed down by their own movements. Breathtakingly beautiful, they bewitched me, drawing me toward them as a mother is drawn to protect her children from danger.

Cecilia reached me and stood a few steps away, her intense blue eyes glaring at me with hatred.

"You're old!" she exclaimed, her voice melodic and chirpy like that of a vampire woman, yet with a boyish tone.

"Cecilia... do you remember?" I tried to speak softly, to calm her.

He didn't let me finish. He clenched his jaws and leaned forward, preparing to attack me.

"No, no, no, my dear. Remember, you have to be nice to humans," the monster interjected, stepping between her and me.

"Please," I pleaded, "they are only children. And you, Cecilia, do you remember your daddy? I'm sure you do... well, know that the monster who created you killed him."

I saw suspicion flicker across the child's gaze, and suddenly, a look of pain overtook her face. She tried to say something but didn't manage it in time.

The monster turned and leapt at me. "Did I say you could talk?"

In his anger, he was even more grotesque. The drowsy, lustful expression of a beast in heat and the nauseating stench from his mouth overwhelmed me, and I lost consciousness.

When I came to, the monster was no longer on top of me, and I breathed a sigh of relief. The echoes from the rock face amplified even the slightest noise.

The monster bounded towards the dark cavern and let out a roar, then froze.

"Come forward, my son, join your little brothers."

"Andrea!" I shouted.

He walked forward gracefully, never taking his eyes off me, and stopped by my side. I heard Cecilia hiss, and the rest of the group mimicked her.

"Let her go," Andrea pleaded, addressing the monster.

"Why should I listen to you?" he replied, smiling devilishly.

"She has nothing to do with your revenge."

"You're right, but she is my passport, and besides... I would never hurt her." He finished his sentence with a melancholy tone.

Then he seemed distracted by a noise and tightened his lips into a grimacing smile. His fists clenched so tightly that I could hear his bones creak.

"No!" he growled, preparing to pounce.

"Don't you dare hurt her!" Andrea shouted, stepping in front of me.

"Or what?" the monster taunted.

"I will kill you."

"You can't do that. I've enchanted you, and maybe... maybe I could even force you to do it," he threatened.

The children began to move slowly, forming a semicircle around us.

"Stop!" Andrea commanded.

Confusion clouded their eyes, but somehow Andrea managed to calm them. The monster bared his teeth, trying to comprehend what was happening.

Andrea moved closer to him.

I heard a piercing scream and saw the monster hurtling through the air, crashing against the rocks with a screech that sounded like steel grinding.

A gust of fragrant wind washed over me, bringing a sense of calm.

"Ludmilla." She picked me up in her arms and carried me out of the cave.

"How are you? Did that unclean creature dare to touch you? Are you hurt?" she asked, noticing the blood on my forehead.

"I'm fine. We need to go back in."

"Calm down... you're not going anywhere."

"Hey, Inspector, I see you're still in one piece," said a voice I recognized well.

"Luca!" I instinctively threw myself into his arms. "We have to go in and help them!" I repeated, sobbing.

"You two stay here," Ludmilla cut in.

"Not even easy to keep her still," Luca said. "If she moves, shoot her."

He disappeared back into the cave.

I remained motionless, my feet heavy, clinging to Luca. I looked around, desolate, broke away from his embrace, and collapsed to the ground, crying.

"Cecilia... did you see her? This is all so insane... tell me it isn't real."

My sobs shook me so violently that I was doubled over in pain.

"Hey... hey... look at me, Maria, look at me," Luca urged, gently lifting my face.

"This is unbearable," I sobbed, wiping my tears.

A noise from the forest, just outside the cave, alerted us both.

"Get down behind this bush," Luca whispered.

She emerged slowly from between the trees. Cecilia. Her eyes scanned everything around her, sparkling like sapphires. She shielded her face with one arm as the sunlight filtered through the leaves, irritating her as it did all vampires.

She stopped, standing still, staring directly at me. Our eyes met, and she caught my gaze.

"You're old," she repeated, chanting the words for the second time.

"Hey kid, you don't have a very refined vocabulary," Luca teased her.

She turned her head and glared at him, the tension in the air palpable. Then she bent down, preparing to leap. She could have torn us apart in seconds, but something in her expression shifted.

"I don't want to kill you... I want Ludmilla."

"You're right, but I can assure you that Ludmilla will face justice for her actions," I tried to reason with her.

"I was a child. I had the right to live."

"Your father wouldn't have wanted to see you like this. He died in front of me. And your mother... she never recovered after your death. This wasn't Ludmilla's doing; it was the monster who created you, who created all the other children and set fire to the disco."

She stood there, tilting her head to one side. I took a step toward her, wanting to console her, to hug her, but Luca stopped me.

"Stay still. Remember, she may look like a child, but she can take your head off with one strike."

We watched as she clenched her jaws and hunched her shoulders. She could have reached me in a single bound, but she stayed motionless. A mocking smile curled her lips, and her gaze shifted past me. Then, in a state of confusion, she let out a heart-wrenching scream. We turned around.

Not far from us, something bounced off the rock and rolled to our feet. Luca and I exchanged horrified looks.

I jumped back in disgust. One of the children lay lifeless at my feet.

"No!" we heard her scream.

She changed her focus and charged at Luca.

"You will die," she growled.

She leapt at Luca, but he was ready, his pistol loaded with wooden bullets. He emptied the entire magazine into her.

"We have little time before she recovers. Run!" shouted Luca.

I stood still, watching as a silhouette swooped down over Cecilia. Ludmilla. "Get to safety!" she ordered.

"Don't hurt her!" I shouted.

"Luca, take her away; we don't have time for this," Ludmilla insisted.

"Leave me alone!" I snapped, turning on Luca, who tried to grab my arm.

I heard Ludmilla snarl like an enraged bull. She seized Cecilia's body and hurled her against the rock face of the mountain.

Then everything unfolded like a macabre sequence. Luca slipped and hit his head on a boulder. The trickle of blood from his wound stirred Cecilia, who freed herself from Ludmilla's grip. She sniffed the air, drawn to the metallic scent of Luca's blood, and pounced on him.

Ludmilla appeared behind her, striking her with a makeshift wooden stick. It snapped in two, and she used the sharpest piece to stab her. Cecilia grasped the piece of wood, trying to pull it out, but Ludmilla didn't give her a chance. She grabbed the stick and leapt onto a ledge. I watched as Cecilia's head rolled to the rocky ground, detached from her body, toward a pool of water left by recent rains.

I tried desperately to look away, but my eyes were fixed on the puddle as tears streamed down my face.

"Maria, don't cry," Ludmilla whispered. "Really. Cecilia was just a monster with no future. If I hadn't killed her, she would have. Charles. There can be no such thing as child vampires."

"But you were a child vampire. Why you and not her?" I shouted back.

"No, I wasn't a child vampire. I adapted as an adult. And anyway, look what I did when I broke free from Robert's control."

"What am I supposed to do now?" I asked anxiously.

"Nothing. You need to forget."

Slowly, I began to regain some clarity.

"What about the others? Andrea?" I asked.

"Everyone's fine, it's over," Robert's gentle voice replied. "It's time to tend to our captain's wound."

He approached Luca and gently began to wipe the blood from his forehead.

Together, Ludmilla and Robert, after seeing to Luca, began to carefully gather the remains of Cecilia and the other child's bodies.

We made our way back towards the entrance of the cave. Charles was there, waiting for us. He ordered his people to take the bodies and place them with the others.

I watched as they all gathered in a circle, not understanding what was happening. Luca came over and hugged me.

"They are performing the funeral rite. Vampires cannot return to the earth; they must undergo cremation. They circle around to protect the ritual from human eyes."

I watched the thick smoke rise, almost seeming to take shape, but the wind that picked up scattered it into the air. What lingered was an intense floral scent, the same that accompanied any of them when they approached. Then, they all joined hands and began to whisper, their voices rising until it sounded like the beating of a thousand wings.

Ludmilla stepped out of the circle and approached the remaining pile of ashes. Robert handed her an urn shaped like an angel with outstretched wings. She collected some of the ashes and poured them inside, then walked over to me.

"Keep this with you. I am sure Cecilia is now at peace, and she will watch over you."

I took the urn and clutched it to my chest, feeling its cool, smooth surface as if it could somehow ease the ache inside me.

I began looking around, searching for Andrea, expecting to see him among the circle.

"Where is Andrea?" I asked, my voice laced with worry.

"There," Ludmilla said, pointing with her finger.

I saw him at the front of a group of vampires, pulling massive chains to drag the monster out.

"You didn't kill him," I said, my voice shaking with anger.

"Do not judge what you do not understand," Charles stated firmly. "Mihail will be mummified deep within the earth, but first, he will be judged by the Council."

"The children weren't judged," I argued, my frustration boiling over.

"Woman, I told you not to judge what you do not understand. They were not children, not anymore. That was not their doing. They were turned into immortal monsters, and their souls will now ascend peacefully to heaven. But they could not have remained here on earth; it is for the good of all mankind." He finished with a finality that left no room for argument, his gaze heavy enough to make me lower mine.

Irritated and utterly drained, I sat down on a nearby boulder and began to cry again, feeling the weight of everything collapse on me.

I felt a pair of hands rest gently on mine, and for a moment, I hoped they were Andrea's, but I no longer saw him. Not that day. Ludmilla understood my silent disappointment.

"He is still under the effects of the sickness; it will take days for him to recover, and right now it is better that the two of you are not alone together. We don't know what Mihail may have commanded him to do."

I looked at her, confused and torn, but I knew well enough that once a decision was made, there was nothing I could do to change it.

18

When the car stopped, I snapped out of the stupor I had willingly immersed myself in. We had returned to Adelheid's house. I begged everyone to leave me alone with my thoughts and locked myself in my room. During the journey, in a state of torpor, I devised a plan. I would go back to Charles and kill the monster with my own hands. Once, he had managed to escape his coffin; I would make sure it never happened again. But I knew that on my own, I could never accomplish this. Only Ludmilla would be willing to join me on such a reckless mission, but I would need to present the plan to her carefully.

I stepped into the shower, trying to picture the scenarios I might face. My thoughts were interrupted by a sudden touch on my shoulder.

"Hey, you've been in there for an hour. Do you plan on melting?"

"Andrea? What part of 'I want to be alone for a while' did you not understand?"

Ludmilla's warnings echoed in my mind, and I felt a flicker of concern. But on the surface, he seemed harmless.

"I need to know you won't leave me," he whispered, wrapping his strong arms around me.

I turned my face against his chest, and after a long, deep breath, I began to speak.

"If you need me, I'll always be there, at least until death parts us… and, as you well know, there's no doubt about who should die. But if you're asking for certainty about our relationship, I can't give you that right now."

"That's not what I was hoping to hear," he replied, his voice heavy with disappointment.

I looked up at his face and, for the first time, noticed the red ring encircling his dark pupils.

"How long has it been since you fed?"

"You're changing the subject."

"Maybe, but I'm worried about you. Today was hard for all of us, but for you, who endured that monster's control, it's worse. So, please, go with the others and feed."

"Does Luca Perri have something to do with this?"

"What are you talking about? Are you out of your mind?"

I looked into his eyes and realized something was different. He tightened his grip on my arm.

"Let go of me, you're hurting me!" I shouted.

Before I knew it, his lips were pressing against my neck, violently.

Ludmilla burst into the bathroom and shoved him to the other side, sending him crashing into the shower glass, which shattered. She draped my bathrobe over my shoulders and carried me out of the room.

"I warned you it might be dangerous to be alone with him."

"He got into the shower without my knowing; I couldn't do anything but go along with it."

"Let me see your neck," she said sternly, tilting my head to the side. "You did well..."

"Thank you," I replied quietly.

"I was going to bring you dinner; I hope you're hungry."

"Yes, I am, but give me a few minutes first."

"Of course," she said, sitting on the bed beside me.

"You have to take me to Charles," I blurted out.

She raised her right eyebrow. "Are you mad?"

I searched her eyes, hoping to find some way to persuade her. "Please."

"I don't understand why you would ask such a thing. Maria, why do you want to go to Charles?"

"I need to know."

"Know what? Charles will kill you—or us—as soon as we walk through his door."

"You know, when I was held captive by the monster, I caught a glimpse of... good."

Ludmilla burst into laughter. "A glimpse of good... I can hardly keep a straight face," she said, still laughing.

"It doesn't seem to me that he's putting much effort into it," I replied dryly.

"Sorry. Maria, there's nothing good about Mihail. But what exactly did he tell you?" she asked, now more serious and suspicious.

"He talked to me for two hours about his life instead of killing me... and he kept hinting that the best part was yet to come. But things didn't go his way."

There was a long moment of silence, and I avoided her gaze, sensing she was trying to read my thoughts.

"Fine," she said finally.

I had the distinct feeling she was hiding something, but maybe it was just the mysterious way vampires perceived humans. "And when would you like to end our lives?" she asked with a hint of sarcasm.

"Tomorrow."

I heard her hiss and swallow hard. "Tomorrow at dawn, I'll be here. Be ready," she said tersely, almost reluctantly.

"Thank you. I knew I could count on you." She left without saying goodbye.

In my heart, I was certain that the monster still had something to say, and before I carried out my plan, I needed to talk to him one last time.

I glanced at my phone lying on the bed. It was almost midnight, an hour earlier in Italy. I felt the urge to call my mother, perhaps for the last time.

"Maria, what's going on?" she answered, startled.

"Everything's fine. I had a spare moment and wanted to say goodnight before going to sleep. How are you?"

"We're fine, but when are you coming back?"

"A few more days. We're close to solving the case," I said, trying to sound reassuring.

"I know you tell me what you want to anyway. You've been like that your whole life."

"Mom, please, it's not that I only tell you what I want. I tell you what I can. You know that investigations are kept confidential until they're solved or closed. I need to go now. Say goodbye to Dad for me. Goodnight."

I heard her sigh and mumble something, but I ended the call. She had always been like that, ever since I joined the murder squad... but she was just being a mother.

I murmured something incoherent and slipped under the sheets.

That night, I kept waking up from nightmares. I couldn't count how many times I saw my head severed, by an unseen hand, lying next to the rock where Cecilia's lifeless body had been.

The alarm on my phone jolted me awake. 05:30 flashed on the screen, and I struggled to silence it without dropping the phone.

Ludmilla knocked on the door soon after. "Are you ready?" she whispered.

I peered through the doorway, and with a finger to her lips, she signaled for silence. She wrapped her arm around me, and we hurried out of the house.

She guided me to a car parked on the street. "Get in," she ordered.

I settled into the passenger seat, wanting to thank her again.

"Don't thank me. Stupid me, I'm going to die before I even reach a hundred years old," she said with mock sarcasm.

"Well, think of me—no matter how things turn out, I'm definitely not going to see a hundred," I said with a faint smile.

She didn't respond to my dark joke, and instead accelerated toward the motorway, taking a side road to enter it.

"But you can't just bypass the toll gates!" I protested.

"Do you think I'm going to pay the toll?"

"Usually..."

The road soon became familiar to me, and I realized we weren't following the usual route.

"Where are we going?" I asked, but she didn't answer. Instead, she pressed harder on the accelerator, speeding up.

"Ludmilla, do you want to answer?" I urged, as she accelerated again. The situation was infuriating. What was that crazy woman doing?

"Ludmilla, stop. Slow down... or stop," I pleaded.

Gradually, she eased off the gas, turning onto the slip road towards Constance.

"Ludmilla, talk to me. If you keep silent, I will..." I threatened, my patience wearing thin.

I unbuckled my seat belt and reached for the door handle, ready to make my point.

"Aside from the fact that you're clearly behind the times if you think the door opens while the car is moving..." she said, her tone dripping with sarcasm.

A sharp, violent pain shot down from the base of my neck along my spine. Then everything went black.

19

A stabbing pain in my head and neck jolted me awake. I looked around and, for a moment, I thought I was still in the bedroom at Adelheid's house. But as I regained clarity, I realized I was in the bedroom at Ludmilla's house.

I turned, sensing a presence beside me. It was Ludmilla.

"Sorry," she said, her face looking genuinely contrite.

"What are we doing at your place? Oh God, did we have an accident?" I asked, alarmed.

"There was no accident, but you... you gave me no choice. Did you really think I was going to take you to Charles?"

Suddenly, everything came rushing back. I had tried to jump out of the car... but why was my neck aching? Had I really done that? Then, a horrifying thought struck me. "You bit me?!" I shouted.

"Of course not!" she replied, offended.

"Speak, Ludmilla, I'm losing my patience."

"We vampires don't have much patience either, and you were starting to be pedantic, not to mention completely out of your mind. I hit you in the neck. Sorry, again."

Anger surged through me, and I clenched my teeth. "How dare you?"

Under different circumstances, I would have grabbed anyone who did that by the throat, but I knew perfectly well that trying to physically confront a vampire would only end badly for me.

"You owe me some explanations, Ludmilla."

"And you will get them, but first drink this herbal tea—it will help with the pain in your neck."

"I'm not drinking anything," I said, folding my arms and scowling.

"Look, I can always force your mouth open," she said with a playful wink.

I glared at her but reluctantly took the cup. I sipped it; it was surprisingly pleasant, with a hint of honey. The pain vanished almost instantly, faster than any painkiller I'd ever taken.

"What am I drinking?" I asked, curious.

"A blend of mountain herbs. Adelheid is the family naturopath. Only the addition of a touch of... honey is my own contribution."

I placed the empty cup on the bedside table, and Ludmilla took my hand. "Are we at peace? Friends?" she asked, extending her pinky. I linked mine with hers. "One... two... three, friends more than kings."

I never really understood what it meant, but it was how we made peace after fights when we were kids.

"You still need to explain why you won't take me to Charles," I said seriously.

"I will give you all the explanations you want, but first get dressed and join me in the living room. We'll talk better over a good cup of coffee."

It seemed a reasonable deal. The herbal tea had been healing, but a coffee would be good for my spirits.

When I joined her in the living room, steaming cups of coffee were already set out, and Ludmilla was waiting on the plush white sofa. She didn't waste any time, and as soon as I sat down, she began to speak.

"Well, you know, having a father like mine makes you ashamed to exist every day. I learned early on that I wasn't the biological daughter of Adelheid and Dorian, but I was told that he didn't want anything to do with me and that my mother had died giving birth to me."

She paused, gathering the courage to continue. I urged her on by gently squeezing her hands.

"But I wasn't born alone... there was another child... my twin," she said, her voice thick with difficulty.

My expression shifted to a mix of irony and disbelief. "But you never had a sister."

"They told me after I finished my adaptation, around the age of eighteen. They explained that my twin didn't inherit the vampirism gene, and she was hidden from me because, as a human, it would have been too dangerous for her."

"And do you know who she is?" I asked, my voice hesitant.

"Yes. When they revealed her identity, I rebelled against Adelheid and Dorian. I was young, and just after finishing adaptation, I was very fragile. From the moment I learned of her existence, not a day passed without me thinking about her. So I decided to go to her house. I showed up at her door; it was her adoptive mother who answered. She recognized me immediately—after all, we had known each other since childhood. She told me she was away at school and would be back the following month. She was very kind and begged me to come back the next day. She wanted to surprise her and would call to arrange it. But I didn't account for my family's reaction. Adelheid was furious. She called me crazy and told me I was the one who would be surprised."

She punished me by enchanting me: she made me forget my sister."

Ludmilla's words echoed in my head, almost as if I were reading them on a page. She wanted to surprise her...

Suddenly, I remembered an event from around thirty years ago, give or take. I had called home, as was my habit every other day. My mother mentioned that a girl, who looked very much like Ludmilla, had come all the way to the house looking for me, and she never showed up again, even though my mother had waited for me the next day by the phone to greet her.

What I was thinking was madness, a trick of my mind, a lie. But deep down, it felt like I had always known.

Gripped by a nervous tic, I let go of Ludmilla's hands and started ruffling my fringe. I was at a loss for words.

Ludmilla moved closer. "You are my sister... Maria."

"I... I... I don't know what to say... but how is it possible that my parents kept something so important from me?" I stammered.

"They are not to blame. When they adopted you, they were charmed into believing your mother had given birth to you."

"That's... that's not possible, Ludmilla. I've requested my birth certificate myself, several times... Did they glamour the registrar too?"

She hesitated before answering, looking at me with an almost pained expression. "I believe that's exactly what happened. Sometimes, fate has a way of twisting lives together in a way that defies logic."

"My whole life, I've been trying to... achieve something. Every action marked by this suffocating feeling of incompleteness... and I never understood why. The psychologists who evaluated me during my time on the police force attributed it to an obsession with pushing beyond... but why were we allowed to meet as children?"

"That was Grandpa Robert's doing. As a former human, his life was still governed by fear, and his greatest fear was that he would lose you if the vampirism gene ever activated. But after the events of 1986, everything changed, and he had to distance himself from you to protect me. Even after I came looking for you, Grandpa wanted to make sure you were safe. He tracked you down and kept an eye on you from afar."

"So that's what the monster was trying to tell me?" I asked, feeling a new wave of anxiety.

"Most likely, yes. When it became clear he hadn't had time to explain everything to you, Adelheid and Dorian insisted—even yesterday—that I keep the truth from you."

"And that's why you agreed to go along with my suicidal plan, just to end up here now?"

"Yes," she said, her voice dropping as she lowered her head.

I tried to keep my composure; there were still too many things I needed to understand.

"How did the monster know about me?"

"Mihail didn't let go, even when ordered to after we were born. He soon found me. Grandpa Robert, fearing for my safety, thought letting him see me from time to time would keep him calm, at least until I finished adapting. He used to visit a couple of times a year, and when he did, he brought wonderful gifts. I called him 'Father Christmas.' I was a little girl, and I actually liked him."

"You never told me about him."

"I was enchanted not to. Dorian made sure I couldn't tell anyone. But then came that damned day. I begged Grandpa to let me attend the event, but he was adamant. That year, Mihail showed up right at the gathering. I begged him to take me to see Grandpa secretly... and he, always seeking the opposite of what was right, agreed. He wanted to spite Grandpa. He took me to the party.

I went alone to the adjoining living room where the parents were gathered, and when Mihail realized how they had treated me, he set his plan into motion. He let me react hysterically; he knew that even though I hadn't begun to adapt yet, my anger could be easily triggered. He convinced me to return, but this time through the main entrance. He hypnotized the bouncers, who let me pass. You already know this part—Cecilia, crazed, threatened me with a broken bottle. When I lunged at her, everyone saw what I did... and how I did it. If Grandpa hadn't arrived, they would have killed me... and maybe it would have been better. But then the fire started, the screams, the doors locking, and it wasn't because of a short circuit from a gunshot but because of Mihail. Grandpa didn't see Mihail there; he only cared about getting me out of that hell. Mihail had himself locked inside so he could carry out his diabolical plan: he bit as many little girls as he could, infecting them so they would hover between life and death."

"My goodness, that's horrible... what about Cecilia's mum?" I asked, still trying to process everything.

"Her only fault was that she saw something she shouldn't have. It disturbed her so deeply that she couldn't recognize herself anymore," Ludmilla replied.

"Are you telling me he could have brought her back to her senses?" I asked, feeling a chill.

"Yes," she whispered.

"Well... I think it's probably best to leave her in her oblivion at this point," I said, but my voice lacked conviction.

"You don't sound convinced by your own words... I can sense it. Think about it: how would you feel today if it all came back to you?" Ludmilla challenged.

"You're right, it's better not to think about it. And then we'd also have to tell her that her husband is dead... killed by the same monster..." I trailed off, staring at her, my mind struggling to grasp everything.

Ludmilla pressed on. "Look, Maria, this is all incredibly difficult, and in my opinion, you need to release the accumulated terror..."

I cut her off. "Don't tell me to delay it; I need to understand, and then I'll try to process it, as you say."

"As you wish," she murmured.

"Ludmilla, please."

She took a deep breath and nodded. "Mihail didn't show up for many years, not until my 20th birthday. By then, my adaptation was complete. I was a fully-fledged vampire, with all the flaws," she added, her tone bitter yet laced with sarcasm. I pretended not to notice.

"The day he came, I was supposed to leave for university. I will remember that day for the rest of my existence. He appeared, as only he knows how, in the train compartment that Adelheid had booked just for me. I was happy to see him, after all, I was still spellbound and didn't remember anything. As I hugged him, he managed to enchant me again. I followed him to Romania. The cave where he held you captive... that was my home for a long time. He wasn't satisfied with merely enchanting me; he wiped my mind and awakened every suppressed memory."

I blinked, trying to make sense of it all.

"He's more than just a monster!" I exclaimed, horrified.

"Oh, I assure you, he wasn't the only monster," she said, her voice filled with a simmering anger. "He left me, for days, tormented by nightmares and guilt, and then decided it was time to 'fix' things. In his own twisted way. He made me sick again, forcing me to forget my family and, above all, forget that I was a benevolent vampire. The thirst returned like a punch to the gut, and I hunted with him for years. To make it seem less traumatic, he set a rule: I would only hunt those unworthy of living. I sought out my prey in the slums of Bucharest—murderers, rapists, paedophiles, and other scum. They met their end under my bite."

I looked at her, clutching my head in my hands. Even though I thought I had understood the essence of vampires, everything seemed so much more dreadful now.

Of course... because now it was Ludmilla. I couldn't imagine her as a monster.

"I was about twenty-five when they captured me," she continued, ignoring my distress. "At that time, my family was living in Germany. Dorian was the police commissioner of a small town in Bavaria, where legends were still welcomed. Someone told him about what was happening in Bucharest, and it didn't take him long to connect the dots. The trail of bodies, though hidden from human eyes, wasn't hidden from those of a vampire. He decided to come and see for himself. He left with Robert and made contact with the local police. He met an inspector, a vampire, who shared his strong suspicions about the killings over the past few years. They decided to investigate on their own and soon found evidence of my presence. An outcast vampire, worse than Mihail, had photographed me and demanded a promise that he wouldn't be reported to Charles in exchange for the photo. That's where Luca Perri came in."

"Luca?" I asked, squinting in surprise.

"Yes, the vampire hunter. But at that time, Dorian didn't know that yet. They met by chance; Dorian's inspector friend had warned him.

Vampire hunters use the blood of Azaras to kill them. But he also told Dorian that Luca, being a member of the Italian Carabinieri and undercover in Romania, was open to accepting the presence of benevolent vampires. And that's how it went. Luca agreed to talk to Dorian. At first, he was skeptical that I was under my biological father's control, but when he realized that the Geoana family consisted of benevolent vampires, he agreed to help Dorian search for me. However, they had to confront Charles and report what was happening. Charles is not a benevolent vampire; he is the oldest existing vampire and the most dangerous. He has been head of the Council for, I believe, over a thousand years. He is a just man, but he follows his law without compromise. He made a pact with both Dorian and Luca, promising my safety upon capture. He only required my imprisonment until I was rehabilitated from the hypnosis Mihail had induced. Only Charles can break the sickness without needing the creature who cast it. And so, on Christmas Day 2000, I was captured and locked in the dungeon of Charles' estate."

I felt a pang of pity for Ludmilla, seeing her relive this story.

She, on the other hand, watched me closely, as if gauging my reaction, and continued speaking.

"The period of rehabilitation was long and painful. But as soon as I stepped onto that path, the veil of sickness began to lift. Memories resurfaced, vivid and relentless, intensifying the pain. Charles helped me through it, and it was inevitable that I fell in love with him."

"You were with Charles... wow!" I exclaimed, caught off guard.

She stared at me, and when she spoke again, her voice was tinged with bitterness. "Wow?" she asked, her tone sharp.

"Sorry, I thought it sounded like a romantic story," I tried to explain. She burst out laughing.

"Well, it was a beautiful love story. The best ten years of my life."

"Ten years... you'll have plenty to tell me if you value our friendship," I teased her, singing the words playfully.

"I remind you that we are sisters," she replied, more seriously now.

"All the more reason to confess everything," I said, tightening my grip on her hand, which she hadn't let go of. We both burst into laughter, just like we did when we were children.

"Go on, continue," I encouraged her.

"What can I say... When Charles restored my goodwill, I couldn't bring myself to kill Mihail or even have him killed, so I didn't report him. Since he was my father, it was my choice. This attitude of mine caused quite a few problems with my mother. She wanted revenge, the same revenge she hadn't managed to get years before. I threw it in her face the day she tried to extract Mihail's location from me, using hypnosis. But Charles intervened and defended me, and above all, he defended the law. I didn't speak to Adelheid for years, which was one of the reasons she moved to Cluj and Dorian to Constance. You see, Dorian, despite not being my biological father, has always loved me deeply, and he couldn't stand to see Adelheid behave like that. As for me, although I love her, I've never felt her as my mother, or even as an aunt—our aunt, I mean. She has a very tough character and rarely indulges in maternal affection. I spent much of my life with Grandpa Robert, and I owe everything to him."

Ludmilla fell silent, and the room was heavy with a surreal, almost suffocating stillness. My demeanor seemed to catch her attention.

"After all, these kinds of problems exist in human families too," she said hesitantly. "It hasn't done you any good, my sister," she remarked, reminding me that she had warned me against listening to the full story.

"There... you see, we are sisters, but hearing you say that still makes me nervous... no, unstable."

"Well... then I'm sorry. I won't call you that, at least not until you're ready," she said, crossing her arms tightly and pouting.

"Don't take it to heart. Just give me some time to adjust to all this. You have to admit, something monumental has happened in my life."

"You're right, and I'm sorry if I was too forward. But now, tell me a bit about your family... I'm curious."

I burst out laughing at how curious Ludmilla was, but she just raised her right eyebrow and looked at me.

"You've been around my parents for several years... they haven't changed. I think I disappointed them the day I decided to join the police force. My mother, in particular, had this vision for me—husband, children... a life that she always described as simple and without excess. Instead, all I've done is give her endless worries. Whenever I call and can't tell her where I am, I can hear the distress in her voice. She feels it physically, like a pain, and she lives in fear of that one phone call she hasn't yet received... the one about my death. The only thing that's ever brought her any peace is my relationship with Andrea. He managed to find a way into their hearts, even my father's. Imagine if I had to tell them he died in Romania..." I trailed off, my voice catching in a sob.

"I'm sure it won't come to that. Andrea will come back with you, and you'll resume your life together."

"I don't think so," I said, my voice flat.

"What?" she asked, her expression darkening.

"How do you think my future with Andrea could be, him as an immortal vampire and me, soon enough, an old woman in a diaper... Don't joke," I said bitterly.

"Is that what you think? So love isn't enough for you. Andrea, as a vampire, could give you a kind of pure love you've never even imagined... and you're rejecting it?"

"You can't understand, Ludmilla," I insisted.

"Fine. Convince me I'm wrong and that you're not just a coward," she challenged, her eyes piercing into mine.

'What if I really am a coward,' I thought. Love is so irrational. The more I loved Andrea, the more I realized I had to distance myself from him. Nothing made sense anymore.

"Human life is complicated," I sighed.

"That's as good a conclusion as any. But I want to know just how much of a coward you are... philosophy doesn't interest me," she replied dryly.

I began to feel irritated; Ludmilla was only adding to my already tangled thoughts.

"Can we talk about something else, please?" I asked.

"Fine. Your choice. Go ahead," she said with a smile.

"You mentioned Dorian earlier, but only a little... If it's not too much to ask."

I saw her face light up, her perfect oval face brightening as her lips curved into a joyful smile.

"Dorian was born in 1100. He was a French friar, turned by another friar he met on the road to Jerusalem. Dorian was part of the Eleven, French friars dedicated to protecting pilgrims traveling to Palestine to pray at the tomb of Jesus."

"You mean to tell me Dorian was a Templar?" I asked, astonished.

"Yes. He devoted the first years of his life as a Templar to defending pilgrims. In those days, people had a blind belief in supernatural creatures; one wrong step could have cost him his life. He dedicated himself to the monastic life until the early 1800s. He describes that period as 'a train of forces waiting to be unleashed.' In 1888, when he entered his home, he found the body of Elisabeth Stride, one of Jack the Ripper's victims. From that point on, he decided to pursue forensic science... and that's how you met him."

"A life truly worth living and telling, if not for the minor issue of being a vampire," I said, my enthusiasm cutting through the heaviness of our conversation.

I leaned my head back against the sofa and sighed, suddenly feeling an overwhelming wave of exhaustion.

"Do you want to get some rest?" Ludmilla asked.

"If you don't mind, I'll just stretch out here on the couch." I felt too tired to make it to a bed.
"As you wish. I'll go prepare dinner," she said and left the room.
I drifted into a deep sleep. I dreamed I could fly, soaring over a forest, seeing nocturnal animals and hearing their cries, so perfectly timed that it felt as though I could understand them.
The scene shifted, and I found myself in the woods, near a giant oak tree. Voices in the distance alerted me; it was laughter. I hadn't walked, but suddenly, I was close to the voices. My mother's face appeared, illuminated within a flickering light. She smiled and extended her hand. "Don't be afraid," she said. I stepped back as she moved out of the light. She was wearing a white dress—one I recognized, the same one she wore when she used to take me to the beach as a child. She opened her arms, but I kept stepping back.
The scene shifted again. I was lying on a bed, my mother sitting beside me, trying to comfort me. I didn't quite understand my fear or her words, but everything changed in an instant. "Drink, my daughter," she said, holding out a dead animal. Terrified, I pushed her hands away. The scene shifted again. Now she was staring at me grimly, her eyes narrowed, and her lips pulled into a sneer. "You will not escape your fate," she thundered. I started to run, glancing over my shoulder to make sure she wasn't chasing me. Then I took flight, and as I flew backwards, I saw all the scenes I had experienced, until I reached the beginning of the nightmare. There, a light swallowed me up.
"Wake up!" Ludmilla shouted, shaking my shoulders.
I jolted awake and sat up, running a hand through my sweat-soaked hair, breathing in sharp, ragged gasps.
Ludmilla's hands clasped mine. "You were having a nightmare; I couldn't wake you up."
I looked at her, bewildered, and the nightmare came flooding back, sharp and vivid.

"How long was I asleep?" I asked, still dazed.

"About three hours," Ludmilla replied, her face creased with worry.

I froze, trying to listen. Someone was speaking, but it was Ludmilla's voice... except she was right there in front of me, observing me silently. I strained to hear more clearly.

"How did you know I was dreaming about my mother?"

"I don't know," she said, the worry on her face deepening.

"You said it again," I snapped, my voice rising with suspicion, "why deny it?"

"So you wouldn't accuse me of being insane?"

I saw her tense up. Her hands gripped mine like someone holding a hot object, and then she bolted from the room as if she had been burned.

Still stunned and trying to focus, I listened for any sound from outside: a car breaking down, the driver cursing; two women chatting about their heartbreaks; a child crying; and birdsong, more melodious than ever. Then a different, unfamiliar noise caught my attention. I concentrated harder. I could hear the waves of the sea.

Why was I hearing these things?

Maybe I was still in the nightmare... maybe I would wake up soon.

"I only gave her a drop of my blood. She was too tired; it shouldn't have done anything to her!" I heard Ludmilla scream, her voice panicked.

I swallowed, and an uncontrollable rage started to replace my exhaustion. I got up and followed her voice.

"Grandpa, hurry!" I heard her pleading on the phone.

She froze as if facing a feral animal.

"You gave me your blood? How dare you?" I growled.

"How did you hear what I was saying? I only whispered it to Grandpa," she asked, her terror visible.

"I don't know, but I heard it clearly. Ludmilla, I'm asking you one last time: did you give me blood?" I asked, slowly, scanning every syllable.

"A drop... in the herbal tea," she murmured.

Without thinking, I lunged at her, but something powerful threw me back against the opposite wall. The impact should have hurt, but I felt nothing.

I looked up and saw Robert standing beside Ludmilla.

"Go away!" Robert ordered Ludmilla. He stepped closer to me and gently took my hand. "Don't worry, everything will be fine," he said, his voice soothing as he stroked my hand.

"I feel a strange tingling all over my body," I complained, trying to make sense of the sensations.

"It will pass," he assured me.

"What has happened to me? What has Ludmilla's blood done to me?" I asked desperately.

"I don't know... I don't know, dear. Things don't work like that; you can't start adapting just from a drop of blood. And believe me, Ludmilla wouldn't lie about this. Such a violation of the law would cost her dearly."

I pulled away from Robert's embrace, bringing my hand to my jaw. I winced as I felt a sharp pain in my gums. My muscles tensed as uncontainable rage surged back. I dug my nails into my palms, trying to suppress it.

Robert wrapped his arms around me, pulling me close. I struggled to push him away, but he was too strong.

I forced myself to focus, shoving the rage down deep inside so it wouldn't explode. Then I leapt over the sofa, putting distance between us.

"What have you done to me?" I growled, my voice low and menacing.

"Nothing, Maria, I haven't done anything to you, but you need to find a way to calm down," Ludmilla said, re-entering the room.

"Don't tell me to stay calm! That's the worst thing you could say. Believe me," I snarled, like a spooked animal ready to bolt.

I saw her lower into a defensive stance. She understood my intent.

I sprang from behind the sofa, leaping toward her with all my strength, ready to attack. She ducked and managed to grab my leg, lifting me effortlessly, as if I were a rag doll. Robert was behind me, and he grabbed me, lifting me up as if I weighed nothing, before throwing me back against the wall.

When I regained consciousness, I found myself strapped to a chair, my arms and legs tightly bound. I wriggled, struggling against the restraints, but they held firm.

I lifted my head and saw him.

"Andrea, are you here?" I murmured, my voice weak.

"Yes, I'm here. You don't need to be afraid anymore," he said, his tone soothing.

"But I'm not afraid. I just have a strong desire to kill Ludmilla," I finished, my voice dripping with malice.

Andrea didn't respond. He just kept looking at me with a gentle smile. But in that instant, the urge to hurt him, to cause him pain, became overwhelming. I started thrashing in my chair, hissing like a wild animal.

Suddenly, my mind was flooded with one thought: blood. My muscles tensed, and in a moment of strange clarity, I felt a wave of nausea, a deep revulsion for myself.

Andrea stepped closer, and even through the fog of rage, I noticed something. His beautiful blue eyes were now a deep, inky black. They glowed with a strange light I had never seen before, as if they were pulling me in, dragging me down into a bottomless abyss. The anger drained away, and I found myself breathing normally again.

I sat there, head bowed, ashamed. I couldn't bear to look at anyone.

"Now you are ready to know," said a voice. Dorian's sensual, serene tone brought me back from the dark place I had been sinking into. I raised my head to face him.

"I can remove the restraints if you're feeling up to it," he said, his voice almost fatherly.

"Yes, please," I said, almost pleading.

Gently, Dorian unlocked the chains that Robert had used to bind me. I moved my hands, letting the blood flow back into them, and sighed deeply. My breath hitched, and I covered my mouth with my hand. For a long moment, I looked around at everyone in the room, noticing that Adelheid had arrived too. Her presence did not bring any comfort. Then, overwhelmed, I began to scream and sob. "Why?" I chanted over and over.

"Maria, please look at me," Dorian said. I felt the same calming effect as I had earlier with Andrea. Dorian's eyes caught mine, and I sank into a sense of total relaxation. "It's okay," he said, stepping back slightly. "Think back to when you were with Mihail. Do you have any gaps in your memory?"

"No, as far as I know... he didn't bite me, if that's what you're asking."

"He must have hypnotized you to make you forget. We need to check your body for bite marks," Dorian said, his voice steady. "You might have them anywhere."

"Then check," I replied without hesitation.

"We'll leave you alone with Adelheid," Dorian said.

I emitted a low, guttural growl, but Adelheid heard it perfectly. She looked at me like I was an insect.

"Fine," I muttered, starting to remove my clothes.

Adelheid inspected me carefully. "You don't have any bite marks... I just don't understand."

"Ludmilla!" I shouted her name with such anger that I barely managed to hold myself back from smashing the coffee table in front of the sofa.

"Don't!" she growled, lowering into a defensive stance.

The rage within me was so powerful, so overwhelming, that I could almost feel it taking shape. A burst of energy shot from my chest, hurling toward Adelheid, who was thrown against the opposite wall with a loud crash.

The exertion, coupled with the shock of what I had just done, left me drained and dizzy.

Adelheid lunged at me, lifting me effortlessly and pinning me back to the chair, strapping me down once more.

The door swung open, and everyone rushed in, alarmed by the commotion.

"What happened?" Dorian asked, his eyes darting between me and Adelheid.

"Something I have never seen in my life, and believe me, I've seen quite a bit," she said, gesturing to the dented wall.

"You hurt her. You're too strong compared to her," Robert scolded.

"It wasn't me who damaged the wall; it was the burst of energy—anger—she released from her chest," Adelheid said, her face twisted in a mix of confusion and disgust.

I pretended to be unconscious, overwhelmed with shame for what I had done.

"Did you find any bites on her body?" Ludmilla asked hesitantly.

"No," Adelheid replied, shaking her head.

Andrea came over and sat beside me, taking my hand. I decided to lift my head and turned to look at him, hoping he could see the desperation in my eyes. How was all of this possible? He squeezed my hand gently.

"When Luca Perri hears about this, he'll hunt us down, and only God knows if he won't manage to kill us all," Adelheid said, her voice full of tension.

She let out a frustrated snort and, thankfully, walked out of the room. I found even her presence unbearable.

I tried to breathe rhythmically, alternating long inhalations with shaky sobs. My heart felt like it was beating everywhere in my body, and the throbbing sound in my ears made it hard to think straight. I needed to calm myself, to learn control—and fast. Self-pity was not going to help me now.

"Now I am lucid and ready to accept," I whispered, almost to myself.

"Welcome back," Dorian said softly, pulling up a chair. "Would you like to share what you're feeling?"

Now that Dorian was sitting directly in front of me, I realized something had changed about him. The almost hypnotic beauty he used to exude was gone, replaced by a more grounded presence. I let out a laugh, surprising even myself.

"I see you're able to enjoy yourself again," Dorian remarked, smiling.

"You're different... you're not like how I saw you before," I said, chuckling again.

"That's because you're seeing things differently, and people too. It's a sharper vision, like putting on the right pair of glasses," he explained.

"How did this happen, Dorian? I didn't want this, or at least I wanted to make the choice myself."

"I don't have all the answers, but I can tell you that even if Ludmilla had made you drink all her blood, it wouldn't have turned you. It doesn't work like that. I believe your vampire gene has somehow been reactivated. After all, you are still the daughter of a blood vampire."

Just hearing the phrase "daughter of a blood vampire" made my stomach turn.

Dorian released the restraints, and I massaged my sore wrists. Ludmilla approached me, tears in her eyes, and hugged me tightly.

At first, I tried to pull away, but then something strange happened. I could feel her thoughts, her suffering, and I realized she wasn't lying. I squeezed her tighter, feeling a connection I hadn't anticipated.

"What was that?" I asked, bewildered.

"You entered my mind and read my thoughts. It's a common ability among vampires... but let's talk about you. I read your mind too. I saw your gift, your ability to shape anger... quite impressive. You'll just have to learn to control it."

Robert approached, taking my hand gently. "My dear, I've spent my life hoping I could protect you from this moment. Destiny, if we can call it that, took a different path... but I am here to help you embrace your new essence. You're with your family now, even though none of us intend to replace the family who raised you. I love you."

I was moved by his words and hugged him warmly. "My parents will always be my parents, I can never see that monster as my family. But knowing I have you and Ludmilla... that makes me proud."

Ludmilla joined in the embrace, and I felt our minds intertwine, a pure, familial love that soothed some of the turmoil within me.

Slowly, we let go, and I wandered over to the two windows in the room. In the middle was a seventeenth-century mirror. I stared at my reflection, searching for any sign of the monster I feared I had become. It was still me—maybe a bit rejuvenated, with smoother, shinier skin, which brought a slight flicker of irritation.

I touched my face, trying to grasp the reality of it all. This had to be real. And now, for reasons I couldn't fully understand, I was a vampire. "I will be one for the rest of my existence," I whispered to myself.

My legs buckled beneath me, and I found myself on my knees. As I fell, my head struck the antique mirror, shattering it.

Terror and shame overtook me, and I fled from the room, out of the flat, and into the street.

The light outside hit me harshly, causing a stabbing pain in my eyes. I desperately searched for shelter, crossing the small square filled with bar terraces, and found refuge in a narrow alley behind a trash bin. The shade was a relief for my stinging eyes.

Voices buzzed in my head, every noise echoing and amplifying, making it hard to keep my balance. Amid the chaos, two voices stood out—Dorian and Ludmilla. They were close.

I huddled against the wall, trying to make myself small.
"Maria, I can hear you," Ludmilla's voice echoed. "Everything you're experiencing is normal. We've all been through it. It will pass, but you need help. Maria..." she repeated, stepping in front of me.
I burst into tears again. I thought vampires were supposed to be strong and composed, but all I had done since turning was cry.
Ludmilla crouched down and lifted my chin, forcing me to meet her gaze. She stared at me intently, and it happened again—I sank into her eyes and felt myself enveloped by a sense of calm.
"How do you do that?" I asked, still bewildered.
"Think about how you shape anger, that's a gift unique to you. But the ability to manipulate emotions, to read minds—that's something shared by almost all vampires," she explained.
"Honestly, I still don't even know how I shape the anger..." I confessed.
"You're looking at eternity, you'll have time to learn. Would you have ever imagined this?" she asked, a gentle smile playing on her lips.
I let out a laugh, seeking some form of self-consolation, like a cat purring to calm itself.
Dorian arrived and helped me to my feet.
"Now, I have to tell you something you're not going to like," he said quietly, a strange smile tugging at his lips.
"What now? Isn't this enough? Just say it," I said, trying to brace myself.
"You need to drink human blood, or the adaptation won't solidify, and you'll risk turning into a real monster."
I studied his face carefully, trying to find the right words to respond, but all I could do was laugh, the sound bordering on hysterical.
"You must be joking. I will never drink human blood, and I won't drink animal blood either. I'm a lifelong vegetarian," I said, emphasizing the last five words.

"I can assure you, you'll never be a vegetarian again," came Adelheid's voice, cutting in with a sharp edge.

She appeared at the mouth of the alley, her usual impenetrable, scrutinizing expression making me tense. I gasped, realizing that my fingers had curled into claws. She always had a way of driving me out of my mind.

It was inevitable. The anger started to bubble and take form.

Help me! I mentally shouted towards Ludmilla.

She grasped my arm and began to caress it, locking eyes with me. I felt the weight of my anger dissolve, and I unclenched my fists, managing a small smile.

"You need to teach her some control, or I swear I will hurt her..." Adelheid began, but Dorian stepped in, pushing her back.

"You're not helping by acting like this, Adelheid."

I screamed in my mind, I will never drink blood! as she turned to leave.

"We'll see, we'll see!" she shouted over her shoulder, disappearing into the distance.

"Let's go home," Dorian said gently.

I emitted a low grunt, but followed, realizing that my fight was far from over.

20

Everything was silent in Ludmilla's house. Through the large window, the first light of evening filtered through the patterns on the glass, creating playful displays of light and shadow.

"You know we have to do this," Dorian was saying. "Luca needs to hear this from us, or we'll be dead before we can explain."

"But I don't feel like it... I don't feel like explaining myself to him, not now."

They insisted on inviting Luca over and explaining everything to him, right away, that very evening. I had only one wish: to go to sleep.

"Tomorrow we have to go to Charles... no complaining," said Adelheid, always so kind....

"Tomorrow we'll go to Charles, and once I have his blessing, we'll tell Luca everything," I replied sarcastically.

"We have a long day ahead of us. Why don't we all go and rest? With a clear mind, we can think better," suggested Robert, whose grandfatherly wisdom helped calm both Adelheid and me.

I said goodnight to everyone and headed to my room.

I immediately sensed Andrea's presence.

"Please don't ask me anything. I still need to figure out what to do with my life. I'm not ready to think in doubles."

He left without a word. He turned inward and disappeared; I couldn't sense any thoughts... it almost hurt.

To distract myself, I rummaged through my bag, looking for I don't know what, but I found my mobile phone. I turned it on. There were twenty-two missed calls from Celeste. As if a sponge had wiped away the reality of the moment, I switched to 'human mode.'

I tapped one of the notifications on the touchscreen and waited for the call to connect.

Tuut...

Oh, damn, I snapped back to reality. I hung up.

What was I thinking, talking to Celeste... what would I even say? "Hey, guess what? I'm a vampire now... oh, and so is Andrea..." Thoughts... thoughts... thoughts.

I started tapping my lower lip with my index finger, a sign that my human tics hadn't left me. Charles, Luca... how many more people would I have to explain my transformation to? My head was pounding, and I tried to listen for thoughts.

Ludmilla? I tried to think.

"I'm coming!" She didn't give me a chance to respond.

I saw her come in through the window. "Where were you? What were you doing out there?"

"Doing what, sooner or later, you'll be forced to do."

"Or?"

"Or you could turn into that monster you know so well."

"I'd rather die."

"You see? You are free to choose," she replied impertinently.

"Alright, I didn't call you to be scolded... my head's splitting..."

"You're no longer human, sister. Aspirin won't do anything for you. You need to feed."

"I'm going to the kitchen to make myself a latte," I said provocatively. "Go to hell. I'm going to bed." She disappeared as quickly as she had come, through the window.

I woke up lying on the bed, still in my clothes. The day was bright, and the sun was shining through the window panes. Instinctively, I brought my hands to my eyes, but to my surprise, the discomfort of the previous day was gone. I threw the window open wide and took a deep breath, filling my lungs until they burned. I felt good, strong, and ready for anything. Charles didn't scare me, nor did Luca Perri.

I went to Ludmilla's living room, where the others' voices were coming from. They were waiting for me to leave.

"Good morning, you look radiant," Andrea complimented as he approached.

He tried to kiss me, but I turned my lips, offering a harmless peck on the cheek. It hurt, but at that moment, I couldn't think of anything but blood. But I'd never admit that.

"I was wondering," I said with a swagger, "why on earth should I go and bow down to Charles... I didn't do it as a human, so why would I as a vampire?"

They all fell silent, stunned. Only Adelheid came closer to me.

"I'd watch my attitude if I were you, unless you want Charles himself to rearrange that cocky face of yours. You have no idea who you're up against."

I could hear Ludmilla's mental giggles, and I glared at her.

"Alright, let's stop the theatrics. Maria, please learn to control your emotions now; they're more intense as a vampire. If Charles finds a crack in your mind, he will make you his, forever. We must be on our way," said Dorian kindly but with a hint of menace. "As agreed, you'll stay here with Robert," he added, addressing Andrea.

"Why shouldn't the two of them come?" I asked suspiciously.

"Charles must think we're there solely to present the facts truthfully and to introduce you in your new form. Too many people might look like we're shielding you."

Robert approached and hugged me warmly. "Don't worry, he won't have any reason to doubt how things happened. Or at least, if he does, he'll read you and see the truth. But you need to present yourself respectfully... is that clear?" he finished, pressing a kiss to my cheek.

Dorian left first. We found him waiting for us, the car already running, just outside the front door.

Adelheid took the front seat, while Ludmilla and I sat in the back. I heard a knock on the window by my side. Dorian lowered it with the button on the door.

"Good morning, everyone. Where are you headed?"

I heard a distortion in his voice that, as a human, he would not have been able to detect.

"Hello, Luca," Dorian replied.

Adelheid waved briefly and immediately resumed her seat. I heard her mentally threaten me: "Get him out of the way." But I didn't have time to say a word.

"Wherever you're going, I'm coming too. Maria is my concern. You deal with the vampires, I deal with the humans. Or has that changed?"

"Get in," Dorian growled.

"I... I... I don't think that's a good idea," I stammered, realising the burning in my throat.

"Maria, keep calm," they urged.

"Get on my side," Ludmilla invited him, making sure he wouldn't sit next to me.

I could smell Luca like never before. It confused me, and the burning pain in my gums intensified.

I touched my mouth.

Goodness, what was happening to me? I had the sensation that my teeth had doubled, and some weren't fitting properly in my mouth.

The canines were lengthening.

"No!" I screamed internally.

I felt them all tense, except for Luca, who, unaware—or so I thought—gazed placidly out the window.

Ludmilla's hand squeezed mine. "Relax," she said.

I felt a wave of calmness spread through me, but it wasn't enough to retract my canines.

Someone needs to hypnotise Luca, I heard her say.

He'd notice, Adelheid replied. You have to keep her calm, it's all we can do.

I tried to calm myself with some autogenic training. I focused on the burning in my gums, imagining the warmth spreading through my body, bringing a sense of mental relaxation. Slowly, my heartbeat settled into a rhythm.

I felt the canines retract.

"I get the feeling I'm not wanted," said Luca sarcastically.

"You're the one who invited yourself," Ludmilla retorted, elbowing him in the ribs.

I heard him groan. I let out a laugh, but it quickly turned back into pain.

The scent of Luca's breath filled my nostrils, my throat parched with thirst, and my gums burned again.

The canines extended.

D'n'zione, I can't resist... I thought in desperation.

You have one second to decide: attack Luca, and he'll likely kill you, or you'll have to do this...

Dorian turned to the trunk and grabbed a bag, which he set at his feet, not before banging it firmly against my head. I grunted.

"Who wants a drink?"

"I hope it's water," Luca said.

"Of course," Dorian replied, tossing him a small bottle.

"Here," he offered me one too. "Drink and shut up," he said grimly.

I took the bottle and opened it. A shocking scent hit my nostrils: blood.

I tried to stay impassive and brought it to my lips. I had braced myself for revulsion, but it never came.

Honey, lavender flowers, but also whipped cream with strawberries... all these flavours overwhelmed my taste buds. I drank greedily, taking care not to spill a single drop.

Feeling better? Ludmilla's little voice echoed in my head.

I want more.

For now, you'll have to make do, or Luca will catch on.

Then I had an idea. I searched my bag for a mask and put it on. It helped.

"Are you not well, Inspector?" he asked, noticing the mask.

"I actually sneezed a lot tonight, so it's better to wear it, you never know. Besides, air conditioning dries out my nostrils. Or maybe I've caught the Coronavirus."

Leaning forward to get a better look at me, I felt Ludmilla stiffen.

"Are you kidding me?" he growled.

Ludmilla grabbed his arm and forced him back into his seat, but Luca, agitated, tried to turn around, pressing himself against the backrest to see me more clearly.

"That's enough!" Dorian thundered, pulling the car over. "It's three against one, you can't seriously think of taking us on," he threatened.

"Dorian, you and I have been friends for years. I know you... I know you well enough to sense something's not right. What happened to Maria?"

We all got out of the car, except for Adelheid, who sat there like a marble statue.

Luca stepped closer and took my hand. Let him do it, Ludmilla warned me in thought.

He looked me straight in the eye. "How did it happen?" he murmured. "I don't know, but it wasn't them. I swear."

"Speak... say something!" he said, his voice rising.

"As she told you, we don't know. We think Mihail somehow gave her his blood and then hypnotised her to forget," Dorian replied.

"So you're off to Charles now, before he kills you all," Luca sneered wickedly.

"You know how these things work; there's no point in being sarcastic. If Mihail's goal was to get us all killed, he's probably succeeded."

Luca's curiosity about what had happened to me was unsettling. I began to swallow back bile.

I felt my canines descend, this time without any pain, and for the first time, I could sense my eyes turning bloodshot.

"She hasn't fed yet," Ludmilla warned him.

"She's dangerous, and you're taking her to Charles's house? She'll kill you all before you even reach the door."

"You can address me. I'm right here, and I can hear you... idiot," I growled.

Someone grabbed me and tossed me back into the car. I couldn't move; something was restraining me. The same damned chains...

"You cannot go without feeding, or you risk becoming violent. It would be difficult to calm you down. Please, drink," Ludmilla urged.

She offered me her wrist, and I stared at her, bewildered and incredulous. Did she actually want me to feed on her? Was she insane?

"You won't hurt me... vampire... sanguine... immortal... and you won't turn into an azara..."

The artery in her wrist was so turgid and pulsing that I could feel the blood flowing. Hunger turned into an uncontrollable craving. I sank my teeth in.

The warm, thick fluid, so different from what was in the small bottle, flooded my throat, and as it coursed through my body, I felt a wave of well-being and calm.

I pulled away.

"That was easy, wasn't it?" Ludmilla asked, smiling.

"Mostly satisfying," I replied, running my tongue over my lips.

"Get back in; the baby's done throwing her tantrum," Adelheid hummed.

Ludmilla unchained me, and we resumed our journey.

Luca remained motionless, silently gazing out of the window, a ridiculous display of stoicism.

We arrived at the cable car park just as it began to drizzle; we waited in the car, watching the line of tourists scurrying back to their cars for shelter.

With the storm on our side, we started up the first path at the foot of the cable car. When we reached the clearing before the forest, Luca was asked to put on a blindfold. I couldn't help but laugh as Dorian hoisted him onto his shoulders.

The run lasted only a few minutes before we stopped in front of a huge oak tree, where Dorian began moving some branches and leaves aside.

"A trapdoor!" I exclaimed.

Shut up, just think. Luca is like a bloodhound; he could find his way to Charles. I'm surprised he hasn't already, but it mustn't happen because of us, Ludmilla scolded.

I followed the others and jumped in, though not quite gracefully. I ended up sitting on the ground.

"You'll need some training..." Ludmilla teased, as she and Adelheid helped lower Luca down.

A tunnel carved through an underground forest led us to the magnificent sinkhole I remembered so well. Here, Luca was finally allowed to remove the blindfold.

21

Adelheid knocked on the door, and it was Charles himself who answered.

"Did we have an appointment?" he asked, his tone anything but friendly.

"I'd say no, but we need to confer with you," Adelheid replied.

From Charles' expression, it was clear what mood he was in: surprised, enraged, and completely on guard. One wrong move, and he would kill us.

"Come in," he said curtly, stepping aside.

It was at the precise moment I passed him that I saw him hesitate, and then instantly stiffen, assuming a devilish expression.

"If you're here to beg for forgiveness, you're mistaken, you understand that?" he spoke in a wrathful tone.

"We are not here to ask your forgiveness. We haven't done anything," Adelheid replied firmly.

"Are you mocking me, woman?" he growled.

Dorian moved closer, blocking Adelheid from Charles' view.

"We're here to figure out, together with you, how this could have happened. You have such powerful psychic abilities... read us, and you'll know the truth," Dorian said.

There was a long silence. He studied us, then made his decision.

"I will speak with her alone, and only after I've heard her side of the story will I agree to talk to the rest of you."

He put his arm around my waist and, like lightning, whisked me into another room. He gestured for me to sit down, and I obeyed without protest.

He looked steadily into my eyes and touched my cheek with one hand. He stayed like that for a few moments.

"So, you would be Mihail's other daughter?"

"So it seems," I replied, lowering my head.

"Look at me," he murmured. "You must never be ashamed of where you come from. Remember that always."

I looked at him, incredulous. "How could I not be ashamed? He's a monster. He's done things that... that..." I couldn't finish the sentence.

"You're right; he has done deplorable, forbidden things. But remember, he is a vampire... and that is our nature. Mastering it is not easy, and not everyone is capable of it... sooner or later, you'll understand this yourself. But now, tell me how it all happened."

I tried to read his predatory, patient, and opportunistic gaze, seeking his true intentions, but it was impossible. So, I began my story, mixing real events with hypotheses. I avoided mentioning the drop of blood Ludmilla had put in my tea; I didn't want to give him a reason to blame her alone. I focused my accusations on the monstrosity of my father.

"Oh, rest assured... a drop of blood... even if she had bled, you wouldn't have turned," he murmured, leaving me puzzled. I was certain I hadn't thought that.

I treated his remark as a provocation.

I didn't respond.

"Stay here. I'll be right back."

I didn't dare move a muscle, but then I heard Ludmilla's voice in my head.

Are you okay?

Yes, and you?

We're waiting for you.

I shut down my thoughts the moment I sensed him returning.

"Drink!" he commanded, handing me a polystyrene cup.

The red, fragrant essence made my gums tingle, but I set the cup down on the table.

"Where did this blood come from?" I asked, suspiciously.

In response, he pulled a blood bag, like those used in hospitals, from the pocket of his sweater.

I brought the cup to my lips and drank frantically.

"Now drink from my wrist," he said, extending his arm toward me.

I looked at him in horror. "Why would I do that?"

"Because I command it. Only then can I truly know you."

Something inside me, against my will, forced me to sink my teeth into his wrist. I sucked until my mouth was full, greedily swallowing over and over, yet never feeling satisfied. I wanted more... and more.

"We're done," he said, yanking his arm away from my mouth. He composed himself and gestured for me to leave the room. "I had a human meal prepared for you. You need it." I thanked him and returned to the main hall.

The laid table awakened a certain human hunger in me.

I was about to pick up a plate to serve myself when Ludmilla's furious voice echoed in my mind.

You're insane to have drunk his blood! she shouted.

What was I supposed to do?! I snapped back.

Finally, she withdrew from my thoughts, grumbling, and I dove into a slice of lasagna, to the disgrace of the finest Italian cooks.

The waiting felt endless, so I decided to wander around the vast hall. The gigantic bookcase, taking up an entire wall, was filled with antique books, but my attention was drawn to a small, locked case containing an open book, resting on a richly inlaid bookstand shaped like two angel wings.

I rummaged through the drawers of the reading table and found a pair of white gloves. I slipped them on and dared to turn the key in the glass door.

I gently took out the book and placed it on the stand. I was stunned. Before me was a Bible... Gutenberg's forty-two-line Bible from 1455.

The complete version; I knew only twenty-two copies existed and never imagined I would hold one in my hands.

The gold-thread binding was almost pristine, as was the red cover. I carefully placed it back with reverence.

"Our inspector has a taste for old books," commented Charles, re-entering the hall with the rest of the group.

"I noticed the gold-thread binding, but especially the forty-two-line Bible. It's practically unobtainable, and the twenty-two existing copies are in the Vatican or the world's most renowned museums and libraries... it's fascinating to find a copy here."

"Few people know that, at the time, the Gutenberg Bible was sold as folded sheets, to be bound according to the buyer's preferences. I thought that using gold threads would bestow timeless value on the book, making it unique."

Of course, how had it not occurred to me earlier that he could have bought it directly from Gutenberg himself...

I noticed Dorian chuckling behind me. I guessed he had picked up on my thought.

The noise coming from outside the hall put us all on alert, except Charles, of course. I turned my gaze, full of suspicion and fear.

There he was, once again facing me. "Monster," I hissed.

Dorian immediately came up behind me, wrapping his arm around my waist, trying to pull me towards Luca, but I resisted.

I began to tremble, and the rage within me grew... hatred... disgust... and then more rage. I tried to harness it, to give it form: an invisible spear.

I lunged forward and struck him in the chest, hard enough to knock the wind out of him. He crashed against the wall, dragging with him the two vampires holding chains. They roared.

The two guards got up, adjusting their chains. I heard the monster groan, but then he slyly looked up at me, a smirk curling on his lips. "Two of my daughters together. Wonderful!"

I glanced at Ludmilla, who looked as astonished as I was. The phrase "two of my daughters" hadn't gone unnoticed...

Forget about it. He only wants to stir things up, to prolong the time he has left before oblivion. Ludmilla sensed my state of mind and tried to calm me down.

"Take him back to his cell immediately!" ordered Charles. Then he turned to me: "You have an important and dangerous gift. You will need to learn how to use it... it would be unpleasant to have to undo it."

So my gift was something that could be undone... but I chose to stay silent. I couldn't wait to leave that place.

Charles looked over my shoulder and gestured for everyone to follow him.

I moved last, pausing for a few seconds to savor the monster's curses as he was locked away again. Then I joined the others.

I sat down between Ludmilla and Luca, with Adelheid and Dorian opposite me. Charles stood at the head of the table and, in an academic tone, began a sort of lecture on his conclusions.

"For more than three thousand years, I have been part of this world, and I have never seen anything like what is happening with Maria. But I have heard the witches speak of it, back when they still roamed among us, their spirits present. I thought only one of them might be able to help us." He interrupted himself, getting up from his chair, and went to the door.

Father Vesta entered.

We all froze, staring at the imposing figure of the priest as he advanced, his eyes fixed only on me.

"I know you've already met Father Vesta," said Charles.

"I would say so," I replied, standing to greet him.

"I warned you," he whispered as he sat down.

Adelheid was trembling, her gaze fixed and ominous on the priest, while Dorian held her hand, squeezing it gently. I understood that, in his way, he was soothing her.

"Father Vesta... Vesta, please, I called you here to assist with this situation. So, please, share your thoughts," Charles urged.

The priest glanced at each of us before he began to speak.

"They are known as Dual Beings: half human, half vampire. In them, the vampirism gene may remain dormant for life, leading to a natural human death, or it can activate, giving rise to the highest genetic rank among vampires: the malier."

I felt a psychic wave wash over me, picking up the emotions of those around me. I noticed Ludmilla's distressed expression.

At that point, Charles rose stiffly from his chair. "What are you rambling on about, witch? The malier died out hundreds of years ago. Or rather, no, it was the likes of you who forced them to that terrible end," Charles thundered, slamming his fist on the table.

"You asked, and I answered. My task ends here," replied Father Vesta, unwavering.

"It's not over," Charles said, his tone menacing.

They locked eyes, challenging each other, but the priest did not show a hint of fear. Eventually, he seemed to concede to Charles' will and continued.

"There were twelve of them, all born from the same vampire. Brothers and sisters, sharing the same father, each with their own gift, paired in twos: two mutants, two rulers of the elements, two wayfarers, two controllers, two ferrymen, and two benevolents. But their abilities could only manifest if all were born and the pairs united. Some witches perceived these beings' abilities as the greatest threat to humanity. They formed a coven and dedicated their lives to hunting them down, but they could never catch the vampire who created them." He turned to Ludmilla, pointing a finger, "You are a controller; you have the power to manipulate emotions, but unlike others of your kind, you can make people feel whatever you wish. As for you..." he said, shifting his finger towards me, "you are a benevolent... but you will still combat any dangerous supernatural being, and sooner or later, they will hunt you down and kill you."

"A fascinating explanation, but lacking in substance," Charles commented, bored.

I felt the tension rising, and all I could think about was how this unbelievable story would end.

"I have said what was asked of me. I will finish by warning you: as long as the malier remain apart, the magic surrounding them will be unstable and dormant. But if, one day, the twelve come together, the magic will be complete, and they will hunt down witches, or rather, any supernatural creature that is not a vampire."

"So, you witches weren't concerned about humanity, but about your own survival. Take him to the dungeon!" Charles shouted.

Father Vesta paled, trying in vain to reason with Charles.

We stood still as some vampires escorted Father Vesta out of the hall.

"He would have killed you. Eventually," Charles declared. "Now I understand why, every time I thought of killing you, I changed my mind. Your ability is very powerful. I can't imagine what it would become if you ever found your other half," he said, turning towards Ludmilla. "And you..." he continued, addressing me, "you are a benevolent. It's unbelievable. Until yesterday, you were nothing more than a mere human..." he smiled, letting the sentence trail off.

"I didn't understand any of this... perhaps the ramblings of an old man... but was it necessary to treat him like that?" I ventured.

Charles stepped closer to me, making no sound but gesturing for me to follow him. He had heard my thoughts. I moved, the rest of the group behind me, but Charles blocked Adelheid and Dorian, preventing them from continuing. "You come," he said, looking at Luca.

The short corridor ended at a security door, which required two keys to open.

We entered a large room, crossing it to reach another corridor. From there, we began to descend. The wide passage gradually narrowed into a low tunnel, forcing us to duck and proceed in single file. Another armored door led us to a large circular space—the bottom of the dungeon.

There were four cells, each sealed with iron bars.

"They are iron bars embedded into the walls and electronically controlled. No vampire can break through iron. It is the only earthly element that can restrain us," Charles explained.

Through the bars of one of the cells, I saw the monster. I approached, but immediately two guards pushed me back with an iron club.

"Leave her be," Charles commanded.

I glared at them and stepped closer to the bars.

"What can I do for you, child?" he hissed.

"You could prove to me that you're not a real monster."

"But I am."

"I'm not convinced. I think you could surprise everyone," I said, trying to flatter him.

"Because you believe the lie."

"Let's say that, having just met my biological father, I'm asking for a favor. You owe me one."

"I don't owe you a damn thing, but I know where you're going... I will help you. As much as I can."

"I guess you know what I need."

"Believe me, the priest's mind is a mess, like a crushing machine, so many are his thoughts that they form an immense, chaotic beach. Yes, I know what you want from me."

"I want to go in to him," I demanded, my tone arrogant.

"As you wish," Charles replied smoothly.

"You are crazy!" shouted Luca.

"Please, Captain, don't interfere. I need you to trust me," I pleaded.

"But I trust you; it's him I don't trust. Do you understand that?"

"He won't hurt me, and besides, I can defend myself well enough now," I reassured him.

He stepped aside, leaving me in front of the bars.

I am coming with you, I heard Ludmilla's voice in my head.

Please, I need to be alone with him.

I saw her lower her head. Be careful, don't trust him.

I smiled at her.

The bars began to slide back into the wall, and I stepped inside. They closed behind me.

The monster sat in a restraining chair, raising his head when he heard the bars lock. His pale face, covered in purulent pustules, seemed to gain some color at the sight of me.

"Remember when I told you about my friend Sebastian?" he asked.

I nodded hesitantly.

"During one of the fantastic parties at Jacques' house, a strange, ancient-looking vampire shared the legend of the Twelve. Believe me, until an hour ago, I thought it was just a tale, the product of a vampire's hangover."

"Go on," I growled.

"At the beginning of the year 1000, when humans and supernaturals still lived in harmony on Earth, twelve women from a village in southern France were kidnapped. They returned a few days later with no memory of what had happened. At that time, magic flowed freely among humans, who saw it as the essence of nature. So, when the women discovered three months later that they were pregnant, the village chief sought the help of witches living in nearby caves. The witches understood that only a bloodthirsty and powerful vampire could have performed such an atrocity. They tried, unsuccessfully, to remove the fetuses. Exhausted from casting futile spells, they decided to protect the women and their children by binding them with a single spell. When the children turned ten, they planned to disperse them. But they didn't account for the vampire who created them. One night, he kidnapped all twelve children, killed their mothers and the rest of the village, and then threatened the witches: if they tried to find him, his wrath would fall upon all humanity, for as long as the Earth revolved around the sun. And so it was."

"Is that all?"

"Yes, that's it."

"Your friend Sebastian, what does he have to do with this?"

"He was obsessed with the story and eventually lost his mind. He searched every corner of New Orleans and found a witch, one who had lost her powers but retained her knowledge... and she told him the rest. That was the real reason he didn't follow me when I was expelled from Jacques'. He believed he could reunite the Twelve. Now it's your turn, daughter," he said, looking straight into my eyes.

I resisted the urge to punch him for calling me 'daughter' again and asked the guards to let me out.

"Did you find what you were looking for?" Charles asked.

"I'm not sure," I replied, uncertainly, "but I might have evidence that someone has tried to repeat the legend. To find out more, Andrea and I need to return to Italy. As soon as possible. I have one more request," I added, taking advantage of Charles' silence.

"Speak," he said, his gaze fixed on a precise spot on my face, as if he intended to burn through me.

"I need Father Vesta. I believe only he can verify whether this is just a fantasy or, unfortunately, the truth... and besides," I continued before he could respond, "I ask that you refrain from proceeding with the mummification of... M... M... Mihail," I stammered out, struggling to say the name I didn't want to utter.

Ludmilla and Luca stared at me with expressions that were hard to decipher, but they probably just wanted to slap some sense into me.

"Do you really think you can ask me for anything?"

Charles' tone sent chills through me, but I pretended not to notice.

"Asking is allowed. I'll still need him later, after which you can carry out the sentence."

"Leave," he said calmly.

I felt my legs tense, ready to spring, but I managed to control my muscles and relax.

I clenched my fists.

"Give me Father Vesta... I implore you."

Charles sharply turned to the guards and ordered them to bring out the priest, then grabbed me by the arm and shoved me against the bars of the cell. I heard the monster gnash his teeth. Charles' grip tightened around my neck. "I could snap your neck right now. You're still so fragile... don't make me regret indulging you."

Then the monster's hoarse, low voice interrupted. "Only I know the face of Sebastian. You'll never find him without me."

I stood there, wide-eyed and puzzled, staring into the cell. I was too shocked to respond to his provocation, and suddenly, that shock morphed into anger. I felt it start to rise, taking shape. Ludmilla noticed, but couldn't calm me down. I managed just in time to push Luca aside, and a mass of energy left my body, crashing into the cell bars. They didn't break, but the shockwave caused a short circuit. The bars began to retract into the wall.

"Wow, you're really strong, but if you don't learn to control yourself soon... I'll have to take care of it," Charles threatened, his smile clearly forced.

The two vampires guarding the cell were caught in the shockwave, sent flying down the corridor like leaves in the wind.

"You bitch," one of them growled.

A barely perceptible movement caught our attention. Charles' expression stiffened.

"He's escaped!" one of the guards thundered.

Charles snorted like an enraged bull and grabbed me by the neck again.

"Look what you've done!" he hissed, squeezing so hard that my vertebrae creaked.

Luca stepped forward, his voice menacing as he addressed Charles: "Hurt her, and the truce is over."

Reluctantly, Charles released me. I didn't flinch and continued to stare him down. He turned away.

We started running back towards the house, racing at breakneck speed through the tunnel and then down the corridor. Suddenly, I stopped—I couldn't hear Ludmilla anymore. I turned around and realised she wasn't behind us.

"Damn him, he's got her!" I screamed, panic rising in my voice.

Adelheid and Dorian were waiting at the end of the corridor, their faces tense, their fists clenched.

"How could this happen? You will pay for this!" Adelheid growled, glaring at me with a menacing intensity.

I didn't even notice when she moved. Suddenly, she was behind me, twisting one arm behind my back and pressing her other hand against my neck, threatening to dislocate my vertebrae.

"You are all guilty of Ludmilla's kidnapping, but she..." she said, leveraging my poor neck even further, "she is the worst. She should never have been among us, but you, Dorian, you always had to indulge Ludmilla's whims. She should have remained human and died... thirty, forty years... maybe even less, and it would all be over. Instead, my poor child is back in the hands of her monster father."

Adelheid burst into tears and released me, collapsing to the ground.

I stood petrified against the wall, struggling to believe I'd understood her words correctly.

"Q... what happened to me was planned to accommodate Ludmilla's whims?" I asked, not sure whether I felt more indignant or threatened.

"I don't think this is the time to discuss that," Dorian replied coldly, helping Adelheid to her feet.

He was right. I composed myself, swallowing the anger that was starting to rise, though my thoughts were now a chaotic jumble of suspicions.

Two of the guards returned and approached Charles.

"Speak."

"Pauline," one of them murmured.

Charles froze, and his mouth twisted into a pained expression. "What happened to Pauline?" he asked through clenched teeth.

"You better see for yourself, boss."

He followed them across the vast hall. I tried to follow, but Dorian blocked me. I shot him a sidelong look, but he waved me off.

Charles returned, carrying Pauline's body in his arms. I covered my mouth when I saw that it was headless. The ghostly silence that greeted the sight of her poor body quickly turned into a murmur of questions as he gently laid her on a couch.

I saw Charles kneel down and take her lifeless hand. He caressed it and brought it to his face, tears streaming down his cheeks.

"He will pay, rest assured... he will pay..." he began to repeat, sobbing.

The two guards returned, one of them carrying a black drape wrapped around something round—Pauline's head.

I didn't know who Pauline was, but I pieced it together, recalling the old woman who had opened the door when I first came to this house.

"Grandma..." Charles whispered through his sobs as the vampire handed him the cloth. He cradled it in his arms and parted the fabric just enough to see her face. He gently caressed it.

I was stunned to hear him call her grandmother. I scanned the faces of those present, searching for answers, but Dorian, for the second time, signalled me to keep quiet.

"Go get Father Vesta," Charles ordered.

"Why Father Vesta? What did he do to you?" I decided I would no longer seek Dorian's approval to speak.

193

Charles turned his head and stared at me for a long, silent moment. "I think you could follow my guards and help Father Vesta walk here."

I was pleasantly surprised and, without waiting for him to repeat himself, I ran down the corridor towards the dungeon. I didn't realise it was a trap until the two vampires who had preceded me stopped, blocking my way.

"Where do you think you're going?" one of them hissed, pouncing on me.

He tried to bite me.

Suddenly, it came back to me: two lousy azaras.

I managed to free one arm, but the other vampire immediately pinned my head, trying to expose my pulsating carotid artery.

"Don't think you can escape, you bitch. If you'd never come here, Pauline would still be alive," snarled the vampire holding my head.

I felt rage building, the weight of the vampire on top of me preventing me from taking deep breaths, but it only fueled the growing ball of power inside me. It burst out with such force that the vampire above me was thrown against the ceiling. I managed to free myself, and as I grabbed one by the neck, I pinned the other with continuous blasts of power, slamming him into the ceiling. I glanced up when I heard the thud as he fell to the floor. I was too tired to keep holding him up there. The other vampire was still squinting at his fallen comrade, making sure he was okay. He loosened his grip on my neck, and I gathered all my remaining strength and threw myself backward, crashing against the wall. The vampire staggered and fell. Then I placed my foot on his neck and pushed until his head separated from his body. I immediately pounced on the other, who was trying to run for help. I tackled him, grabbing his legs, and he went down. I dragged him along the corridor until a voice stopped me.

"Don't dirty your hands. Stay pure," said Father Vesta.

"Too late. I've already killed one."

"He would have killed you," he replied in a fatherly tone.

I released the vampire, who slumped to the floor, too afraid to look at the priest. I realised he was trembling. I didn't understand what was happening. Father Vesta stood over him, then drew a dagger from within his robes. When the blade struck the vampire, I watched in shock as he dissolved into dust.

I looked at Father Vesta, still trying to make sense of what had just happened. I stepped closer to help him sheathe the dagger.

"What happened?" I asked hesitantly.

"Charles thought I'd use it against you and Ludmilla... poor fool," he said, shaking his head.

"That's not exactly what I asked."

"This dagger," he said, showing it to me, "was forged under a spell by the witches who once protected humanity from the Twelve. It has been passed down through generations. I am the last descendant of Tiara, the witch who led the coven that killed the Twelve."

"Charles will kill us. We annihilated two of his men."

"He won't. He'll see it as collateral damage... at least until he gets his hands on this dagger."

"You think he doesn't know who possesses it?"

"He knows I have it, and he also knows he can never take it from me."

"How is that possible?" I asked, but we were interrupted by noises from the corridor.

Dorian and Luca approached.

"Charles sent us to see why you hadn't returned with Father Vesta," Luca said, sounding annoyed as he glanced at the headless vampire on the ground. "Now I see..." he murmured with a small, knowing smile.

"And the other one? Weren't there two guards?" Dorian asked.

"I took care of it," Father Vesta replied.

"Well, now that we're certain of our end, I suppose we can return to the hall," Luca grumbled defiantly.

"No one will die, rest assured, Captain." Father Vesta unzipped his robe slightly, revealing the dagger.

Dorian trembled, taking a step back.

22

We returned to the salon. Adelheid was standing in a corner, but she came to life as soon as she saw us, or rather, as soon as she saw Dorian.

Have you heard from Ludmilla? she asked me telepathically. I looked at her in surprise and pretended not to understand. Did this hideous vampire, sister of a monster, want to get me in trouble with Charles?

Idiot, we can only communicate with the person concerned, others can't hear us, and for Charles to read us, he would have to want to.

I glared at her, filled with resentment. Be that as it may, I haven't heard her.

Then, clear and overwhelming, Ludmilla's thought entered my head.

"Don't look for me. Mihail is on our side. The kidnapping was a decoy, we're already out. I'll hide Mihail, and I'll wait for you at my place with Luca. My mother and father must not suspect a thing."

"How did you escape? According to Charles, it should be impossible. And why did you kill Pauline?"

"We didn't kill anyone. The vampire—the one Father Vesta turned to dust—did it. You must tell Charles."

"He will never believe it."

"Father Vesta will make the one who brought back his grandmother's head confess. I must leave you now."

I squeezed Father Vesta's arm, and he turned towards me, just long enough to nod.

Charles returned, followed by two other vampires. "Get her!" he commanded.

Immediately, Father Vesta stepped in front of me. "Stop, and let no one dare."

"How dare you, priest, defy my will!" Charles shouted, his tone dark and threatening.

"You dared to send Maria into an ambush. You knew your two azaras would kill her."

"They died at his hands. He will pay for that," Charles snarled back.

"You are mistaken. I was the one who killed them. Self-defense is not a crime."

My God, the priest was taking the blame, even though it wasn't entirely true. I heard Dorian's voice in my mind. "Don't respond. Father Vesta knows what he's doing, and Charles won't harm him."

Charles furrowed his brow and glared at the priest defiantly. Father Vesta spread his arms and began to speak, his voice rising.

"You, who preach justice, mercy, and benevolence, you who created an army of cursed azaras, believing you've bent them to your will... you dared to send a benevolent malier to her death, and now you are ready to take her life without even understanding the situation. Beware of your own creations!"

Charles moved towards the vampire who had brought back Pauline's head, staring at him so intensely that the vampire bent over, almost crumpling into a bow.

"I didn't want to... it was a mistake, but she got in my way... you know... we can't resist... it was a mistake," the vampire pleaded, never daring to raise his head.

Charles seemed to rise, his figure towering as he raised his arm and brought it down hard on the vampire's neck. The force was so brutal that the head rolled right to my feet. I stepped back, letting it roll to the wall.

"Justice is done," Charles declared. He glared at us. "You will bring Mihail back to me, and if you fail, I will kill you instead. You are free to go." He picked up his grandmother's body and disappeared.

"Let's go!" ordered Adelheid.

Luca took my hand, and we all left the house.

"I'll take Luca," I said, intending to explain everything to him on the way back to the car, as Ludmilla had asked.

"Ludmilla has made a deal with Mihail? He must have bewitched her..." Luca exclaimed as the wind from my swift pace whipped his face. "That may be, but I have a clear idea. And I need you and Andrea. Do you trust me?"

He didn't hesitate. "Of course I trust you."

We reached the car a few seconds after Adelheid and Dorian.

"Sorry, I need to practice running with a human on my back."

"I don't think that will be necessary," Adelheid replied tersely.

"Father Vesta, get in the car. We'll drive you home," Dorian said.

"I'll return as I came. Don't worry about me."

We all got into the car, but this time Ludmilla wasn't there to separate me from Luca. The scent that assaulted my senses provoked my thirst. I had to hold my breath repeatedly to avoid it. Dorian rolled down the window, despite the air conditioning—he understood my discomfort.

"Is something on your mind? Do you want to share it with us?" he asked.

"About ten years ago," I began, "my team was involved in a peculiar case: ten women were found naked on the street... they were trying to cover themselves with whatever trash they could find. A passing patrol car noticed them huddled near a bus stop outside the city. They were disoriented, with no memory of what had happened. All they could say was that they found themselves naked in the street for no reason. We brought them to the station, clothed them, and started questioning them. It was all useless—they remembered nothing except what they were doing before everything went blank: they were preparing for a party. That was it. They were all students living on the university campus. At first, we suspected drug use, but toxicology tests came back clean, and there were no signs of sexual assault. We investigated for a few days but had no leads. The families, wanting to protect their daughters, persuaded them to withdraw their complaints."

"Why ten women, if this was an attempt to bring the Twelve back to life?" Luca asked.

I shrugged. "I don't know."

"Unless... someone already knew about the existence of two other pairs: Maria, Ludmilla, and who knows who else," Adelheid interjected.

"I can't bear the thought of my little girl being in the hands of my deranged brother. He could bewitch her and turn her into a murderer again."

"He won't hurt her, will he?" I asked, worried.

"Of course not. She's too precious to him, and now we know why," Adelheid replied, tucking her hair behind her ears.

A phone rang. It was Adelheid's. "Ludmilla?" she shouted into it.

She put it on speaker.

"I'm fine. I'm home."

"Where is that monster?" Adelheid growled.

"He used me to escape, but he didn't hurt me. I'll wait for you here." Ludmilla ended the call.

"Your daughter," Adelheid snapped at Dorian, "always thinks this is a game. He will have already bewitched her."

"We'll know as soon as we see her," Dorian tried to reassure her, squeezing her hand.

As soon as Andrea saw me, he rushed over and hugged me tightly.

"I was scared. For a moment, I feared the worst," he murmured.

I pulled back slightly and looked at him. "Do you remember the case of those ten girls found naked in the street? About a decade ago?"

"Yeah, I remember... Damn, who knows what they were on... but what does that have to do with this?"

"I'm not sure," I said, turning to the others, "but if my suspicions are correct, we might have ten families in danger. The little vampires are growing up and starting to adapt... and I don't think their families have any idea."

"Damn monster!" Robert exclaimed.

"No, he didn't know anything about this. Or rather, he thought it was just a legend until today," I replied, and then I moved closer to hug him. Dear Grandpa Robert.

"Honestly, I don't care about my monster brother's ramblings," Adelheid said sharply. "You let him escape, and you will have to find him," she said, pointing her finger at me. "My daughter is safe, and that's all that matters. I'm going back to Cluj, and I never want to see your face again," she finished, glaring at me with contempt.

She kissed her daughter and left the house.

"Don't mind her. Rather, tell us: what's your plan?" Dorian asked.

"It's hard not to mind her... Anyway, Andrea and I need to return to Italy, but more importantly, we need to find a way to tie our investigation to my suspect."

"We'll need time. Meanwhile, I'll talk to your commissioner," Dorian replied.

I remained doubtful. A few days earlier, I had inferred from something Dorian said that some humans knew about our existence, but the thought of Spatafora being one of them seemed ridiculous.

We are busy, remember? Ludmilla's voice echoed in my mind.

I can't hide Mihail from Andrea.

You're out of your mind. Mihail will never cooperate with anyone not on his trusted list. Only you and Luca.

Then find a way to distance yourself from all of them... I nudged her.

In fact, Ludmilla, already in agreement with Luca, had gone ahead with the lies. A true marvel.

"I just received a message from Captain Perri; he says Father Vesta hasn't returned yet," she said, reading from her phone, or rather, pretending to read something from it.

"He wouldn't get back in the car with us. I assumed he'd hidden his own somewhere," Dorian replied, worry evident in his voice.

"Well, either way, Luca's down here. I'm going with him to find that crazy priest-witch."

"Ludmilla, it's dangerous," Dorian warned her.

"I want to help Luca."

She vanished through the door without waiting for any further arguments.

"I'm going with them," I said quickly, not giving anyone a chance to question or stop me.

I caught up to Ludmilla, who was waiting in the car. "I was afraid Andrea would follow you."

"We'd better go before we see him coming out the door."

"Mihail is with Luca at Father Vesta's house."

I nodded, not answering. I was anxious, and the thought of facing Mihail again filled me with dread.

When we entered Father Vesta's house, Mihail was strapped to a restraining chair, his head hanging down. He straightened up as soon as he sensed us.

"Myyyy daughters!" he exclaimed, his voice dragging out the words.

I glared at him with hatred, and he responded with a mocking smile. I wanted to smash his rotten teeth in, but I knew he was a hundred times stronger than me. So I accepted his presence, knowing it wouldn't be for long.

I recounted the incident from ten years ago.

"Why only ten women? It makes no sense. It's an accident, unrelated to the rebirth of the Twelve," Mihail said.

"Take it easy, bully," Luca interjected. "Couldn't there be another pair of malier? Besides, it didn't seem like you supernatural creatures were even aware that you already had two of them in your midst."

"That may be," Mihail replied with a shrug.

"Listen, you psychopathic monster," Luca shouted, pointing Father Vesta's dagger at his neck, "you're only here because you claimed to know that other psychopathic monster, but if, for even a moment, I think you're messing with us, then this dagger will cut your throat before you get a chance to say anything."

Mihail remained calm, a smirk tugging at one corner of his mouth. He didn't say another word, just kept staring at Luca.

Suddenly, the door opened. It was Charles.

We all froze, but Mihail was the one who quickly dropped his smirk and lowered his mocking gaze.

"Did you really think I wasn't listening to your thoughts? How naive...," Charles said, his voice filled with amusement.

Then the door opened again.

This time, Dorian and Andrea entered.

I avoided the stern gazes of both of them.

"Well, well, well... I see you've been enjoying playing with fire," Dorian said, casting a reproachful look at Ludmilla. He then turned to me: "You... I thought you were smarter, but clearly, I was wrong."

Charles approached Mihail, looking him straight in the eye. "You might have fooled these idiots, but not me... and not even the good Dorian. There is no Sebastian, and you know it."

He had deceived me! I felt the anger rise, but something prevented me from hurling it at Mihail.

Father Vesta intervened, sensing my distress.

"You are a benevolent malier, darling. Your essence will never allow you to kill your kin or a human." I felt my frustration melt away.

"But it was easy to kill that vampire in the dungeon," I muttered, confused.

"I told you, you were defending yourself. You didn't attack him; you could never have done that."

I continued to glare at Mihail with hatred, but I shifted my demoralized gaze to Dorian.

"If this monster made it all up just to buy himself a few extra minutes, then who should we be looking for?" I asked.

"I've already spoken to Spatafora. Tomorrow morning, we have seats booked on the first flight to Italy," he replied.

I turned to Andrea, seeking his understanding, or at least a sign of forgiveness for pushing him aside, but his expression remained impassive. He met my gaze without emotion, and doubt started to creep in.

"Who do you mean by 'we'?"

"You and Luca," he replied.

"No way, Andrea has to come back with me," I demanded, trying to sound firm.

"Andrea can't go back just yet."

"Why not?"

"Remember he tried to kill you in the shower?"

"Yes, but that was before I was a vampire."

"Exactly," he said dryly.

I searched Andrea's eyes for reassurance.

"Everything will be fine. You'll go tomorrow and finish this investigation, even if it has taken a peculiar turn... I know you will. I'll wait for you here."

I couldn't argue anymore; perhaps they were right. I saw Andrea for what he was, not for what he had become.

"I will leave with them!" Ludmilla declared, her voice loud and defiant.

"Absolutely not. You've caused enough trouble, my child. You will go to your mother while your sister and Luca finish their task."

"Make me..." she challenged.

"You know I could," Charles said, his tone menacing.

"You asked for it," she hissed, turning her gaze to each of us.

"Atten..." Father Vesta began, cutting off before finishing the word.

I felt it... we all felt Ludmilla's power. The sensation was like plunging into a sea as green as emerald, sinking into a clear, pure abyss where every thought was stripped away, leaving us feeling so free and light that we didn't want to resurface. Then I came back to the surface, my gaze peacefully resting on Ludmilla. We all did, even Charles, who was clearly trying to resist the manipulation but with no success.

"You'll find your ticket at the airport," Dorian said, his tone almost fatherly.

"Thank you, Dad," Ludmilla replied joyfully.

Charles, aided by Father Vesta, took Mihail and disappeared from the room.

"Ludmilla," Dorian hissed, "don't ever do that again."

Slowly, I emerged from the state of ecstasy Ludmilla had placed us in. I understood her power better now. She didn't just dominate; she cleansed your mind of thoughts and implanted her own. It was a vast power, but still limited by the absence of her counterpart.

I sighed, thinking about my own power: benevolent for eternity... Saint Rita of Cascia! Seriously...

Dejected, I watched Ludmilla jump around joyfully like a child, shaking my head as I smiled at Andrea.

I approached him. I felt the need to talk, to bridge the gap that, because of me, was widening between us.

"You stay here and follow Robert and Dorian. They'll help you, and I promise I'll be back so fast you won't even notice I was gone."

He gently placed his hands on my shoulders. "I don't know how to make it up to you for what I almost did to you that night," he murmured.

"But it didn't happen. Don't dwell on it... I'm not the same as before either, or rather, I am, but with a different essence. I understand you; I know you didn't mean it. That's why you need to stay here and let them help you. Promise me you will."

"I promise," he replied, his eyes glistening.

He gave me a gentle, chaste kiss on the lips and then disappeared with Dorian.

23

Ludmilla was elated about the flight that would take us to Italy.
"What makes you so happy?"
"Being with you, my sister. A trip together—I never expected it."
"Thanks for the consideration," grumbled Luca, eavesdropping from the back seat.
I glanced through the gap between the two seats and winked at him. Then I disconnected, using an ability I'd discovered as a vampire—to shut out the world from my thoughts and turn into a statue. It was unmatched. I slipped on my earphones and, with the volume cranked up high, I enjoyed AC/DC.
We landed at Turin airport on time. After collecting my luggage in the half-empty area, I was stunned to see Commissioner Spatafora among those waiting for passengers.
"Weren't we supposed to be incognito?" I asked Luca.
"Not really. Dorian informed Spatafora of our arrival," he replied.
"You could have at least told me," I muttered, giving him a dark look.
Spatafora scrambled to be seen, not knowing he was already being talked about.
"Welcome back, Inspector," he said, holding out his hand. I shook it just enough to make his eyes water. He swallowed and turned to Ludmilla with his usual melancholy manner.
I believe he received the same handshake from her, as his face turned red, and his eyes teared up.
"Captain Perri, what a pleasure to meet you in person," she said, giving him a hug.

"Maybe his hand hurts too much," I thought, amused.

"Something strange is going on. Mrs. Donadio..." Spatafora murmured darkly.

"What happened to Mrs. Donadio?"

"Since yesterday, she's regained consciousness and started remembering many things... too many."

"Now we're in deep trouble," I thought, immediately regretting it.

"Well... that's good news," I whispered.

"But it's not over," Spatafora continued, his head bowed. "Other witnesses to the events of 1986 are suddenly remembering things. For several hours now, police stations across half of Italy have been swamped with people reporting incidents they'd forgotten for years."

I put my hand over my mouth, glancing at Ludmilla with concern.

"This is not good for you. Your name will surface, and they'll hunt you down," I told her telepathically.

"Nobody knows we're here."

"For now. But it's too dangerous—you have to go back."

I closed the telepathic link and turned to Spatafora. "Ludmilla must leave the country immediately."

"I agree," Luca added.

"Let's move away from here first; we're still inside an airport," Spatafora suggested, heading for the exit.

We followed him, with Ludmilla sulking like a child whose sweets had been taken away.

I looked at Spatafora and wondered how it was possible that this man knew the supernatural world—and especially why.

"For now, you'll all come to my house. You'll be safe and away from prying eyes."

"We must arrange to send Ludmilla back immediately," I insisted.

"I understand, Maria, we will. But I need to consult with Dorian Geoana first," he replied, clearly tired of my persistence.

"Does nobody care about my opinion?" trilled Ludmilla.

"Go on," I replied, resigned.

"I'm here to help. If there's a vampire trying to reassemble the malier, only I have the strength and power to find and fight him. Certainly not you, my sister, who's been adapted for only two days."

I tried not to lose my patience. I decided to postpone the argument for another time, especially not in front of Spatafora. I remained silent, even ignoring Ludmilla's mental nudges.

Spatafora lived in a villa in the hills of Turin, nestled in a forest he owned. He had recently separated from his wife, so the house was at our complete disposal. The knot in my throat, which had been there since landing at Caselle, tightened even more. I thought about my parents and how I wouldn't be able to see them—at least not yet.

"I've prepared a list of the women who filed a complaint that day. It's up to date. Unfortunately, two of them died in accidents, one within three months of the other. I assume there are relatives who might be helpful."

"Actually, we're looking for possible children. Didn't Dorian tell you that?"

"No," he said, shaking his head. "I thought you were after the maniac. What do children have to do with it?"

"I need to ask him. I never imagined he could be friends with the supernatural, with vampires. If I may ask, why is that?"

Spatafora, bold as he was, hadn't expected my question—certainly not so early, and so bluntly, in front of the others.

"My wife is one of them... of you."

I was stunned, scrambling to mumble an apology while Spatafora looked at me, satisfied that he'd silenced me.

Luca spoke up. "Are we sure the women's abductions were intended to procreate?"

"Even if they were, it's not certain that all of them got pregnant. And this is the modern age—abortion exists. But why are you looking for children?" Spatafora asked again.

"If they're the result of a human-vampire relationship, ninety percent will be unadapted vampires—dangerous to those around them. They don't yet know their essence, and if no one guides them, countless innocents could be harmed. And then there's the risk of someone discovering what they are."

"That makes sense. If you think my wife could help, I don't think she'd refuse."

"Yes, we'll need an extra hand. As Ludmilla said at the airport, Maria doesn't yet have the strength of a seasoned vampire, and Ludmilla... should go home," Luca said confidently.

"But I'm not going home," Ludmilla roared, storming out of the room.

"Leave her be," advised Luca, sensing my intention to follow.

As tough as I was, I had an emotional breakdown. I slumped in my chair, overwhelmed by the psychic exhaustion that had plagued me for days, which I'd only managed to suppress with great effort. How hadn't I realized it? Ludmilla had been controlling my emotions, and now, in revenge, she had cut me off, leaving me in chaos.

"May I ask how Deputy Inspector Pancaldi is doing?"

I looked at Spatafora and could barely articulate a response.

"Not well. He was transformed against his will, violently. Whoever found him had to complete the adaptation so he wouldn't die. But his self-control... it's fragile. That's why we thought it best to leave him with Dorian and Robert."

I stopped mid-sentence as Spatafora's phone rang. He apologized and stepped away. I could have easily eavesdropped, but I chose to respect his privacy.

"We need to find her," I told Luca.

"She's around, somewhere in the garden. Don't worry."

"I'm not worried about her; I'm worried about what she might do..."

"What am I supposed to do?" she hissed, storming back in. She stood before me, arms crossed, her gaze sullen. "Tell me, what should I do? Do you think of me as the same as our father?"

Ludmilla's expression made me feel guilty, but I certainly didn't see her as a monster.

"What are you talking about? I'd never think that. But, sister, please go home—you're in danger here," I pleaded.

"You called me sister, that's a first."

I saw her face light up with joy. She hugged me so tightly I could hardly breathe. Then, suddenly, a veil dropped over my painful thoughts, restoring my mental balance.

"Thank you," I thought.

Spatafora returned, his expression blank. He sat down, fiddling with a pen—click, click, click. He brooded, moving his lips left, then right.

"There's some news," he said cryptically, before falling silent.

"Are you going to tell us, or is it a secret?" I asked, sarcasm creeping into my voice.

"Right, sorry," he said, adjusting himself in his chair. "I was on the phone with Commissioner Celeste. There was a domestic incident. Apparently, a television fell off a wall, landing on a cleaner's head. She works for a family whose name matches one on the list."

"Bingo!" I shouted.

"Luckily, the woman wasn't seriously injured. But she claims a ten-year-old child—yes, it seems that young—threw it at her in a fit of anger, yanking it off the wall with his bare hands. Celeste warned me because the case will be passed to juvenile services."

"This is just the beginning if we don't act," Ludmilla said.

The worst was unfolding, and I was sure the two deaths weren't mere accidents.

"We need to move. I'll call Malvina," Spatafora said, dialing.

I watched him, his face pained as he made the call. This situation was beyond the understanding of most humans, even one who knew the supernatural side of the story.

"She's coming," he said, putting his phone away.

"It must be hard to deal with your ex-wife in such matters. I'm sorry."

"Don't be, Maria... It's time we were on a first-name basis, don't you think?"

"It is," I nodded, surprised.

"As I said, don't be sorry. We parted on good terms. And I was the one who left her. I may be a coward, but I couldn't take it anymore. She's immortal, and I'm just a mere human who, soon enough, won't even be able to go to the bathroom on his own."

The same thought had haunted me ever since Andrea's transformation. I noticed Spatafora watching me, as if he'd read my thoughts.

"But now you're one of them. Tell me, what's it like knowing you have an eternal life ahead of you?"

It was clear his partner had once asked him to accept the adaptation. I sat on the sofa, and Spatafora—Giovanni—did the same.

"We're going for a walk in the lovely garden," Luca said, taking Ludmilla's hand. I watched them for a moment as they left, feeling a twinge of annoyance at their hands touching, but I suppressed any thoughts that Ludmilla might pick up. "When I found out about Andrea's transformation, I couldn't accept it. I selfishly thought the same thing as you: 'No way, soon he'll be changing my diapers.' But then adaptation happened to me. I guess you know I had the vampire gene, dormant. I don't want to digress. The issue is that you need to do some soul-searching. Do you truly love her? Are you willing to endure her sympathy? If she loves you, she'll be devastated by your death. Vampires have heightened emotions. She'll suffer for decades, maybe centuries, but she's willing to take that risk. I think it's the ultimate show of love.

Otherwise, if your love was merely fascination with her supernatural essence, then yes, let her go. It's your choice."

"But you didn't answer my question."

"You know, it's still early, but I can tell you this—anger and confusion are giving way to acceptance. Immortality is a great responsibility, but it's one worth experiencing and sharing with humanity."

"Well, I mean... you have to feed on humanity..." he said cautiously.

"You don't have to kill to feed. Unless you choose to."

His gaze softened, and he smiled, staring past my shoulder.

"I am Malvina," she said, introducing herself.

She stood, gazing at me with wide, girlish blue eyes. She must have been transformed young or was a sanguine.

I got up to greet her.

"Darling, welcome back," Giovanni said, his eyes filled with affection. "My love," she replied, embracing him.

They must have loved each other deeply, choosing to part rather than hurt each other. I watched them caress and exchange sorrowful glances. I was still processing the idea of Giovanni as Commissioner Spatafora—still not the most pleasant man. I smiled at the thought.

"How... do you plan to proceed?" he asked, gently releasing her from their tender embrace.

Ludmilla and Luca re-entered, but Malvina suddenly hissed and leapt back, colliding clumsily with an old console against the entrance wall. She smashed it, falling to the floor.

"You've brought a hunter before me!" she roared.

"Calm down, my love," Giovanni rushed to her side. "He's a friend. He's helping us," he said, trying to soothe her.

"He's a bloody hunter, what friend?"

"He's a friend, trust me. Without his help, I'd probably be ashes by now," I said, stepping closer, extending my hand. She hesitated but took it. "Nice work," I added, laughing at the shattered console. I winked.

212

I felt a veil of serenity wash over us. Malvina's eyes reflected realization; she sensed someone in the room had great power. She relaxed.

"I apologize," she said, regaining her composure.

She blushed slightly but began to speak calmly.

"You sought my help, and I will give it. I'll also try to understand why a vampire hunter would befriend... vampires. My apologies again for my reaction. Now, if you'll explain..."

Giovanni poured strong drinks into glasses and handed them to us.

"We need these, ladies and gentlemen," he declared enthusiastically.

The potent liquid slid down smoothly, leaving a slight sense of intoxication. Ludmilla watched me, amused.

"What?"

"You can drink all you want, but you won't get drunk. Just a mild... buzz. Quite nice," I said, returning her amused look.

"I'll go to the hospital to check on the woman attacked by the child," Giovanni said.

"Yes, but we'll take a different approach—not entirely human. We can't allow anyone to remember what happened."

"Do you plan to bewitch everyone?"

"It's not my favorite thing, but it has to be done," I replied dryly. I then turned to Malvina. "You'll accompany Giovanni to the hospital and implant a story in the woman's memory, something... adjusted, enough to clear the child and keep social services at bay. Meanwhile, we'll visit the family. We'll need to do this with everyone. The only way to control these children is to manipulate the minds of their families. We have no choice. Do you agree?"

They all nodded.

"Good. Giovanni and Malvina to the hospital, and the three of us will go to the family."

And so we did. The families were unaware of the essence of their children, but they'd likely defend them to the death—even if they were wrong, and perhaps even without any sickness clouding their judgment. We'd play on affection, acting as manipulative as we had to, because we were vampires helping our own kind.

24

The Testori family welcomed us warmly, shaking hands, completely unaware of Ludmilla's power. I felt a pang of guilt, but as Luca expressed indignation over the accusation made by the babysitter, not the maid, of little Lorenzo, I asked to see the child.

Lorenzo Testori appeared to be a typical child, petite and curious. I found him absorbed in a video game, but as he sensed my presence, he turned, showing the angry eyes of a vampire.

"Who are you? Mamaaaa! Who is this?" he shouted in a melodious tone that no longer surprised me.

"My name is Maria," I whispered cautiously, approaching him.

He stared at me for a moment, then set down the steering wheel he was holding.

"Did you come here to take me away?"

"No, honey, I came here to help you."

"What do you mean?"

Suddenly, my hands grew warm, and instinct told me to take his. He let me.

We sat down on his racing car-shaped bed, and I continued to act on instinct, not fully understanding what was happening. I saw his angry expression soften.

"You are good, and you are here to help me," he whimpered.

I hugged him tightly, feeling all his anger and fear over his uncontrolled strength flow into me. Was this what it meant to be a benevolent malier? Absorbing the suffering of vampires and humans alike? I tried to stay calm, but I was just as scared as Lorenzo.

I called for Ludmilla. It would be her task to explain his essence.

I returned to the other room where Luca was with Lorenzo's parents.

"Is Lorenzo okay?" his mother asked, her tone relaxed.

"Of course, I left him with Ludmilla. She knows what to do."

"Nothing must happen to our special child. We trust you," said the father.

"Nothing will happen to him in the years to come, until his adaptation is complete. Your task will be to keep his essence hidden from human eyes and to help him manage the pains that will come during his transformation."

"He won't hurt anyone anymore? He is just a child. It will be difficult to shelter him from his own instincts, and he will suffer greatly during the transformation," his mother added anxiously.

"Nothing will happen again, I swear," I said, taking the woman's hands in mine.

From the bedroom, we could hear Lorenzo and Ludmilla laughing, absorbed in a Formula One race.

I knew it wasn't humane to tamper with the psyche of people unaware of our abilities, but we had no choice. Too much time had passed without anyone suspecting the diabolical work of an unscrupulous monster. My phone vibrated in my pocket.

"Giovanni?"

"The babysitter has filed her version of the events and withdrawn the complaint. She's better, but the wound on her forehead is pretty bad."

"I'm sorry to hear that. We need to continue with the list, but I think we'll need Father Vesta."

"The witch?"

"You know him?" I asked, surprised.

"Yes... no... I've heard about him a lot from Malvina. Apparently, he's a cornerstone of the supernatural world."

"Hell yes. Only he will be able to determine the powers of each child."

"Do what you need to," he replied, resigned.

I ended the call and turned to Ludmilla and Luca.

"Let's go. We still have a lot of work to do."

They agreed, though Luca hesitated slightly.

"Staying silent won't get you answers," I prodded him.

"Why would Father Vesta come here? If Charles's fears are justified, he might try to kill you all."

"I really don't think Charles is right. I'm convinced the priest knew about my essence even before the transformation. He even tried to tell me... in his own way. And anyway, he never harmed me."

"Maybe..." he nodded doubtfully. "I need at least a short break and a couple of hours of sleep. I'm not a vampire."

"Go rest, but maybe avoid being alone with Malvina."

"Fine, I'll lock myself in my room... I'll avoid killing her."

He left, his expression disapproving. I would have preferred him to confront me, to throw his doubts at me. But he did nothing.

"Don't beat yourself up over him. I've known Luca for a long time, and I can tell you that his instincts as a hunter override any friendship with vampires right now. He has to suppress them," Ludmilla said, hugging me.

I pulled out the list from my pocket.

"We need to visit the family of the first woman who died in the accident—Sonda Wood. She never married, and her daughter has been living with her grandparents since her death. Her name is Deborah Wood, and she's ten years old."

The grandparents hadn't lived in Turin since their daughter's death; they moved to a village in the province where their other son lived.

Lawyer Jeremy Wood was a man in his forties, with the look of a studious, bookish type. His office smelled of book dust and cherry tea. He worked in a small studio on the top floor of a quaint house in classic

Canavese style, with a Bed and Breakfast on the ground floor. The view from the garden towards Monviso was enchanting.

"Inspector Diletti, I presume. My parents told me you were coming."

As we shook hands, I noticed a flicker of admiration in his eyes—the same admiration I'd felt the first time I met one of us. I took advantage of that moment of mental distraction to ease my way into his thoughts. Ludmilla targeted his emotions.

"Please come in. I'll call my parents to bring Deborah."

He straightened the criminal law books scattered across his desk and called his parents through an intercom.

"Would you like some herbal tea?"

"Not for me, thanks."

Ludmilla also declined but helped herself to a candy from a dish on a small table.

"Could you tell us about the accident?"

He sat down and sighed. "It still feels like yesterday, yet... it's already been three months. I miss my sister. But forgive me, I know your time is limited," he said, sipping from a cup. "Sorry. The incident... it happened around seven o'clock in the evening on that dreadful Wednesday. I was about to see off my last client when the intercom buzzed. It was the carabinieri, notifying me of what had happened. I rushed to the hospital. My parents were still living in Turin then; they had only been here a few weeks. I found them sitting outside the ER, waiting for news about Deborah. There was nothing to be done for Sonda—she died instantly. But you're here because of the circumstances of the accident, right?"

I nodded, leaning in.

"Well, I never believed a word written in the carabinieri's report on the circumstances of the crash," he said abruptly, with a mix of pride and disdain.

"I'm listening," I said, more interested than ever.

"I know from experience that when they blame a non-existent hit-and-run, it just means they have no idea what happened. That day, by coincidence, the camera at the city centre entrance wasn't working, which is very unusual. We get fines all the time from that camera, and it's never been off. Nor did any witnesses see the lorry that supposedly didn't give way. The car mysteriously ended up on the opposite carriageway, jumping the guardrail. Sonda didn't stand a chance. Deborah, however, was found wandering along Corso Regina Margherita, unharmed but confused. To this day, she still says her mother killed her because she made her angry. Poor child."

A long silence followed, broken only by the arrival of Deborah. She ran in, throwing herself into her uncle's arms. But it was fleeting—everything changed in a moment. She turned towards us, trembling, her eyes red with anger.

I stared at her, disoriented by her fury. I searched for Ludmilla, who rose and approached the child.

"It's okay," she said, placing a hand on Deborah's shoulder.

I saw Deborah flinch, then turn to Ludmilla, throwing her arms around her neck.

"You know, don't you?" she asked tearfully.

"Yes, but Maria needs to greet your grandparents now. Okay?"

With a slight nod, Ludmilla gestured towards the two figures standing by the door, frightened and speechless.

They stiffened as I got up from my chair. I took their hands and led them out of the studio.

I absorbed all their anxieties, fears, and doubts, leaving them only with the knowledge that they had a special granddaughter to protect for many years. "Tell these two ladies what you do at night," Grandpa prompted.

I glanced at Ludmilla, waiting to hear what the girl did at night.

"I see Mum, but she's not angry with me, even though I killed her. She takes my hand, and when she touches me, I'm in another world. Not a different world, really—it's this world, but everyone is dressed differently, and there are no cars, only horses. I can walk with my mum and talk to her, but then the dream ends, and I wake up scared."

Holy hell, Ludmilla's voice echoed, a wayfarer.

I stood still for a moment, staring at that small, powerful creature. A wayfarer—a vampire capable of traveling through time. I wondered ecstatically what wonders she could do once she learned to understand and use her power.

With the conversation done, we left with the promise that we would return soon and that they would be contacted by a peculiar priest—Father Vesta.

However strong I'd become, I was pushing myself too hard. The mental strain was exhausting me.

"You need nourishment," Ludmilla said, sensing my state, "and not food," she added.

"Let's stop and get something to take home."

"Stop pretending you don't understand. If you don't feed properly, you'll end up doing something you regret."

"I'll grab the first one I see on the street... no, actually, I'll go back up for a moment," I replied, tired of hearing the same lecture.

"Look, I'm not joking, stubborn one. Accept it—you're a vampire now. Sooner or later, you'll have to feed, or your instincts will make you do it at the expense of some innocent. It's your choice."

She turned to the window, sullen, not saying another word the rest of the drive back to Giovanni's house.

As soon as we pulled into the garden, Ludmilla snapped back to life and jumped out of the car before it even stopped.

I saw three figures standing at the front door: Malvina, Giovanni, and Luca. Ludmilla paused midway, as if waiting for something even she didn't know.

"Looks like you've decided to hold a meeting outside... well, with this heat, why not..."

"Always sarcastic, our inspector," grumbled Giovanni.
"What's going on?" I asked suspiciously.
"What do they have?" Ludmilla echoed, coming out of her sulk.
"I have no idea, they look like statues."
Then they broke ranks, like good soldiers. Out stepped Celeste.

In that moment, I made more mental calculations than Einstein did in his entire career, but I couldn't find any logical reason for Celeste's presence or what to say to him.

"Hello, Maria," he said, his tone genuinely disappointed.
"H... h... hello..."
"Don't stutter; it won't work this time. Explain: what the hell are you doing here, and where the hell is Deputy Inspector Pancaldi?"
"I can explain everything," I replied, desperately searching for complicity in Giovanni's gaze, but his face remained unreadable.

Of course, Giovanni Spatafora wouldn't dare ask Malvina to tamper with Celeste's mind. I shot a glare at Luca, who met it with a devilish grin.

I lost my patience, and to prevent the day's accumulated rage from bursting out, I approached Celeste. I took his hands, and his face looked stunned as he felt their warmth. I didn't speak, avoiding eye contact. I closed my eyes and absorbed all his despair. The emotions were purified of their negative energy, but they became so powerful that he collapsed. I caught him just before his head hit the ground.

Ludmilla approached, placing a hand on his shoulder.
"Maria, I'm sorry. I've been fasting since this morning; I forget that age is catching up with me," Celeste said as he regained consciousness.
"We can grab a good dinner from the restaurant downstairs," Giovanni suggested.
"Good idea. You and Luca are staying too, right?" Celeste asked, massaging his neck.

I glared at Ludmilla, wondering what she had done to him.
The truth, I heard her think as she ran inside.

"I can't remember what we were discussing," Celeste said, embarrassed.

"Andrea's... the deputy inspector, remember?"

"Of course, of course. So, he stayed in Romania to get help after his transformation... I'll figure out a good excuse for the superiors if anyone asks."

I watched poor Celeste babble on, knowing he would forget everything once he stepped out of the garden. I hated doing this to people I respected, people I had known my whole life.

It was an evening to forget, at least for me. It was a night of lies and misdirection, hoping Celeste wouldn't recall the truth.

"What were you thinking, bringing Celeste here?" I hissed at Giovanni as soon as we were alone.

"I had no choice. He showed up at the door a few minutes before you and Ludmilla arrived. He wanted an explanation about the new statement filed by the babysitter. And I, as you know, don't have any bewitching or persuasive powers."

"Of course, I'm sorry."

"We're all tired," said Luca. "How about we get some sleep and resume the search in the morning?"

"I agree. Good night, everyone."

As soon as I was in my room, I sat by the window and picked up my phone. I dialed Andrea's number. It was past midnight in Romania, but he answered on the first ring.

"Maria?"

"Hi, Andrea. How are you?"

"I'm fine, don't worry about me. What about you? How is the search going?"

"If it weren't for the fact that I was face-to-face with Celeste tonight, I'd say everything's fine."

"In front of Celeste? Look, Maria, I have to tell you something you won't like."

"Go ahead."

"Mihail has managed to escape again."

"That's impossible. I thought... we all thought he was dead."

"Why do you say that?"

"Do you remember Mrs. Donadio?" He murmured a faint yes. "She has regained her memory, completely. And she's not alone—other witnesses from 1986 are also remembering and pressing charges."

"We'll be with you tomorrow. We think Mihail is looking for you; it won't take him long to find you. I'll let you know as soon as we're on the plane."

"Who's 'we'?" I asked, but he disconnected. A noise distracted me. It was Ludmilla.

"What's going on? I sensed your fear and, sorry, but I overheard you. The line was closing by then."

"Mihail escaped."

"He might have, but something happened to him. And not a good thing."

"They think he's headed here."

"I repeat, that's impossible. Subjugation can only be broken if the creature who initiated it dies, or by their own will. And in the latter case, they have to do it themselves... it's not like sending an email."

"What if someone killed him during the escape?"

"That could be, but we can't rest until we know for sure."

Ludmilla connected with Malvina and asked her to bring Giovanni down to the salon. I did the same with Luca. I had to knock insistently, as he was asleep.

"Maria, what's going on?" he mumbled, opening the door.

A giggle escaped me when I saw how crumpled and sleepy he looked.

"Did you come here to laugh at me, or do you have something important to say?"

223

"Mihail has escaped. We're all gathering downstairs." I cut it short and headed for the stairs, casting a teasing glance at his lean, muscular form.

When I reached the bottom step, Ludmilla was already close by.

"I spoke to Dad. They're waiting for Mum to arrive, and then they'll get on the first flight to Turin. He doesn't want us going to the airport. The less we show ourselves, the better." I nodded and sat next to Giovanni.

"Why are all those people suddenly remembering?" he asked bluntly.

"I don't know, Giovanni, I don't know," I replied, burying my head in my hands.

A noise from outside startled everyone.

"I'll check it out," Malvina whispered, gliding toward the front door. I followed her.

"I come in peace; I mean no harm," said a voice from the hedge.

"Who are you?" Malvina shouted.

We stood still as a figure emerged from the hedge. The man had long, bronze-colored hair, perfectly cropped, framing a stunningly handsome face. His shirt, made of fine Scottish thread, revealed abs so sculpted they looked chiseled from marble. But what left us speechless was the beautiful black cat by his side, staring at us with yellow eyes as bright as a Ferrari's headlights. The cat sat on its haunches and began licking its paw.

"I am Jacques, and this is Miss Nimue," he said with a thick French accent.

"Why do I know you?" asked Ludmilla, standing at the doorway.

Malvina moved like a panther, fluid and menacing, positioning herself beside the man. The cat's reaction was immediate: arching its back, puffing out its fur, its eyes flaring like tongues of fire, and baring sharp teeth.

"Ssssh... good, Miss Nimue. That's no way to behave," Jacques scolded softly. The cat hesitated, then resumed washing its paw. "Forgive her, but Miss Nimue is... rather protective."

"Then you'd better explain why Ludmilla knows you... and quickly," I said, feeling my patience wear thin.

I felt compelled to touch him, to understand his intentions, and absorb any negativity, rendering him harmless. I moved closer, surprising him by taking his hand. I closed my eyes.

"Wow, you are a malìer. I thought that sadistic madman Mihail had made it all up," Jacques said, looking at me with astonishment.

I released his hand; there was no malice in him.

"Either you're a great liar, or you really mean no harm," I murmured.

"Vous n'avez qu'à me mettre à l'épreuve," he said softly.

We stepped aside to let him in, accompanied by Miss Nimue, who strutted proudly beside him.

Malvina walked over to Giovanni and took his hand. "This is Jacques; he seems to be a friend."

Hesitantly, Giovanni introduced himself.

"A human!" Jacques exclaimed, his eyes sparkling with curiosity.

Then his expression darkened when he looked at Luca. "Do you really have a hunter for a friend?"

Miss Nimue hissed at the word "hunter."

"She's a friend," I whispered, crouching to pet her. She began purring and leapt into my arms.

"She's never done that with anyone," Jacques muttered, watching the cat jealously.

"You and I are going to be great friends, tell your daddy," I cooed, scratching her head. Luca approached, and Miss Nimue, with utmost reluctance, allowed him to pet her. She calmed down and started purring, while Jacques watched with a faint frown.

"Okay, I get it—you're good with hunters. But stop the flirting. And you, Miss Nimue, hop!"

The cat took a precise leap and landed on Jacques' shoulder, nestling between the strong muscles of his back. She remained vigilant, her eyes scanning us.

"I think it's time for this kind gentleman to explain what he's doing here," said Ludmilla, who had been standing back, observing the scene.

Jacques settled into an armchair, and Miss Nimue curled up on the headrest, hiding her head under a paw.

"We have met, ma cher, il est vrai, though you should not remember... or did Mihail lift the spell?"

"Maybe he's dead," Ludmilla replied, watching his every move.

"Ah, what a tragedy... I can hear the church bells already," he said with a chuckle. Then, regaining composure, he continued, "I knew you when you wandered, hypnotized by your father's will. Do you remember the man in the woods?" he asked, rising from his seat.

Ludmilla's eyes met mine, her expression troubled, as if she were piecing together forgotten memories.

"It's you?" she asked, scanning him from head to toe.

"It's me, petit étincelle."

We all watched, stunned, as Ludmilla ran to him and hugged him.

"Miss Nimue," she addressed the cat, "I'm sorry I didn't recognize you earlier."

The cat seemed to understand, lifting her head to be stroked and purring softly.

Could it really be the same cat Ludmilla was referring to? I did the mental math—the cat had to be over twenty-five years old... Why did I still find myself surprised by these things?

Meanwhile, Ludmilla had pulled back and stood before Jacques.

"How could I have been without you all this time?" She hugged him passionately. Then she froze, dramatically. "And you, my love, I can't imagine the suffering you felt, knowing the truth while I forgot everything. You damned monster!" she cursed Mihail.

The two parted from their embrace, and Ludmilla, with her usual childlike air, ran over and dragged me in front of Jacques.

"Meet Maria, my sister."

"Ta soeur? I never knew you had a sister..."

"Neither did I, until a few weeks ago. And, just to clarify, I wasn't even a vampire until then," I replied, filling in for Ludmilla.

"Mon dieu, did you transform her?" he asked, looking deeply into Ludmilla's eyes.

"We would never do that. I'm surprised you'd even think it... of me," she replied, hurt. "We're twins," she added, "her vampire gene remained dormant until recently. We still don't know what triggered it."

Jacques, still bewildered, continued stroking Miss Nimue.

"She's a malièr, probably unrelated to the vampire gene, but I prefer not to speculate. As I said, I always thought it was Mihail's fantasy. However, I believe I know someone who can help us. But now, will you tell me what's happening here?"

"We're trying to save the fruits of Mihail's madness from themselves," I replied in a single breath.

"He's tried many times in his despicable existence, but he can't have succeeded..." he muttered.

"Oh, he succeeded," Luca said dryly.

"Mais, c'est pas possible..." Jacques exclaimed in disbelief, "malièr are the result of an ancestral spell. They can't be created on a whim."

"We met one today. A ten-year-old with the ability to travel through time. A wayfarer."

"Wow, that's incredible!" he exclaimed.

"It would be, except that her family, like nine others, has no idea what they're dealing with. Two women were killed—one of them the wayfarer's mother."

Jacques clenched the armrests of his chair, the wood creaking under his grip.

"How do you plan to save them all?" he asked.

"We plan to subdue the families, so they'll protect them until the transformation is complete."

"It sounds reasonable but dangerous," he replied cautiously. "They should stay together, under the guidance of a witch."

"That's absurd," I replied sarcastically.

"I wish it were, but believe me when I say it's the only way."

"How do you propose we take ten children away from their human families? The police would be on us in no time. And don't forget that many humans, in the right places, know about our existence."

Jacques turned an amused gaze to Giovanni, who shivered.

"Stop showing off," Ludmilla scolded, snuggling against him.

"It's time, dear Jacques, to tell us why you're here," Malvina asked, still skeptical.

"Someone told me Ludmilla was in Italy. We met while she was imprisoned by her father's will. When he realized we'd fallen in love, he enchanted her to forget me. He made her believe I was using her for revenge against him." He took Ludmilla's hands and continued, "A century ago, Mihail appeared at my New Orleans mansion with his friend Sebastian. I always thought he was a dangerous lunatic, but I wanted to give him a chance. He knew how to behave in society; his aristocratic background showed. I introduced him to high society in New Orleans, but his cruelty was beyond anything I'd seen in my six hundred years. One night, he recognized his stepfather among my guests—the man who had locked him in a coffin for centuries. Mihail took revenge by beheading him. I banished him from my home, but his friend Sebastian stayed behind. It was Sebastian who told me about Mihail's plans. I never believed in the malier story; I thought it was just Mihail's signature on a string of corpses."

"Damn monster," I growled.

"One thing I'm certain of: Mihail couldn't create malier from thin air... He has a powerful witch on his side."

"According to Charles, witches no longer exist, or they've been powerless for centuries," I said, feeling less sure.

"Charles... Charles... a pompous self-proclaimed judge, closer to a god," Jacques mimicked spitting. Ludmilla squeezed his hand. "He didn't hesitate to use my beloved, binding her to his cravings for years, even knowing she was under a spell to forget me. What does he know of the world around him... witches have only set aside their powers, to amplify them for when the time is right."

"Charles will kill anyone who uses magic," Ludmilla said, distressed.

"Death doesn't scare witches, not when it's the price for a good cause... and you have no idea how much you need them," Jacques replied grimly.

"Tomorrow Dorian, Charles, and Father Vesta are arriving," I said, but Jacques cut me off.

"Tomorrow... I will be far from here," he said in a raspy voice.

Ludmilla gasped. "Don't leave me!" she pleaded, her eyes shining. Jacques simply held her tight, his mind shielded. It could only mean one thing: he intended to leave her behind.

Jacques, I sent a mental plea, don't do this, don't make her suffer... she just remembered you.

He looked at me, startled.

I won't stay where I can even smell Charles.

I'll try to stop them from coming.

How do you think they'll listen to you?

They will, you'll see.

I closed my mind and slipped out of the salon, quickly concocting a plan to stall Dorian and the others. I picked up the phone.

"Maria, what's happening?" Dorian answered, sounding tense.

"You can't come. The monster just returned to Romania."

"And you... how do you know?"

"We found his friend Sebastian. Or rather, he found us. He warned us about Mihail's intentions."

"What are Mihail's intentions?"

"To kill all of you and then carry out the malìer ritual. Please, stay where you are and keep yourselves safe... and, if you can, my fiancé as well. We'll hide the children here."

"I'll discuss it with the others and get back to you. How is Ludmilla?"

"She's fine. Don't worry, she can handle herself."

"Oh, I know... I'll be in touch." He ended the call.

I wasn't thrilled about the lies I had spun to delay their arrival, but we needed Jacques more than ever, and I couldn't let Ludmilla lose him again. As I turned, I saw Luca leaning against the doorframe. He'd heard everything.

"Why?" he asked simply.

"I can't let my sister suffer, and if Charles shows up, she will. Besides, I'd rather not have your ally here either," I replied curtly.

"As you wish," he said with a mocking bow. I brushed past him and headed back to the salon.

"I think I've convinced Dorian to stay in Romania for now," I announced, meeting Jacques's eyes.

"I have just the person for you," he said after a moment of silence, "but don't ask questions about it. I'll go talk to her right away."

"I'll come with you," Ludmilla pleaded.

"Darling, it's better if I go alone. I'll be back soon, and if we're lucky, she'll agree to help us."

Sulking, Ludmilla let go of Jacques's arm. Accompanied by Miss Nimue, he disappeared into the night.

I looked tenderly at Giovanni, asleep on the sofa. Malvina draped a blanket over him and snuggled close. Luca, also quite sleepy, stretched out on another sofa and drifted off.

Ludmilla stood motionless in the doorway, staring into the darkness. I could feel her mind ablaze with the fear of losing Jacques again.

Hey, don't worry. You won't lose him again, I tried to console her telepathically.

I hope you're right. Just remembering what was hidden from me is already painful. But if I lost him again, I don't think I could recover. When Dad finds out about your lie, he won't forgive you. But thank you.

I walked over and hugged her tightly.

25

It was almost seven o'clock in the morning when Jacques returned. Ludmilla ran towards him, but I saw her stiffen and take a few steps backward. I stood still, trying to figure out what was happening. Then I saw her: Miss Nimue, moving fluidly, her tail straight, friendly eyes fixed on me. She came and rubbed against my ankle. I was too shocked to bend down and pet her.

Ada Garzina, Sr. appeared, entering silently like a ghost. I could only stare at her, eyes wide, unable to utter a single word.

I will never be able to make sense of this world, I thought, a constant refrain echoing in my head, as persistent as the tinnitus that, despite my transformation into a vampire, still haunted me during moments of mental confusion.

"Courage, you can recover," Ada said as she approached.

"And what role do you play in all of this?" I asked, more bewildered than ever.

She took my hand, and suddenly, like a series of snapshots, forgotten memories began to emerge from my mind. The pain was so intense it left me breathless, and in that instant, what felt like a series of images became clear awareness. The veil of confusion lifted, and I leaned against the wall for support, but Ada steadied me.

"I didn't know I was a vampire, a malier, because someone compelled me from birth to forget. Now everything is clear," I murmured, feeling the pain.

What I had intended to do to those children, I had suffered myself. They didn't deserve it. Tears streamed down my face, and I clenched my fists. I must not let the pain overwhelm me, or it would crush me. Slowly, shakily, I stood up.

Ada watched me carefully, trying to gauge my state of mind. "It will pass, and everything will feel normal again. You just need to give yourself time."

"How did you lift my confusion?" I asked, giving her a doubtful look.

"All in due time," she replied.

"Well, I think I have every right to know," I retorted stubbornly.

I hated appearing vulnerable, especially in front of someone I could barely tolerate as a child. So I turned and strutted toward the entrance, entering the house. Ludmilla, still clinging to Jacques' arm, followed me. I tried to connect with her mentally, but for some unknown reason, she blocked me out.

I sat on the sofa next to Malvina, who, as still as a statue, kept a vigilant eye on Ada's every move. "Don't you dare," I heard her growl.

"He is a human; he must not know of these matters," Ada replied coldly. She extended one hand toward Malvina and the other toward Giovanni. I saw Malvina struggle to move, while Giovanni sighed and slipped into an even deeper sleep.

"There is someone else in the house," she said, glancing toward the stairs.

"Captain Luca Perri," said Ludmilla, "a good friend."

"A vampire hunter…" Ada sneered. "Always useful to have around," she hissed, glancing at me.

I tried not to think anything, knowing she would hear, but the urge to curse her was strong. She smiled, tilting her head, and began to recite an incomprehensible chant. The first rays of sunlight streaming into the room surrounded her, making her black habit shimmer as if covered in tiny pearls. She spun around and then fell to her knees. Instinctively, I tried to reach out and help her, but Jacques stopped me. "You cannot touch her!"

I looked at Jacques, confused, but he simply motioned for me to wait. Luckily, Ada's strange ritual ended quickly. She rose and, without a word, sat in the only free armchair.

"The children will remain under my protection until they adapt. You and Ludmilla will be their guardians, and Father Vesta their teacher," she decreed, without looking anyone in the eye.

"And why should we do as you say?" I challenged her, tired of pretending everything was fine.

"I thought we were all here for the same purpose: to save those children and others from them. But maybe I was wrong," she replied, fixing me with a serious look.

A witch-nun and a witch-priest... I didn't know you had to take vows to do magic, I thought with amusement, meeting Ada's gaze.

"I'm not a witch, anyway," she commented, of course, after reading my thoughts.

"If you're not a witch, how will you help those children?"

"Listen, Maria," she said, moving closer, "there has never been good blood between us, but I knew your essence, and I couldn't risk approaching you. I might have unintentionally lifted the veil of confusion."

"You were a child too; how could you have known?"

"I am a phoenix, but a bit different. Every time I die, I am reborn as a newborn, carrying the knowledge of all my past lives. My powers allow me to recognize any supernatural being I encounter, and if they're dangerous, I eliminate them. But these are psychic powers, not magic."

I stared at her, trying to comprehend, but I was still puzzled.

A noise from the stairs signaled Luca's arrival.

"Good morning, everyone," he greeted, then froze upon seeing Ada.

"Anqa?"

He bowed.

"Up, up... what are these formalities?" Ada replied, hugging him. "It's been so long since we've seen each other."

"Everything okay?" Luca asked, looking at me with concern.

I nodded with a faint smile.

"You've been up all night; wouldn't some rest do you good? You look exhausted, and you're hungry. Eyes don't lie," he said, approaching.

The last thing I wanted was sleep. I needed only one thing: to know the end of Mihail.

"There are blood supplies in the cellar. Help yourselves," Malvina offered.

"N-n-no, thank you," I replied, my voice barely audible.

"Maria, you need to feed. That's why you're tired," Ludmilla admonished.

"What's all this about?" asked Ada… or Anqa…

"She's determined to be the first vampire who doesn't drink blood," Ludmilla said mockingly.

"Are you mad?" Ada grabbed my arm, forcing me to stand. "Accept Malvina's offer and drink, before you do something you'll regret."

I felt Ludmilla's emotional withdrawal keenly. I followed Ada to the cellar.

"Drink," she commanded, handing me a blood bag.

I finished it quickly.

"More," she insisted, opening another.

I obeyed and drank.

I looked at her and whispered, "Thank you."

"You are a vampire, Maria. You always were. Your father enchanted you at birth, so you wouldn't go through the transformation, and he lifted the enchantment when it suited him. No one will ever have to deal with him again. That vile creature is condemned to hell for eternity. But you must feed regularly, do you understand?"

"Do you know where the monster is?"

"He planned to kill you all, satisfying his sick thirst for amusement by lifting the enchantment from as many people as possible. Poor fool… he hadn't counted on my presence here in Turin," she said, staring at me.

"No, you're not allowed to see him," she declared, looking deep into my eyes.

"I didn't mean to ask," I murmured, averting my gaze, trying to blink away an apology.

"Ssssh," Ada hissed, disturbed by a noise from outside. "It's like a seaport in this house: people coming, people going... Vesta!" she exclaimed, heading toward the front door.

Didn't you convince them to stay home? Ludmilla asked, opening a mental channel.

Clearly, I didn't succeed.

But Jacques will leave if Charles arrives.

If he loves you, he'll stay. And anyway, it might just be Father Vesta outside.

Ludmilla disconnected and went to the door as well. I braced myself, expecting to see Dorian's grim face and Adelheid's feral glare. Fortunately, things turned out differently.

I watched the door until the towering figure of Father Vesta appeared. Miss Nimue hissed and leapt behind me.

"Miss Nimue... it's not like you to hide," the priest teased, stepping inside.

Father Vesta's eyes sought mine, and he moved closer. I rose and embraced him, and he hugged me back with tenderness I hadn't felt before.

"You've endured so much. Anyone else would have been broken, but you... your eyes show strength. Learn to use it, Maria."

"Dear Father, I'm so tired, and there's so much in my head that I can barely breathe. What strength?" I replied, smiling at the thought of my eyes betraying me.

"Did he come alone?" I whispered.

"Yes, although no one believed your random lies," he said, amused.

"Um," I muttered, hiding my face in my hands.

Ada returned, taking Father Vesta's hand, and led him to the center of the room.

"Why does Giovanni still have to sleep?" Malvina asked irritably.

"I thought I was clear," Ada retorted, "humans must be kept out of supernatural matters."

"Giovanni has always known and has never betrayed me. Leaving him in the oblivion you forced on him feels like a betrayal on my part."

Ada clenched her fists, clearly agitated, but calmed herself. She was about to respond when Ludmilla tested her power, subtly forcing Ada's emotions to surface.

"Don't you ever dare," Ada snapped once she regained control. Ludmilla didn't even flinch.

"Come on, girls, stop fighting like children," Luca said, trying to calm the tension.

We all fell silent. Malvina sat next to Giovanni, her eyes fixed on Ada. Father Vesta clutched his rosary, muttering prayers. Ludmilla watched Ada intently, nervously. Luca and Jacques exchanged knowing glances. I felt a torrent of words rising in my throat, desperate to spit them out, but common sense kept me silent. And so, we all remained quiet.

Father Vesta was the one to break the silence. He began reciting a litany, his voice strange, neither male nor female, devoid of intonation. It made my skin crawl. When he finished, he took out some objects from his pockets: rings with red stones. Twelve in total. He placed them on the ground while Ada scattered white powder in a circle around him. Kneeling, he passed his hands over the rings, reciting a few more prayers.

"Done. I have blessed and enchanted these rings. The malier must wear them at all times. They will protect you," he said, addressing Ludmilla and me.

Ada picked up the rings and put them in a small bag, blowing on it before walking over to us.

"Wear them on your right middle finger," she instructed, handing us each a ring.

I took mine, admiring the fire opal set in an antique gold band, with intricate engravings inside.

"They're runes," said Ludmilla.

"Celtic runes, engraved by Tiara herself," Father Vesta added.

I slipped the ring on my finger, and it was loose at first. But then it adjusted itself, molding perfectly.

"Damn... that's awesome!" Ludmilla exclaimed, admiring her hand.

"At the moment, they're just rings. But once all the malier are united, the magic will activate. It's ancient magic; no one will be able to remove or alter it. The rings will help each pair recognize and unite. You must place them on the children's fingers immediately."

I frowned. "But they're children. How will the rings fit, and won't it make them targets? Any malicious supernatural being will recognize us easily."

Ada shook her head, and Father Vesta smiled at my concern.

"Without faith, you'll get nowhere. Your job is to raise these little vampires, help them understand their abilities, and teach them how to use them. Right now, you're the benevolent malier. Don't forget that," Ada said, her tone almost threatening.

Then, without waiting for a response, she left, disappearing into the woods. I swore I heard a flutter of wings.

I sighed, trying to release the tension she had caused since we were children. I never imagined she was a phoenix, a creature who remembered all her past lives. I couldn't fathom what that would be like.

"One euro for every thought you have," Luca said, approaching.

I did not reply, but I returned the handshake, slipping my fingers between his. The atmosphere in the house was finally calming down, and Giovanni woke up.

"How long was I asleep?" he asked, rubbing his eyes with his fists.

"You were tired, my love, and I let you sleep," Malvina replied, stroking his hair.

I looked at the pairs around me: Ludmilla and Jacques; Malvina and Giovanni. Then I realized, as I came out of my thoughts, that my hand was still clasped in Luca's. I withdrew it as if I had been shocked.

I got up from the sofa and approached Father Vesta. "I want to know what happened to the monster. It is my right, considering it is my father," I said, playing the family card.

The priest widened his eyes, staring at me for a few moments, then shrugged his shoulders and in a firm voice replied, "To hell, as Anqa told you. Fear not, he will never harm you again. Not to you, nor to anyone else."

"That's not enough for me," I replied in an icy tone.

If his gaze had been lightning, it would have struck me down. Everyone was staring at me as if I had blasphemed.

"Well... have you been spellbound looking at me? Is there something wrong with me? Is it so absurd to want to know about that monster? Or are you all bewitched by witches and phoenixes?" I finished, emphasizing the last word.

"Alright," said Father Vesta, "sit down." He gently pushed me into a chair.

He placed his hands on my temples, and with terror, I felt my mind detach from my body. I began to descend down a spiral staircase, and as I moved, waves of energy penetrated me. The staircase led to what felt like the entrance to hell. A blast of humid heat hit me, making me cough and struggle to breathe. Another surge of energy flowed through me, allowing me to breathe and continue. The heat grew so intense it felt like it was burning my skin. I felt deep, excruciating pain and had to sit on a step to avoid fainting. Another wave of energy came, and I forced myself to keep going. As I reached the bottom, I found myself in front of a massive pool of flames.

Strangely, the pain disappeared.

A small gap opened in the flames, revealing what lay within. There he was—Mihail, submerged in the hellish fire, burning, healing, and emitting gut-wrenching screams in an endless, horrific cycle. The flames would consume him, but then relent just before turning him to ashes, allowing him to regenerate, only to start again... and again... and again.

The more I watched, the more the macabre display filled me with an eerie sense of peace. He was finally getting what he deserved.

Suddenly, a wave of power pulled me into a bright tunnel. I inhaled deeply, and everything faded away.

Father Vesta was there, smiling. "You have been granted your wish. Now, complete your task."

I looked into his eyes, nodded, and slumped back on the sofa, utterly exhausted.

I felt Ludmilla's presence in my mind. She had seen what Father Vesta had just shown me. She said nothing, but I read in her eyes a freedom she had been denied for so long.

"We cannot afford any breaks," said Father Vesta. "We must bring the young malier together. Anqa, or Sister Ada as you prefer, is setting up a private boarding school for special pupils in a wing of the institute. The little ones will live there; they will attend regular classes, and their other education will be up to you two, and me. Remember that together, you are very powerful. Even if you do not share the same malier gift, you are sisters by blood, both on your mother's and father's side. Your indissoluble, magical bond will make you indestructible, protecting you from any creature, even humans, who might try to annihilate you."

He raised his hands, instructing everyone to stand and form a circle. Standing in the middle, he addressed Giovanni first. "You are human; you should not involve yourself in supernatural matters. Anqa was right about that. But you have a vampire wife, and you have always protected her from exposure, just as you have avoided exposing yourself..."

Giovanni interrupted, "I've thought about it for many years, but the fear of eternity made me weak and foolish, to the point that I risked losing the love of my life. Now I am ready. I want to be one of you."

Malvina turned, her face stricken. "You don't have to do this. You never wanted to; what changed your mind? As Vesta said, this isn't your fight."

"But I've made up my mind," he replied firmly.

Giovanni's pleading eyes met mine. "Ohhh... don't even think of it. Besides, I wouldn't know how."

"It is up to you alone to decide, but if I may say so, Malvina dear, you should have kept human love away rather than nurturing it," Father Vesta declared, pointing at her.

Malvina tried to respond, but the priest turned away, denying her the chance to object.

"Let no one dare turn another human," Luca growled.

"Your threats won't scare me," Giovanni taunted.

Luca's eyes narrowed, scrutinizing him deeply, as if trying to see through to his soul. They exchanged challenging glares, Giovanni's dark eyes against Luca's blue ones, but then something unexpected happened.

Giovanni's expression changed, and he suddenly clutched his chest, struggling to scream, but only a gasp came out. Then he collapsed onto the sofa.

"Giovanni!" Malvina cried out, her face contorted with panic.

A moment later, Giovanni's body started convulsing violently. We were frozen in shock for a few seconds, then rushed to his side.

"Call an ambulance!" Malvina shouted.

Giovanni's face was pale, his body motionless. He stopped moving entirely.

"He's not breathing!" Malvina screamed, her voice desperate.

Ludmilla stepped forward, moving Giovanni's body to the floor. She tried to resuscitate him, but it all seemed futile. Giovanni stopped breathing.

"Make a decision, Malvina," urged Father Vesta.

"How many times had I imagined this moment? But now I can't... I can't do it," she murmured in despair.

Ludmilla leaned closer to Giovanni. "You asked before you died." Then she looked up at Malvina. "There is no more time. If we wait any longer, the adaptation process won't begin."

Malvina shook her head and ran from the room. I stood there, stunned and horrified, as Ludmilla bared her fangs and prepared to bite.

"Wait!" I shouted. "He asked me yesterday what the right thing would be—whether to adapt or not. I may not be the one to decide to restore a life, but Giovanni chose eternity with Malvina. If anyone should adapt him, it should be me."

"I'll do it. Excuse me," thundered Malvina as she rushed back, kneeling beside Giovanni.

She bit him several times, in different places, until a faint pulse returned. He began breathing again, raggedly and unevenly. Malvina took him in her arms and carried him to a room, ready to watch over his transformation.

"Did we make the right decision?" I asked Ludmilla hesitantly.

"He was convinced and asked for it. Fate only sped things up," she replied calmly.

"Still... when I think of Andrea and the struggles he has, I wonder if it's fair to condemn a human to such suffering."

"Come here, little sister," she said, hugging me and planting a kiss on my cheek. "It'll be okay."

In all the commotion, we had forgotten about Luca. Jacques had taken him outside and restrained him.

"What are you doing to him?" I shouted, seeing him tied to a tree with chains.

"What? I'm just trying to reason with him. Hunters can be stubborn, so I had to use some... stronger methods. But I didn't kill him..." Ludmilla and I exchanged incredulous glances.

"What do you want, Luca?" Jacques asked contemptuously.

"Justice. Vampires aren't supposed to turn humans. You know the penalty," Luca hissed.

"He was dying," Ludmilla roared.

"So what? That was his fate."

"You're wrong, hunter," Jacques interrupted, forcing Luca to look him in the eye. "I'll untie you, but you will listen to me. Or you will die, here and now. What will you choose?"

They stared at each other for a moment, and then Luca nodded, letting Jacques untie him.

"He wasn't just dying. I sensed dark magic on him," Jacques continued. "He was killed by a spell, and I doubt Malvina could adapt him."

"What are you saying?" I cried, horrified. "Why would anyone want Giovanni dead?" My mind flashed to Ada. "Damn her!"

"Calm down, Maria," said Ludmilla. "Who are you thinking of?"

"Ada, Sister Ada..."

"That's impossible. Anqa is a phoenix, without any magical power," Jacques replied.

"But she was the one who insisted humans shouldn't be involved," I snapped, growing more agitated. "But this isn't the time for speculation. Giovanni could still die if the adaptation doesn't take. We need to act."

The scream from inside the house chilled me to the bone.

"Oh, God!" Ludmilla sobbed.

"Giovanni didn't make it," Jacques muttered.

We ran frantically towards the room. Giovanni was lying still, his heartbeat gone. I had to cover my mouth to stop the sobs, but it was useless. Malvina's eyes were red, filled with rage. She stared at him, fists clenched so tightly that her knuckles cracked.

"My love... my angel. What have they done to you?" she whispered over and over.

"Everyone out!" thundered Father Vesta. "Even you, Malvina. Please."

We stood outside the door, waiting for any sign from inside, but there was nothing. It felt like hours before Father Vesta emerged.

"The magic made him think he was having a heart attack, but it wasn't real. I managed to suppress the spell. Giovanni is in adaptation. He will live."

We all rushed to embrace Father Vesta.

"You're suffocating me," he joked, smiling.

Malvina was the first to rush back to Giovanni's side. I tried to follow, but Father Vesta stopped me.

"It hurts to tell you this, but it was your father's last act before the flames of hell took him."

I couldn't understand what he had said. I stared at him, shocked, then ran. I locked myself in my room and threw myself on the bed, sobbing uncontrollably.

I felt Ludmilla's presence.

He... the beast... it was his doing, I thought, opening a psychic channel.

Impossible.

Father Vesta told me.

He doesn't have magic.

Jacques must have mistaken subjugation for magic. He must have met Mihail, and Mihail gave the command.

Dear God... what else did he set in motion?

Ludmilla climbed into bed beside me, hugging me tightly.

I relaxed, drifting into a peaceful state. *Thank you, little sister.*

"Oh God..." I said aloud, waking from the calm.

I looked at my phone. Damn, I'd slept for over three hours. I rushed downstairs, listening for voices and laughter.

"Good morning!" Giovanni greeted, smiling.

I ran to him. "Are you okay?" I whispered, tears flowing.

"Hey... hey... why are you crying? I'm fine."

"I thought you were gone. I'm just so happy you're okay."

I stared into his eyes and sensed his aura. He had adapted, but his essence was different—benevolent, yet stronger, as if encased to contain his power. I looked sharply at Father Vesta.

"He's my double. How?"

"We don't know. We were waiting for you to tell us. Only you could connect with his essence."

"And the children?"

"It's the witch, your father's accomplice. She follows his plan, and we don't know where it will lead. We need to bring the children together; we can't wait any longer."

"This situation is impossible..." I began, but Malvina cut me off.

"I've seen too much to entertain legends. Let's stop this charade," she said, darkly.

"Calm down, my love," Giovanni soothed.

Jacques approached Malvina, with Miss Nimue at his side. "I know everything about you, sweet lady. Witches were supposed to vanish centuries ago, but they persevered. The malier were meant to aid them, not fight them. But the time wasn't right, and they were abandoned. They became dangerous, and the witches sought to destroy them. But magic alone couldn't do it."

"How did Mihail fit into this?" I demanded. "He's not two thousand years old. And how is Giovanni a malier? Help me understand, Father Vesta."

"Mental chaos feeds an ancestral witch," he replied.

I reflected on how my life had changed, and all the doubts I had carried. Father Vesta's words cut through my thoughts.

"Maria Diletti," he said sternly. "Do not create chaos in your mind, or you will become the witch's feast. You must have faith, strength, and a clean soul. Only then will you prevail."

I knelt down, calling Miss Nimue. She purred, bringing me comfort.

"You know, I always wanted to have a cat," I whispered.

End of Book One

INDEX

Preface 3
1 6
2 10
3 12
4 16
5 21
6 26
7 31
8 35
9 41
10 50
11 57
12 67
13 76
14 84
15 103
16 120
17 125
18 147
19 152
20 173
21 181
22 197
23 206
24 215
25 232

Youcanprint
Finished Printing July 2023